A Twelfth Dan Master of Dimac and Magus to the
Illuminated Order of the Celestial Sprout, Robert
Rankin has also had a total of thirty-nine jobs,
including illustrator, off-licence manager, market-stall
trader, rock singer and garden gnome salesman. He
lives in Sussex with his wife and family.

Robert Rankin's previous novels, the *Armageddon*
trilogy, the *Brentford* quartet and *The Book of Ultimate
Truths* are all available from Corgi Books.

What they say about Robert Rankin:

'One of the rare guys who can always
make me laugh'
Terry Pratchett

'To the top-selling ranks of humorists such as
Douglas Adams and Terry Pratchett, let us welcome
Mr Rankin'
Tom Hutchinson, *The Times*

'A born writer with a taste for the occult. Robert
Rankin is to Brentford what William Faulkner was
to Yoknapatwpha County'
Time Out

'One of the finest living comic writers . . . a sort of
drinking man's H. G. Wells'
Midweek

'An irregular genius'

RAIDERS OF THE LOST CAR PARK

Robert Rankin

CORGI BOOKS

RAIDERS OF THE LOST CAR PARK
A CORGI BOOK : 0 552 13833 9

Originally published in Great Britain by Doubleday,
a division of Transworld Publishers Ltd

PRINTING HISTORY
Doubleday edition published 1994
Corgi edition published 1994

Set in 11 ½/13pt Monotype Bembo by Kestrel Data, Exeter

Corgi Books are published by Transworld Publishers Ltd,
61–63 Uxbridge Road, Ealing, London W5 5SA,
in Australia by Transworld Publishers (Australia) Pty Ltd,
15–25 Helles Avenue, Moorebank, NSW 2170,
and in New Zealand by Transworld Publishers (NZ) Ltd,
3 William Pickering Drive, Albany, Auckland.

Reproduced, printed and bound in Great Britain by
Cox & Wyman Ltd, Reading, Berks.

For

DAVID A. DOVESTON,

laudator temporis acti,
and why not . . . ?

RAIDERS OF THE
LOST CAR PARK

AS IF YOU HADN'T GUESSED

We are not being told all of the truth.

There are truths. And there are *Truths*. And then there are

ULTIMATE TRUTHS.

Allow me to explain.

If you have ever attempted, in the spirit of scientific discovery, to glue a rectangular map of the world onto a sphere of the same scale, you will soon have realized that it cannot be done. There is simply too much map.

Now, why should this be?

Well, the greybeards of The Royal Geographic will spin you a lot of jargon about 'orthomorphic map representations' and 'parallels and meridians' and 'scale being exaggerated in increasing proportion to the lessening proximity with the equator'.

But then, they would say that, wouldn't they?

That would be what *they* call a truth.

But it's not a *Truth*. And it's certainly not an ULTIMATE TRUTH.

The *Truth* of the matter is that the map *can* be made to fit. All you have to do is increase the size of your sphere by one third.

The ULTIMATE TRUTH is, that the entire planet is really a great deal larger than we have been led to believe. And a considerable amount of it still remains uncharted.

At least by the human population, that is!

Allow me to explain.

There exists, right here, in our very midst, a race of evil beings that secretly manipulate mankind. They plunder its wealth, screw up its progress and nick its Biros. In short, they control the world as we know it.

This dark, malignant and altogether bad-assed bunch have, throughout history, infiltrated every level of our society. They lurk, unseen, unsuspected and seemingly unstoppable. Growing ever in number, bent upon the ultimate downfall of the human race and ruled over by a merciless tyrant, known to his minions as the Hidden King of the World, and his gofer, Arthur Kobold.

Their pest holes are everywhere; hundreds across London alone. Each stacked high with a boundless fortune in stolen booty. But you won't find the locations on any atlas or street directory. They are well concealed.

Because these vile beings inhabit all those bits and pieces you had to snip off your rectangular map of the world to make it fit onto the sphere.

They inhabit the FORBIDDEN ZONES.

And *that* is an ULTIMATE TRUTH!

The discoverer of this ULTIMATE TRUTH, and of many more besides, was a most remarkable man. His name was Hugo Artemis Solon Saturnicus Reginald Arthur Rune.

He was a mystic, magus and master of the arts magickal. Poet, painter and prophet. Guru to gurus and best-dressed man of 1933.

Hardly anyone remembers him today.

When at the height of his celebrity, between the wars, Rune was lionized by high society and held the ear of princes and popes. He could be found dancing the night away with Greta Garbo. Fly-fishing with Franklin Delano Roosevelt. Sharing a joke with Haile Selassie, or leading the conga line at a Buck House garden party.

But for all this, Rune was ever a man with a mission.

Having discovered the existence of the FORBIDDEN ZONES, he set out to enter them, to expose the truth about the beings that dwell within, to liberate the plundered wealth of ages, to free mankind from its secret oppressor and would-be destroyer, and to raise upon high his banner of ULTIMATE TRUTH.

But he did not succeed.

Although, with the aid of his acolyte Rizla, a compass and a tape measure, Rune plotted the location of every FORBIDDEN ZONE in London; and even formulated a means of breaking into them by playing certain 'restricted' notes on a reinvented ocarina, he did not succeed.

On a dark and stormy night some eighteen years ago, Rune and Rizla set forth upon a heroic mission. Fearlessly they penetrated to the very heart of the FORBIDDEN ZONES, there to beard the evil lion in his den. To confront The Hidden King of the World.

Exactly what happened on that fateful night may never be known. Rizla escaped, a broken man.

Hugo Rune was never seen again.

INTRODUCTION

Cornelius Murphy is the Stuff of Epics.

He is seventeen years of age, a tall boy with big hair, a quick wit and an astonishing sense of smell. He is also the illegitimate son of Hugo Rune.

Cornelius has just returned from an epic adventure.

He was employed by a certain Mr Arthur Kobold, to seek out certain missing chapters from a certain missing book.

The Book of Ultimate Truths. Penned by a certain Hugo Rune.

During the course of his epic adventure, Cornelius, accompanied by his best friend Tuppe (who is also the Stuff of Epics, although to a somewhat lesser degree), and travelling in a suitably epic nineteen-fifties Cadillac Eldorado, discovered his true parentage.

He also learned of the existence of the Forbidden Zones and that Rune is still alive and kicking, held captive inside one of the Zones by the stinkers that dwell within.

Being an epic adventure it was naturally fraught with peril and Cornelius found himself risking life and limb on numerous occasions. As might well be imagined, the Hidden King of the World, determined to destroy any threat to the security of his secret kingdoms, was prepared to go to any length to prevent the tall boy passing on what he had learned.

As well as being fraught with peril, the epic adventure was not without complications. There was a Scotsman, the Campbell, who was not really a Scotsman at all, but a malevolent chimera. Part man, part something-else-entirely. And there was a train, THE TRAIN OF TRISMEGISTUS, which wasn't really a train at all, but a Satanic-style agency of despatch, unleashed by The Hidden King of the World.

Cornelius did not return from his epic adventure altogether unscathed. He lost a good deal of his big hair in a life-and-death struggle with the Campbell. Had his Cadillac Eldorado mashed to pieces by falling masonry. And was tricked out of Rune's missing chapters by Mr Arthur Kobold, writer of dud cheques, eater of cake and evil cat's-paw of The Hidden King.

But if you are the Stuff of Epics, then you just have to take this sort of thing in your stride. And if, like Cornelius, you find yourself at the end of it all in possession of Rune's annotated A-Z and the plans for his reinvented ocarina, then the way ahead is clear.

You must enter the Forbidden Zones.

You must free your father.

You must wage war upon the Hidden King of the World and expose the truth about the evil beings who secretly control mankind.

You must become a warrior in the cause of ULTIMATE TRUTH.

And if you happen to come across any of that boundless wealth stored up inside the Forbidden Zones along the way . . .

Well, that wouldn't go amiss either.

1

There are exactly twenty-three really wonderful things in this world, and to be in the right place at the right time is one of them.

Happily this still leaves twenty-two others for the rest of us to share. And amongst these is Rock 'n' Roll.

Now Rock 'n' Roll may not be to everyone's taste. Some speak highly of Classical Music. In fact, some speak highly of Classical Music and say things like, 'Of course, Classical Music was the Rock 'n' Roll of its day.' Which is frankly a load of old tucket. Classical Music was the Classical Music of its day. Bawdy ballads were the boogie. *Let me make the ballads and who will may make the laws*, wrote Andrew Fletcher in 1703. And two hundred and fifty years later Jerry Lee Lewis would drink to that.

And so today would Mickey Minns. Not that Mickey needed too much of an excuse to up-end a pint pot. Mickey was an old rocker and the downing of large quantities of beer, went, as they say, with the territory. He'd once jammed with Jeff Beck at The Marquee and had Mickey been in the right place at the right time he would have played bass on 'Hi Ho Silver Lining'. But he wasn't, so he did not. Minns had been draped across a saloon bar counter during

17

the recording of that particular Rock Anthem. And he was currently draped across one now. Different counter, different decade, but the song remains the same.

Back in the Sixties he'd had a full head of hair and a twenty-eight-inch waist and he'd owned a guitar shop. He still owned a guitar shop. It was situated just off the high street and called Minn's Music Mine. Mickey had considered changing the name on many occasions over the years. But the way he saw it, fashions come and fashions go, yet the British still love a shop with a stupid name. And his was slightly less stupid than most.

The part-time barman called last orders for the lunch-time session and Mickey raised his head from the counter to order another. He didn't have to rush back. Not now he'd got the new assistant and everything.

The new assistant's name was Anna Gotting and she was a rare beauty. Blond of hair. Blue of eye. Independent of spirit. Seventeen years of age and five foot eight of height. Valid arguments against the inclusion of such a being in the list of the twenty-three really wonderful things have yet to be heard. Mickey Minns, for one, could find none against employing her. He considered Anna ideal for the position. Ideal indeed for any number of positions, several of which sprang immediately to his lecherous mind. After all, it was just remotely possible that the teenage siren might harbour a secret passion for balding old musos with beer bellies and bad breath. Well, almost anything was possible. Almost.

But the tank top of stupidity did not hang in the crowded wardrobe of Mickey's failings. He had a teenage daughter of his own. And he had a business to run. In Anna, he saw a valuable asset. She'd only been with him a month and the weekly takings had already doubled. Never had so many guitarless young men purchased so many plectrums.

Mickey sighed inwardly, belched outwardly and stumbled away to the Gents whistling 'Beck's Bolero'.

He was blissfully unaware that this parting pee and that postscript pint were about to cost him very dearly indeed.

Because at Minn's Music Mine, the first link in a fantastic chain of events was about to be forged. A chain which would lead from the mundane to the miraculous. From the humdrum to the phantasmagoric. From *taedium vitae* to *terra incognita*. From the *crambe repitita* . . . and so on and so forth. The way some of them do. And it would all begin with the tuneless ting of Mickey's old shop doorbell.

Now it must be stated fairly and squarely, that Minn's Music Mine was a proper guitar shop. A guitar shop in the grand tradition. The genuine article. If asked to describe itself to some young and impressionable customer-to-be and suddenly finding itself with the wish and the ability to do so, it might well have said something like this. In a rich American accent, no doubt.

'Hi there. My name's Minn's Music Mine and I'm a guitar shop. Like me to show you around? Don't be shy. Step right up.

'OK. So this is my door. Note the steel cage bolted across it. And the signs. See these signs? *"Stolen guitar? No thanks!"* and *"Shoplifting is theft! We always prosecute!"* and *"Beware guard dog! Got the balls to break in? You won't have 'em when you break out!"* See all those exclamation marks? I am a security-conscious establishment!

'Now. Let's step inside. Mind the step there. OK. Allow me to draw your attention to the carpet. Note the cunning arabesques woven into its quality fabric. These are musical notes. A carpet not dissimilar to this once featured on *Six Five Special*. You never heard of *Six Five Special*? You weren't even born? No, I guess not. Never mind.

'And you can't see any musical notes anyway? They're there. Under all the stains and the cigarette burns and stuff. They're there! I'm telling you. Now see here, these, to your right. Amplifiers. And speakers. Lots of speakers. The tall ones are WEM Vendettas. You've never heard of WEM Vendettas? Yeah, well, they're quite old. They're on special offer. Have been for some years.

'But these are new. See these? Japanese guitars. You get the whole works for less than £100. Axe, strap, lead, plectrum, amp, speaker, play-in-a-day handbook. The whole works. Bottom of the range, these guys. We sell plenty. They're crap as it happens.

'What? Your mate has one? He says it's "excellent"? Fair enough.

'OK. Now, careful where you stand, or you might step in a saucerful of cigarette butts. You'll see quite a lot of those in here. All the saucers are, you will

20

note, full. And lying all around and about amongst them, see these? Coffee mugs. And in them. Precisely one quarter of an inch of congealed black gunk. No more, no less. That's the way we do business.

'Why? Why what? Why all the full ashtrays and the coffee mugs with exactly one quarter of an inch of congealed black gunk? *Why?* You're asking me *why?* Well, that's what you have in guitar shops. That's *why*. It's a tradition, or an old charter. Or something.

'Look, forget about the ashtrays. Come and see these. Here. All over this wall. Polaroid photos. Rock stars. Rock stars past and present. Mostly past, I guess. But they've all been in here. You can see my owner, Mr Minns, in many of them too. There's one of him with Charlie Watts. He bought a practice pad in here once. Watts. Charlie Watts. You never heard of Charlie Watts?

'Never mind. Now. Guitars. Do *we* have guitars. The racks here. These are your "Spanish beginners". Boxwood. Narrow necks, so kids can get their little fingers around them. And the rack up on the wall. Your £200-plus acoustics. Up out of the way where the bloody kids can't get their fingers around them. And right up there. Top of the world, Ma, as we say, is an original Les Paul Sunburst. The pride of my owner's collection. He'd never sell it, of course. Check out the patina. And the frets. See these frets? Tasmanian porcupine quill. And the inlay on the finger-boards. Mother-of-pearl. You can almost taste the sustain. A Les Paul original. Les Paul. *Les Paul?* You're standing in a guitar shop and you have the

21

gall to ask who is Les Paul? For Chrisakes, fella, I can put up with so much and then no more! You have a crack at my carpet! You snub my saucers! You poo-poo my polaroids!

'But Les Paul! What the hell did you come in here for anyway?

'The *Who*? There's a polaroid over there of Mr Minns being beaten up by Keith Moon. Not that Who. What who then?

'Oh. I see. The who with the blue eyes and the blond hair. The *Gandhi's Hairdryer World Tour 93* T-shirt and the tight blue jeans. The who sitting on the stool playing the Stratocaster.

That who. Ah yeah. That who.'

'That who' was practising her guitar licks. If you're going to work in a guitar shop, you must know your licks. And your riffs, of course. Your licks and your riffs. If you can't wield your axe and blast out a passable 'Stairway to Heaven' or 'Sunshine of your Love', then forget it. Take the checkout job at Tesco's.

Anna's licks were greatly admired locally. As were her riffs.

And so, on this particular day, the lunch-time guitar fanciers having purchased their plectrums and drifted back to their checkouts at Tesco's, Anna had the shop all to herself. So she cranked up the volume and let riff.

She knew full well that she wasn't cut out for a lifetime of shop work. She was destined for greater things. Although exactly what these greater things were, she did not know. But there was plenty of time yet to find out. And during this period she really loved playing the expensive guitars that no-one was ever likely to buy.

She didn't hear the tuneless ting of the old shop doorbell as it tolled the knell of her passing interest and it was some moments before she realized that she had an appreciative audience.

Before her stood a brace of young men. They had evidently arrived together. But there all similarity between them ended. One was tall. Very tall. The other was quite the opposite. The tall one wore a black shirt, buttoned at the neck. A light, pale cotton jacket with long lapels, drooping padded shoulders and one-button-low. Black trousers of the peg persuasion. Canvas loafers. No socks. The entire ensemble had that 'lived-in' look about it.

At the high head end there were points of interest. A fine aquiline nose. A noble brow in the making. A mouth made for smiling. Gentle eyes. The head was swathed in bandages and topped off by a cap with the words *Ultimate Warrior* printed on the front.

The short one, and he was a very short one, scarcely reaching the knee of his companion, sported Mothercare dungarees, a tartan shirt and red jellies. He had the face of a cherub.

Anna switched off the expensive guitar, unplugged it and set it carefully aside. Then she climbed down from her stool, tucked the rear of her T-shirt into the twenty-three-inch waistband of her jeans, stroked back her hair and pounced.

She plucked up the fellow in the dungarees and

23

cradled him in her arms. 'Watchamate, Tuppe,' she laughed, lowering her cheek for a kiss.

'Great licks, Anna.' The small one applied his lips to the allocated beauty spot.

'And watchamate, Cornelius.'

The tall boy stood and he sniffed.

'I bet you can't get it.' Anna grinned wickedly.

'I bet you I can.' Cornelius took another sniff. '*Chanel*,' said he.

'But which one?'

One more small sniff and one big smile. '*Chanel No. 19*.'

'Correct, as ever.' Anna carefully set down the Tuppe, then fell upon the lowered neck of Cornelius Murphy and kissed it. It was the kiss of an old friend. Cornelius kissed her hair. It smelled wonderful. He could easily have identified the shampoo. But he did not. He closed his eyes and savoured the subtle fragrances which composed the olfactory identikit that was Anna Gotting. It was all quite wonderful.

'So where have you been?' Anna stepped back and glanced him up and down. 'I haven't seen you since we left school a month back.'

'We've been working,' Tuppe said. 'But it didn't work out,' he added.

'So what are you doing here? Starting a band? I'm getting the hang of lead guitar, if you are.'

'We'd like to buy an ocarina,' said Tuppe brightly.

'A what?'

'An ocarina.' Cornelius mimed the playing of one. 'It's an egg-shaped wind instrument with a protruding mouthpiece and six to eight finger holes. It produces

24

an almost pure tone. Do you have one in stock by any chance?'

Anna eyed the tall boy. 'What happened to your head?'

Cornelius gingerly fingered his cap. 'Car accident,' he suggested.

'Oh. I'm sorry.'

'About the ocarina?' Tuppe grinned up.

Anna smiled down. 'I think I've seen one somewhere. Do you want me to look for it this minute?'

'Please.' Tuppe nodded vigorously. 'It's quite urgent.'

Anna shrugged. 'OK. You can play the guitars if you want. But don't touch the Sunburst. It's an original.'

And with that said she swept away to the storeroom, laying down a trail of *Chanel No. 19* that Cornelius could have followed with his nose bandaged.

Tuppe gazed wistfully around the shop and sighed. 'I wish I could play the guitar.'

'You could learn.' Cornelius strapped on the Stratocaster and did Pete Townsend windmills with his right arm. Then he stooped hastily to pick up the rack of sheet music he'd overturned. 'Why don't you take lessons?'

'I couldn't reach the fretboard. My arms are too short.'

Cornelius did not apologize for his thoughtless remark. And Tuppe did not expect him to. They were best friends. Each saw the other as an equal. The glaring difference in their heights did not enter into it.

'Is this an ocarina?' Anna returned with an item resembling a tiny bullet-pocked mahogany submarine.

'That's the fellow,' chorused her customers.

Anna turned the instrument between her delicate fingers and perused the faded price tag. '£5.18s.6d. Is that a fair price for an ocarina?'

'The price of a thing bears no relationship to its value,' said Tuppe wisely.

'That depends whether you're buying or selling,' replied Anna, wiser yet.

Cornelius shuffled his loafers. 'We weren't actually thinking of buying it.'

'You mean you just want to have a blow or something?'

'Well no.' Cornelius chewed his lip. 'We were hoping to steal it.'

'Why?'

'Because we don't have any money.' Tuppe pulled out his pockets. 'We're stony broke.'

'So you want to nick *this*?'

'I don't *want* to.' Cornelius held down his cap and shook his head. 'Dishonesty does not dine at my table as a rule. But the present circumstances are somewhat exceptional. Might I perhaps borrow the ocarina?'

'I could ask Mickey, but I don't think he'd be keen. What do you want to do with it? Busk?'

'I want to drill holes in it.' Cornelius smiled painfully.

'Then forget it. Listen, are you two on something or what?'

'Certainly not.'

'Then why do you want to drill holes in an ocarina?'

Cornelius looked at Tuppe. And Tuppe looked at Cornelius.

'Tell her,' said Tuppe.

'I can't,' said Cornelius.

'Of course you can. If we succeed in this thing, everybody in the world is going to know about it anyway.'

'Everybody in the world?' Anna looked from the one to the other of them.

'All right.' Cornelius smiled a little less painfully. But not much. 'You see,' he began, 'Tuppe and I have just returned from an epic journey. And during the course of it we learned a great and terrible secret. A secret which we have sworn to reveal to the world.'

'Oh yes?' Anna put her hands in her back pockets (Bette Davis style).

'Oh yes. We learned that all across London there are Forbidden Zones. They are cunningly concealed and only a very few people know of their existence. Inside these Zones exists another order of being.'

Tuppe whistled the theme from *The Twilight Zone*.

'Another order of being?' Anna spoke the words in a toneless tone.

'Another order of being, yes. A secret civilization. And it has apparently been orchestrating the progress of mankind for centuries.'

'Screwing it up,' Tuppe added.

'I see.' Anna turned up her eyes. Bumblies hung from the ceiling. She'd never noticed them before.

They were constructed from the rolled-up foil of Woodbine packets, *circa* 1965. 'Go on,' she said.

Cornelius went on. 'We also learned that it is possible to enter the Zones by playing certain notes on an ocarina. Notes which cannot normally be played. You have to drill new holes. I have the plan here in my pocket, on a map. We plan to drill the holes, enter the Zones—'

'And grab the booty,' Tuppe put in.

'What booty?' A note of interest entered Anna's voice.

'Riches.' Cornelius made expansive gestures. Then he stooped once more to clear up the sheet music. 'Untold riches. The stones from engagement rings. Missing art treasures—'

'Biros,' Tuppe put in.

'Biros, umbrellas, odd socks, yellow-handled screwdrivers, supermarket trolleys, all the stuff that unaccountably goes missing. We'll only be going in for the untold riches to start off with.'

Anna studied the ocarina and then the face of Cornelius Murphy. 'And you really expect me to believe this?'

'No. Not at all. I only want the ocarina. You asked me why and I told you. I'd prefer it if you didn't believe a single word. *I* wouldn't, if I was in your place.'

'You really are on something.' Anna prepared to return the ocarina to the spot it had occupied for the last twenty-three years.

'No wait,' Tuppe blurted out. 'His dad's trapped in one of the Zones. *They* captured him.'

'Now I know you're lying. I saw Jack Murphy going into the bank this morning.'

'He's not my real dad.' Cornelius sighed. Explaining the unexplainable is always a problem. 'My real dad is a great magus called Hugo Rune.'

'And mine is Elvis Presley. So long, guys.'

Cornelius fluttered his fingers. 'Could I just look at the ocarina, before you put it away?'

Anna hugged it to her bosom. 'What will you do if I give it to you?'

'Well, I thought I would say something like, "Can I take it outside to see the colour in the daylight?" then just sort of run off with it.'

'Sound plan,' said Tuppe.

'I can't let you do that. I'd lose my job if Mickey found out.'

'I suppose you're right.' Cornelius rammed his fluttering fingers into his trouser pockets. 'I wouldn't want that. We'll go elsewhere. Listen, it was really nice to bump into you again, Anna. And smell your perfume. If Tuppe and I survive in one piece, rescue the daddy, return with the riches, best the blighters in the Forbidden Zones and reveal them to the world, then I'd like you to bear my children. Bye for now then.'

'And be lucky,' Tuppe added.

Anna watched the odd couple turn and make for the door. She'd known Cornelius for five years. He was a friend. Eccentric perhaps, weird even, certainly not like the rest. But he *was* honest. And he was really quite handsome. Although Anna did harbour a secret passion for ageing musos with baldy heads, beer bellies

29

and bad breath. Well, anything was possible. Almost. But the tall boy's story was clearly ludicrous. An insult to her intelligence.

Anna glanced around the interior of Minn's Music Mine, seeing it all as if for the first time. Which is sometimes the way when you see something for the last time. Or even, when you discover yourself to be in the *right* place at the *right* time.

'Perhaps', she said, as the tall boy reached the door, 'you'd like to take this outside. To see the colour in the daylight.'

Cornelius turned back. And he smiled a most winning smile.

'Perhaps you'd like to see it too,' he suggested.

2

Mr Thompkin, who ran Thompkin's Tools in the high street, was a canny fellow. But not quite canny enough. If he hadn't found himself suddenly prey to erotic fantasies, he would never have let the beautiful seventeen-year-old girl in the *Gandhi's Hairdryer World Tour 93* T-shirt take one of his nice new electric drills outside, to see the colour in the daylight.

When she hadn't returned after fifteen minutes, he dutifully, if somewhat regretfully, telephoned the police.

The line was engaged. A Mr Michael Minns was on it. Apparently, he had returned from a late business lunch with Japanese clients, to discover that his assistant had, like the Elvis of old, left the building. But this time leaving the door unlocked. He was calling to report the loss of twenty-three expensive guitars. Including an original Les Paul Sunburst, valued at around five thousand pounds.

'There's no point in just claiming for an old ocarina,' his wife had told him. 'Go the whole hog, do it in one, and we'll sell up the shop and move to Benidorm.'

As Mickey was far too pissed to argue, he had agreed. He wrapped the precious guitar in an old kaftan and hid it in the wardrobe. 'Is this *my* tank top in here?' he asked.

Anna, Tuppe and Cornelius Murphy sat on a bench in the park. They were sharing the large chocolate cake that Master Bradshaw, the baker's son, had actually allowed Tuppe to take outside to see the colour in the daylight.

'I feel', said Tuppe between munchings, 'that the "see it in the daylight" ploy might be subject to the law of diminishing returns. I only outran young Bradshaw by the skin of my teeth.'

Cornelius dusted chocolate crumbs from his lap. 'I don't think we're really cut out for a life of brigandage. We must remember to pay everyone back as soon as we're able.'

'So where do we go from here?' Anna licked her fingers.

'Back to my house,' Cornelius told hcr. 'We'll have to walk I'm afraid. I had a car, but it got—'

'Dumped on,' said Tuppe. 'From a great height. A crying shame so it was.'

'We were tricked,' Cornelius explained. 'By a villain called Arthur Kobold. He employed me to find the missing chapters from a great book. Tuppe and I were almost killed doing so. Come on, let's go. I'll tell you everything that happened on the way.'

Anna shrugged. 'I'm still not certain I should believe anything you've told me so far.'

'It's all true.' Cornelius stood and stretched.

'It is,' Tuppe agreed. 'There's no plug on that drill, by the way.'

'Stuff the plug,' said Anna. 'Tell me again about the booty.'

'Tell me again about the booty.' These words, although spoken at exactly the same moment, came from another mouth altogether.

Coincidence? Synchronicity? The chromium-plated megaphone of destiny? The speaker of the words didn't know. Neither did he care. All he knew about and all he cared about, above and beyond everything, including the call of duty, absolutely everything, was the science of deduction. The art of detection.

And why should it be otherwise?

For this man was a detective. And not just any old detective. This man was *the* detective.

This was he of the Harris Tweed three-piece whistle.

He of the albino crop and the ivory ear-ring.

He of the mirrored pince-nez, the black malacca cane and the heavy pigskin valise.

He of the occasional affectation.

This was the man, the legend and *the* detective.

Inspectre Hovis of Scotland Yard. (*Who?*)

The man, the legend and *the* detective straddled a single regulation police-issue chair and carefully re-phrased his question.

'The booty,' he boomed in a deep baronial bari-tone. The voice of one whose social class is scheduled to be first up against the wall come the revolution. 'Tell me about it.'

Terence Arthur Mulligan, known regularly as 'the

33

accused', made a surly face at the great detective. 'I've told you all I know,' he muttered in fluent working class.

'Then tell me again.'

'Look,' Terence gripped the edge of the regulation police-issue interview table, 'I was driving me cab, right? And I'd just dropped off me fare, right? Old bloke, white hair, looked like Bertrand Russell.'

'Bertrand Russell.' Hovis breathed on to the silver pommel of his cane and buffed it with a monogrammed handkerchief.

'Bertrand Russell, 'cept it weren't him, because he's dead. Though I did have him in the back of me cab once. D'you know what I asked him?'

'About the booty.' Hovis examined his reflection in his cane's gleaming pommel. It was immaculate. As ever.

'Nah, it weren't about that. I asked him—' But the flow of Mulligan's discourse was unexpectedly staunched by the sudden introduction of a polished silver pommel into his gob.

'The diamonds.' Inspectre Hovis rattled Mulligan's teeth, withdrew the cane and cracked it down on the interview table. 'Tell me about the bally diamonds and tell me now.'

'Just you see here . . .' Mulligan fell back, flapping and spluttering.

'No.' Hovis rose to loom above him. 'Just *you* see here. You were pulled in for exceeding the speed limit. When asked to turn out your pockets, what should the arresting officer find but a veritable king's ransom in diamonds. Now, I am going to ask you

34

just one time more. Where did you get them?'

'I found them. I was having a fag, right? Sitting in me cab and then there was a bloody big explosion and this dirty great sort of train thing came steaming out of this hoarding. Lights flashing and stuff. And it flew by, right? And then I saw the diamonds. They were lying all over the road. So I scooped them up and I was just driving to the nearest police station to hand them in, when two of your blokes stopped me, right?'

'Wrong,' said Inspectre Hovis.

'It's the truth,' pleaded Mulligan. 'Except for the last bit. I wasn't really taking them to the nearest police station.'

'No,' said Hovis. 'I thought not.'

'No,' said Mulligan. 'I was going to distribute them amongst the poor and needy.'

Hovis raised his cane to smite Mr Mulligan, but thought better of it. There was always the chance that the video camera, supposedly recording the interview, might actually be switched on. 'Tell me some more about this train,' he said wearily.

'I only saw it for a moment. It was like a ghost train or something. It made this sound . . .'

The great detective lifted a quizzical eyebrow.

'Yabba dabba do,' said Terence Arthur Mulligan.

'Where did you steal those diamonds?'

'I didn't steal them!' Mulligan drummed his fists on the table. 'How many more times? I found them. They were lying all over the road. Just like I told your blokes.'

'Yet when they drove you back to the scene of this

outré occurrence, they could find no broken hoarding. No evidence of any train.'

'I can't explain that.' Mulligan slumped in his chair. 'But I didn't steal them. I found them. I swear.'

Hovis shook his head. 'No,' said he, 'and again no. I put it to you that you are telling me a pack of lies. Spinning me the *crambe repitita*.'

'What *is* that, by the way?'

'The *crambe repitita*. The warmed-up cabbage. The old old story.'

'Ah,' said Terence. 'That.'

'That.' Inspectre Hovis removed his mirrored pince-nez and fixed Mulligan with a baleful stare. 'I regret to inform you, sir, that you are, as we say in the trade, bang to rights. In the frame and up the Swanee. *Flagrante delicto*, or as near as makes no odds.'

'I wanna see my brief,' growled Terence, who knew his rights.

'And so you shall,' replied Inspectre Hovis, who knew them also. 'But you are going down this time, chummy. There's bird in this for you. Your goose is cooked.'

'Your goose is cooked, dear,' called the mother of Cornelius Murphy to the adoptive father thereof. Her words travelled through the open kitchen door of the family home, down the length of the back garden and fell upon the intended ears of her large and sorry-looking spouse.

Jack Murphy sat in the doorway of his shed. The very picture of despair. His wig was off and his great head was down. A multiplicity of chins rested upon

36

his befairisled chest. The bepatched elbows of his shirt rested upon the bepatched knees of his corduroy trews. His hooded eyes were fixed upon the dud cheque that he held between prodigious fingers.

The once merry mouth was turned down at the corners and a low murmur arose from it, as a rumble of distant thunder.

'Woe unto the house of Murphy,' murmured this rumble. 'For lo it has become undone.'

The daddy held up the cheque and let the late afternoon sun play upon its evil edges. Twelve hours before it had read, *Pay Jack Murphy the sum of £5000. Signed Arthur Kobold.* But no longer.

When he had presented it to the bank, a terrible transformation had occurred. The words of joy had vanished away, to be replaced by those which glowed there still. *Pay this fat fool one hundred laughs, then kick him into the street.*

The junior bank clerk had been pleased to do so. 'Your son was in here earlier with one of these,' he smirked.

The elder Murphy scowled at the rogue cheque. He'd been done. His son had been done. Kobold had stitched them up like a pair of the proverbials. It was too much to bear.

'Are you coming in to eat this goose?' called his wife. 'The cat's already had two of its legs. You'd best hurry before it gets the others.'

Inspectre Hovis returned to his office. It was a long haul from the interview rooms of Scotland Yard, but he knew the way well enough by now. He strode down a corridor. Marched up a staircase. Strutted along a passageway. Strolled through the typing pool. Sauntered past the forensic labs. Plodded down a back stairway. Stumbled through a fire exit and finally staggered across the car park to the Portakabin.

The Portakabin!

Hovis gazed up at the abomination and chewed at his lower lip. And the same evil thoughts entered his mind as ever they had done for the last twenty-three days. The days that he had been exiled here. And the same name came once more to his lips. The name that he loathed and despised with every natural fibre of his expensively clad being. The name of Brian 'Bulwer' Lytton.

Chief Inspector Lytton. The new broom that was sweeping clean the department.

And a fresh young broom he was. Ten years the junior of Hovis. And an influential broom also. One which held sway with those of the high echelon. One which had had Hovis 'Temporarily Relocated'. And who now occupied his former office in a manner that seemed anything but temporary.

'Lytton.' Inspectre Hovis uttered the name as the profanity it was and, turning momentarily from the prefabricated door of the Portakabin, he raised a defiant fist towards the distant window of his erstwhile domain. 'I'll be back,' said he.

He didn't see the flutter of the venetian blinds, nor the satisfied smile on the face of Brian 'Bulwer' Lytton as he fluttered them. Which was probably all for the best really.

The temporarily relocated detective pressed open the prefabricated door and entered the disagreeable confines of his new abode. They were crowded. Very crowded.

Elderly filing cabinets flanked the cabin, standing where the removal men had left them. Their drawered faces to the walls, as if in disgrace. Files, once impeccably indexed, were now piled in unmarked boxes, cartons and crates, along with the inspectre's personal effects. His pictures, commonplace books, fencing trophies, awards for bravery, bits and bobs and fixtures and fittings.

But where was his desk? Where his precious Louis XV ormolu-mounted, kingswood and parquetry kneehole desk? With its painted leather-lined top and its channelled border? With its kneehole flanked by drawers with rococo handles and ram's mask escutcheons? The desk presented to him by the royal house of Windsor, in gratitude for his sensitive handling of a tricky little matter concerning an heir to the throne, a homeopathist called Chunky and a Dormobile named Desire. Where that?

Still in his old office, that was where! Too large to get into the Portakabin and now commandeered by Chief Inspector Brian bloody Lytton!

Hovis glowered about his temporary accommodation, regarding it with a face of foul contempt. Taking in its each and every hideous detail, before releasing his pent-up fury in a silent primal scream.

This done, he straightened his regimental necktie, placed his cane by the door, removed his pince-nez, folded them into a sleek tortoiseshell case and slipped this into his top pocket. And then he smiled upon his second in command.

His second in command smiled back at him from her place behind the knackered trestle-table, which now served both she and Hovis as a desk. Her name was Polly. Polly Gotting. She was Anna Gotting's twin sister. And she was the inspectre's *new* second in command.

His old second in command, of ten years standing, reliable Ron Sturdy, had been temporarily relocated. And although Polly was quick on the uptake, willing, eager and helpful and possessed of an IQ far in excess of reliable Ron's, she just wasn't the same.

'Any joy?' Polly asked.

'Joy?' Hovis had almost forgotten the meaning of the word. 'Joy?'

'With Mulligan. Did he respond positively to questioning?'

'No.' Hovis negotiated his way between the boxes, cartons and crates. 'He remains adamant. A train emerged from nowhere and showered the street with diamonds. He just picked them up.'

'You'll have to let him go then.'

'I know.' Hovis sank on to a cardboard box. Something valuable within fractured with an alarming crack. The inspectre was deaf to the sound. 'Have you rechecked all the witnesses' statements?'

'The independent witnesses? Yes. There were a lot of reports. Some kind of weird train. Three people have come forward to say they saw a taxi-driver picking up what looked like diamonds after it passed by.'

'A curious business.' Inspectre Hovis rapped a brisk tattoo on the prefabricated floor with the heels of his hand-stitched brogues. 'Something happened last night. Something momentous. Half the force out in pursuit of a spikey Volkswagen. A ward full of chase casualties. A train from nowhere and a cache of diamonds. Did you check on the diamonds? Was I right?'

'You were right.' Polly passed papers. The inspectre inspected them. 'Amazingly they were still on record.'

'I knew it.' Hovis scanned the papers, nodding all the while.

'But how did you know? How could you possibly recognize the cut of diamonds stolen before you were even born?'

'The great unsolveds.' Hovis returned the papers, then tapped the portside of his skull. 'All in here. They are the staff of life to me. There is crime and there is classic crime. I have it within me to solve the Crime of the Century. It is my destiny. I know it and I will fulfil it. When I saw Mulligan's diamonds my heart rose. I recognized them immediately to be part of the lost Godolphin hoard. If those diamonds had not been stolen in 1914, it is probable that the First World War might never have taken place.'

'Really?' Polly shook her head. 'I always thought that the war was precipitated by the assassination of Austria's crown prince, Archduke Franz Ferdinand, heir apparent to Emperor Franz Josef I, at Sarajevo on 28 June 1914.'

'Did you indeed?' Hovis examined his fingernails.

They were immaculate. As ever. 'Then let me tell you this, history is rarely written up by those who actually make it.'

'Oh I do so agree. As Gibbon remarked in *Decline and Fall*, Chapter Three, *History is indeed little more than a register of the crimes, follies and misfortunes of mankind.*'

'Quite so,' said Inspectre Hovis.

'And wasn't it Napoleon who wrote, *What is history but a fable agreed upon?*'

'I believe it was,' said Inspectre Hovis.

'And Sir Robert Walpole. *All history is a lie*, he said.'

'Polly,' said Inspectre Hovis.

'Yes, sir?'

'Put the kettle on.'

Polly smiled once more at Inspectre Hovis. First up against the wall, come the revolution, she thought.

3

O Lucifer, Son of the Morning
And Lord of the Bottomless Pit,
Roll back your celestial awning
Thy thurible is lit.

Hail thee that riseth in the east
Behold the sacrificial feast.
                    Amen.

'Amen to that,' agreed Tuppe, tucking a napkin into his shirt neck and rubbing his knife and fork together.

'Does your adoptive daddy usually dedicate his dinner to the devil?' Anna whispered into the ear of Cornelius Murphy.

'Oh no.' The tall boy gave his bandaged head a careful shake. 'I suspect he's just buttering up the Prince of Darkness in the hope of a favour.'

'Damned right!' Murphy Senior was seated at the head of the Murphy kitchen table. His lady wife at the foot. Tuppe, Cornelius and the lovely Anna ranged variously between. 'It is my intention to summon forth all manner of banshee, bugaboo and bogybeast. To raise divers demons, dibbuks, ghouls and gorgons. To conjure pigwidgeons and

43

pandemoniacs from those regions which are forever night. And things of that nature, generally.'

'To any specific end, Mr Murphy?' Tuppe enquired.

'Indeed yes.' The master of the house raised up his great chest and glared at the ceiling. 'To unleash a great and terrible pestilence upon the head of Arthur Kobold. Bad cess be unto him.'

'Amen to that also,' said Tuppe.

'Shall I be mother then?' Mrs Murphy rose, brandishing an electric carver. 'If I'd known the daddy was planning to invoke His Satanic Majesty tonight I'd have got a goat in, rather than this goose. Leg, anyone?'

'Excuse me, Mrs M,' Tuppe cast a wary eye over the hapless fowl which graced the greater part of the dining table, 'but am I right in thinking that this goose is somewhat over-represented in the lower-limb division?'

'You've a lovely way with words, young Tuppe.' Mrs Murphy leaned over and gave the small fellow an affectionate chucky-cheek, nearly putting his eye out with the carving knife. 'I wonder what they mean.'

'He's asking why the goose has so many legs,' her husband informed her. 'Bred that way, would be my guess. A chap I once knew used to breed chickens with four legs, so all his family could have one. I said to him, "What do they taste like?" And he said, "I don't know, I've never managed to catch one yet."'

Anna laughed politely.

Mrs Murphy hacked at the avian multi-ped, raising a fine cloud of feathers. 'I knew I should have plucked this before I cooked it. But I was afraid to open the oven door, in case it got loose again.'

'You cooked it alive?' Anna was horrified.

'Of course not, dear. I had the gas on for half an hour first.'

'Ah,' said Cornelius. 'That would explain the smoke-blackening on the walls and ceiling.'

'The firemen were very nice.' Mrs Murphy passed legs around. 'They said the house should be condemned. Your father ran them off with a mattock.'

Tuppe examined the leg on his plate. 'About the goose.'

'It wandered into the back garden this morning. Well, trucked in really. I think it must have escaped from Polgar's Pet Shop last night.'

Tuppe pushed his plate aside. A recent near-fatal encounter with a furry fish was still fresh in his memory. 'Did I tell you I've become a vegan?' he asked.

'Oh,' went Mrs Murphy. 'I didn't know you could *become* a vegan. I thought you had to be born there.'

'That's a Venusian,' said her husband.

'As in Venusian blind?'

'I expect so.' Jack Murphy shrugged.

'Well, that's very nice, Tuppe. I'm glad you've got yourself a proper job. Do you commute between the planets, or are you in the office?'

'In the office,' said Tuppe. 'By the radiator.'

'That's nice. More goose, did you say?'

'No thanks, but I'll have some of those sprouts, please.'

'Help yourself. You'll have to use your fingers, I'm afraid. My friend Mrs Cohen is having her son circumcised, so I've lent her my serving spoons.'

'For the do afterwards,' Jack Murphy explained to the open-mouthed Tuppe.

'It's very kind of you to invite Tuppe and me to share your dinner,' said Anna, raising her hand against another helping of goose. 'I'll just stick to the broccoli, if you don't mind. I'm on a diet.'

'I was on a diet once.' Mrs Murphy loaded up her husband's plate. 'You had to eat nothing but soft furnishings. It was called the G Plan, I think.'

Cornelius forked up some spinach. 'Your cheque bounced also then?' he asked the daddy.

Murphy Senior nodded gloomily and speared an asparagus tip with his fork. 'It's not the principle of the thing that troubles me, it's the money! I was actually planning to pay Mike the mechanic for the car I gave you.'

'The Cadillac Eldorado.' Cornelius chased peas around his plate. 'About that . . .'

'It got dumped on,' said Tuppe. 'From a great height. Would someone pass the *petits pois*, please?'

'*Dumped on?*' Jack Murphy fell back in dismay. 'You lost the Cadillac?'

'In as many words, yes.' Cornelius nodded sadly.

'Kobold?'

'In as few words, yes again.'

'That does it! Roll back the lino, Mother, we're raising Behemoth tonight.'

'Not until everyone's finished eating, dear. Have some more courgettes, Anna. Try the yellow ones. I know they look like Chinamen's willies, but they taste delicious.'

'Thanks,' said Anna. 'These aubergines are excellent, by the way.'

'The beautiful Cadillac.' Jack Murphy sighed. 'Arthur Kobold must pay for his transgressions.'

'He will.' Cornelius munched upon a parsnip. 'He can run, but he can't hide.'

'Can't he?' The daddy helped himself to more cauliflower.

'He cannot.' Cornelius forked up some greens. 'I have the plans for the reinvented ocarina. I intend to free Rune and bring Kobold and his cronies to justice.'

'And grab the booty,' Tuppe put in. 'Pass the pimentos.'

'Good lads.' Murphy Senior gave his adopted son a hearty shoulder-pat. 'This news cheers me up no end. Now, if there is anything I can do to help, don't hesitate to ask.'

'Is that anything, as in *anything*?' Cornelius didn't hesitate to ask.

'Anything.'

'Then I need an ice-cream van please. And I need it by midnight.'

The daddy's eyelids didn't even flicker. 'Naturally,' said he, finishing up the last of his green peppers. 'I shall see to it that you have one. More carrots?'

'No thanks, I'm fine on carrots.' Cornelius smiled broadly. 'But you might pass the *crambe repitita*.'

'About the ice-cream van?' Anna asked. She, Cornelius and Tuppe were now ensconced in the daddy's
garden shed. The meal had reached a successful
conclusion, with three puddings, a cheese tray, brandy
and Turkish cigarettes. Unaware that her husband's
cheque was going to bounce, Mrs Murphy had cast
aside her normal ecological convictions and spent
lavishly at Safeway. 'I don't think I could manage any
ice-cream. I'm full.'

'It's the van I want. Not the ice-cream,' Cornelius
told her. 'The van has a public-address system on the
top. For playing music. And if we pull out all the
interior fixtures and fittings, then there'll be plenty of
room.'

'For what?'

'For the booty.' Tuppe rubbed his tiny hands
together. 'We've got Rune's A-Z, with all the
entrances to the Forbidden Zones marked in it. We
drive up in the van. Play the magic music through
the speaker system. A portal opens. We roar in, grab
whatever we can, then make our getaway. A sort of
inter-dimensional ram raid.'

'Mrs Murphy was right, Tuppe. You *do* have a
lovely way with words.' Anna turned to Cornelius.
'She's an interesting woman, your mum. Did she
really play bass for Jeff Beck on "Hi Ho Silver
Lining"?'

'She told you that?' Cornelius had the ocarina in
the vice on the daddy's workbench and was worrying
at it with the electric drill. The drill still lacked a plug,
but as there were no power sockets in the shed, this

didn't create too much of a problem (eh?).

'She also said she was the fourth Beverly Sister.'

'She told me she was one of the Five Tops.' Tuppe rooted about amongst the interesting things beneath the workbench. 'Why is there always a half-empty bag of solid cement in every shed?' he enquired.

'It's a tradition,' Cornelius told him, 'or an old charter, or something.' He undid the vice, took up the ocarina and blew drill dust from it. 'All done, I think.'

Anna leaned over to take a look. 'And you really truly believe that when you play this thing these secret portals will open?'

Cornelius checked his handiwork against the route map. 'They'll open.'

'They will,' Tuppe agreed. 'Trust Cornelius, he knows what he's doing.'

'Thank you, Tuppe.'

'Don't mention it, Cornelius. But harken, harken. What is that I hear?' Tuppe cupped a diminutive palm to an ear of a likewise confection.

'It's "I'm Forever Blowing Bubbles".'

And indeed it was. It issued from the speaker system of a smart new ice-cream van. A smart new ice-cream van which was even now drawing up outside twenty-three Moby Dick Terrace. Home of the family Murphy. And stepping down from the cab was none other than the father of the house.

'Fortune's always hiding,' he sang.

And he smiled as he sang it.

* * *

49

The taxi went west towards approaching midnight. The unmarked police car followed it at a respectable distance. The taxi took the slip-road from the fly-over and cruised down to the Chiswick Roundabout. The unmarked police car followed it. The taxi turned left on to the Kew Road, went through green lights at Kew Bridge and rolled on towards Brentford.

And the unmarked police car followed it.

The taxi-driver, one Terence Arthur Mulligan, checked his driving mirror. Same unmarked police car. Same upper-class git at the wheel. Was this police harassment? No, not yet. The unspeakable inspectre was probably just checking to make sure he'd given the correct home address. Well, he wouldn't be disappointed. Terence was homeward bound.

Because, after all, he hadn't committed any crime, had he? OK, he had a bit of previous. OK, he had a *lot* of previous. But he was innocent of all charges here. He'd just been in the wrong place at the wrong time. Seen a weird train, picked up some diamonds. Got nicked. He'd told all this to Hovis and Hovis had released him. So now he was going to go home and get his head down.

And get his socks off, of course. Because his feet were fair giving him gip. What with all those diamonds he'd stuffed into his socks, once his pockets were full. Terence was genuinely grateful that the boys in blue had failed to search his socks.

Terence indicated correctly and turned into the back doubles of Brentford, careful not to lose his follower. He didn't want any trouble. He was a free

50

man. The way he saw it, he had told the police the truth. He just hadn't told them all of the truth.

For instance, he hadn't told them that he had actually been in the *right* place at the *right* time. Nor that he had actually been acting under orders to clear up all traces, after the Train of Trismegistus passed through on its dreadful mission. Nor, that he, Terence Arthur Mulligan, was actually a member of BOLLOCKS, the Black Order. London's Legion Of Cab Knights. A top-secret organization, sworn to serve the hidden masters of the Forbidden Zones. Nor that it was now his duty to return those diamonds currently in his possession, and those in the hands of Inspectre Hovis, to these very hidden masters.

Actually, the more Terence thought about it, he hadn't told the police the truth at all. But then there are some things you tell to policemen, and some you don't.

Terence turned into Moby Dick Terrace and was nearly driven right off the road by an approaching ice-cream van.

'Bloody Hell!' Terence swerved aside and bumped on to the pavement. He slammed on the brakes and drew to a halt right outside his own front door. Number twenty-seven.

'You bastard, Bruv!' Terence gripped the steering wheel and uttered a number of profanities. All ended with a reference to a certain 'Bruv'.

There was good reason for this, as it happened. Because the smart new ice-cream van, the smart new *stolen* ice-cream van, which was now vanishing into the night, belonged to none other than Terence's brother. One Reginald Bohemian Rhapsody Mulligan.

Coincidence? Synchronicity? The chromium-plated megaphone of destiny? Who knows? And frankly, who cares? Just as long as it meant that something really exciting was about to occur.

And it was. Oh yes indeed, it really truly was.

4

Hi Ho Silver Lining and away they went.

Mulligan's Ices hit the open road. Cornelius was at the wheel. Anna and Tuppe were gutting the van and chucking all the bits and bobs out through the serving window.

Now, it could well be argued that this might better have been done back at the Murphy residence. Possibly so, but it wouldn't have been nearly so much fun. Nor would it have offered the opportunity for that extra bit of plot-complication which makes it all worthwhile.

A tray of cornets arced through the serving window, caught upon the mild night breeze, danced prettily along the open road and finally came to rest on the bonnet of a parked police car.

This was a 'marked' police car. All state-of-the-art technology: the big number on the top for helicopter recognition during 'riot situations'; the regulation police-issue revolver, that they always swear blind they never carry, in its usual clip beneath the glovey; the speed trap monitor thingy; and an unholy host of computer-assisted in-car crime-busting paraphernalia. The whole bit. And in this sat two police officers. One was young and lean and pale and pimply. He munched a Big Mac, between sucks on a strawberry milkshake. The other was solid and stocky, military-moustached and in the middle of his years. He tugged ruefully upon a corned beef sandwich and sipped from a flask of Earl Grey tea.

Now, it could well be argued that the introduction, so soon, of yet another police car, be it marked or unmarked, was pushing credibility just a tad. Possibly so, but then if that's pushing credibility, just wait until you cop the identity of the rueful tugger.

'Did you see that, Sarge?' asked the pale and pimply police constable, Ken Loathsome.

'I did, son,' replied reliable Ron Sturdy (for it was none other). 'Radio-in our position and we shall give chase forthwith.'

The unmarked police car now lurked on the corner of Moby Dick Terrace. The lights were out and the driver's window down. At the wheel and all alone, Inspectre Hovis stewed in a black fug and a green tweed suit. The dreadful aspect of his shadowed stare was a real brass bed-wetter and no matter how you viewed him, the Inspectre was not a happy Hovis.

Oblivious to alliteration, the dour detective delved a discreet digit delicately down and drew a diamond-decked dandy case from the pocket of his waistcoat. Flipping this open with a practised thumb, he teased out a hand-rolled cigarette, tucked it between his lips and prepared himself to be oblivious to pseudo-Shakespearianisms also.

For lo, within that darkling car a match did flame and swiftly fled sleek plumes of smoke as wraiths toward the star-strewn canopy of night.

Oblivious also to the ever-present possibility of ruination to his career, Inspectre Hovis drew deeply on his tailor-made. Savouring his favoured blend, Virginia Plain, cut with ambergris, dried persimmon, flaked peyote button and Egyptian hashish. An acquired taste, but a really decent blow, once you had the measure of its mellow fruitfulness.

And Inspectre Hovis had. He was something of a connoisseur when it came to the use of restricted substances. Holding strongly to the conviction that, when the going gets tough, the tough should get stoned out of their boxes. And, at the present, the going did seem to be getting irksomely tough.

Relocated to Portakabin purgatory. Bereft of reliable Ron. Banged up with a seventeen-year-old pragmatist and now this. Here. This here. Hovis glared out at the night. Here. Here of all places. Back here in bloody Brentford!

With the entire Metropolitan district and most of the known world to choose from, with crime rampant up every street and down every alleyway of every town and every city, with criminals hailing from the far-flung corners of God's good earth, why did he always end up here? Here in bloody Brentford?

Of course Hovis could find no specific fault with the borough. Who could? The cradle of civilization. Hub of the known universe. 'When a man is tired of Brentford, he is tired of life,' as Samuel Johnson *actually* wrote. No, you couldn't knock the place. Not really.

But be all that as it may, and very well it may be, Inspectre Hovis was sick of the sight of it.

He had always imagined that his career as an Inspector of Scotland Yard would be set against a backdrop of sailing yachts, swank casinos and country houses. Rubbing his immaculately clad shoulders with the tit-and-tiara set, bedding svelte heiresses and blasting the fur and feathered with his matched Purdys on the moorlands of the gentry, whilst solving The Crime of the Century.

Not numbing his bum in a clapped out Morris Minor on the corner of a Brentford backstreet! Not at all!

It was so damnably unfair. Why couldn't life imitate art just once in a while? He wasn't asking for much. Certainly for nothing more than he rightly deserved. All he wanted was the opportunity to solve The Crime of the Century. With the other perks thrown in, of course.

He could see it all in his mind's eye. The accolades. The press interviews. His eight favourites on *Desert Island Discs*. The call to the palace. The light tap on the shoulder. The 'arise Sir Sherringford Hovis'. It was his birthright.

Hovis sighed dismally. Of course, to solve The Crime of the Century, that crime had to be committed first. And the chances of it being committed in Brentford were somewhat less than likely. Following Mulligan home had been a waste of time. Curious though the recovery of the Godolphin diamonds had been, their theft was eighty-year-old news. Were they part of something? That ever elusive big one? Hovis shrugged. Probably not. He'd give it another fifteen minutes on the off chance, then head off home to bed.

Inspectre Hovis offered up another 'heartfelt', finished his smoke and flicked the butt end into the street. 'To paraphrase the dying words of the late lamented King,' said he, 'bugger Brentford.'

'This is car twenty-three,' called Police Constable Ken Loathsome. 'Am in pursuit of suspect vehicle travelling east on Great West. Target is a good–humor truck.'

'A what?' asked reliable Ron.

'An ice-cream van.' Constable Ken chewed upon his bottom lip. 'Licence plate—'

'Registration number,' growled reliable Ron.

'Registration number.' Ken cupped his hand over the microphone. 'What is the registration number, Sarge?'

'I don't know, son. We'll have to get a little closer and have a look see, won't we?' Sergeant Sturdy viewed his youthful associate from the corner of a world-weary eye. The boy was a buffoon. A bottom-feeder in the great gene pool. Hand-reared on American cop shows and donuts that go dunk in your decaffeinated. Not his cup of tea at all.

'I'll get right back to you.' Constable Ken signed off with the inevitable 10.4. 'Shall I make with the si–reen, Sarge?'

'If you must.'

'Excellent!'

'There's a police car following us,' cried Anna.

Cornelius glanced into the driving mirror. 'We'd better try and lose that then.' He put his foot hard down, as one does, and the ice-cream van shot forwards.

Anna and Tuppe shot backwards. They gathered in a struggling heap at the rear of the van, much to the joy of the small fellow. 'Nice acceleration,' he remarked.

And indeed it was. Surprisingly so for an ice-cream van. Or perhaps not, considering the Mulligans. Rotten apples to the core, the whole family of them.

'They're trailing. Which way should we go, Tuppe? Tuppe?'

The sound of a slim female hand striking a small male cheek was quite discernible, even above the roar of the van's engine.

'Ouch!' Tuppe disentangled himself from Anna and crawled forward. Cornelius leaned around and scooped him on to the passenger seat.

'My thanks.' Tuppe rubbed his cheek and grinned foolishly.

'Which way?' Cornelius passed him Rune's A–Z.

Tuppe leafed carefully through it. 'I think we should go out a bit. Not start too close to home.'

'Agreed,' agreed Cornelius. 'Where then?'

'There's one marked in Hammersmith. Indicate left and when we go round the next bend, take a sharp right.'

Cornelius did so.

Terence Arthur Mulligan had emptied out his socks and now he crept barefoot up the stairs to the darkness of his bedroom. His wife Valentina was snoring soundly, but it wasn't the usual fear of waking the nymphomaniac twenty-three-stone ex-women's shot-put champion of Romania that kept him from switching on the light. Terence tiptoed over to the window and peeped between the curtains. He was still there. The unspeakable Inspectre. Parked on the corner.

Terence smiled and rubbed his hands together. 'You'll get yours, copper,' he whispered.

The fully marked police car screeched to a halt.

'Shit!' cried Constable Ken. 'We've lost the motherf—'

'I am well aware of that, son. And kindly keep the language down.'

'Sorry, Sarge. So what should I do? Call for backup? Get a chopper in here?'

'I would suggest you put the car into reverse. Chummy indicated left before we lost him on the bend, did he not?'

'He did, Sarge.'

'Then reverse up and turn right.'

'Eh, Sarge?'

'Just do it, son.'

'Is this it?' Cornelius asked.

'This is it.' Tuppe studied the A–Z. 'Down at the end of this cul-de-sac.'

Anna leaned between them. 'That can't be right. There's just an overgrown old wall down there. And you can see lights from a road shining on the other side.'

'X marks the spot,' said Tuppe.

59

'So what is your plan?'

'Same plan as before.' Cornelius took the A–Z from Tuppe and slipped it back into his pocket. 'We drive down to the end here, play the ocarina through the van's speaker system, then, when the portal opens, we storm in, grab whatever booty we can grab. And then we drive like the clappers.'

'And that's the plan.'

'That's it.'

'Sad.' Anna shook her head. 'That is a very sad plan.'

'You liked it well enough when Tuppe told you it back in the daddy's shed.'

'Well I don't like it any more.'

'Well I do,' said Tuppe. 'I think it's a damn fine plan. And if it's good enough for Cornelius it's good enough for me.'

'Thank you, Tuppe.'

'Don't mention it, my friend.'

'It sucks,' said Anna. 'And would you like me to tell you why it sucks?'

Cornelius looked at Tuppe.

And Tuppe looked at Cornelius.

'No,' they both said.

Terence Arthur Mulligan crept back down the stairs and entered his kitchenette. It was a glum kitchenette. Glum and gloomy. And dank also. And malodorous. *Penicillium* flourished in its sink-tidy and a grey primordial soup bubbled in the crisper of its fridge. The only thing that kitchenette had going for it was the twenty-three thousand pounds' worth of

60

diamonds laid out on its table. Which was something.

Terence quietly closed the door, tugged a cheerless chair from beneath the table and, having first carefully examined it for errant lifeforms, seated himself there upon. Then he opened the table drawer and took out a toy telephone. Clearing diamonds aside, he placed it on the tabletop, lifted the foolish plastic receiver and put it to his ear. And a chill ran through his bones as he did so.

The toy telephone, as he knew full well, was hollow and disconnected, and could not, by any stretch of the imagination, be actually expected to work. But work it did. Every time.

Terence shuddered as he heard the dialling tone and his finger trembled, not a little, as he dialled the three digits on the silly little dial. Somewhere another phone began to ring.

'Hello,' snapped a voice which had the cabby's bowels a-loosening.

'H . . . hello,' replied Terence.

'Ah, Mulligan,' went the voice. 'And what do you have to say for yourself?'

'I done my best, right? But I got nicked. It wasn't my fault.'

'I see. And what of the diamonds?'

Terence gazed down at those before him. It would be just the work of a moment to say 'the police have them *all*'.

'The . . .'

'Yes, Mulligan?'

'The police . . .'

'Spit it out, man.'

61

'The police have got . . .'

'Got?'

'Got some of them. They tried to beat the truth out of me. But I stood up to them, right? I managed to nick some diamonds back off 'em. I done my best.'

'And do the police intend to charge you with theft of the diamonds?'

'Nah, just with speeding.'

'We'll take care of that then.'

'You will?'

'Naturally. After all, you done your best, right?'

'Right,' said Terence. 'I did done my best.'

'Of course you did. Is there anything else you'd like to tell me?'

'Yeah,' said Terence, 'there is. The geezer who beat me up, followed me home. He's a right nutter. He's parked on the corner watching my gaff.'

'Well just you go off to bed like a good fellow. There's nothing more we wish you to do.'

Terence breathed a very large sigh of relief.

'For now,' said the voice of Mr Arthur Kobold.

5

It was a quiet, unassuming little cul-de-sac. Late-Victorian terraced dwellings, in the early Vernacular style. Angled stone bays and boxed sashes. Carved brick sunflowers set between storeys and the complex coloured glazing of the front doors which is emblematic of the Aesthetic Movement. Here and there a fretworked porch displayed elements of the Domestic Revival and the elaborate plasterwork on the gables and eaves, based on the traditional pargetting of East Anglia, combined with the Arts and Crafts rising-sun fanlight motifs, to give that refreshingly eclectic mixture, much typified in the work of the now legendary architect R. Norman Shaw.

The modern additions of stone cladding and satellite dishes buggered the whole effect to kingdom come.

The ice-cream van moved slowly down the cul-de-sac and stopped at the end, its headlights fixed on the overgrown brick wall, where X marked the spot. Cornelius switched off the engine, but not the lights. And took up the reinvented ocarina.

'Right,' said he, massaging the newly drilled holes with his long fingers. 'Let's have a crack.'

Anna shook her head doubtfully, but Tuppe

switched on the speaker and tapped the microphone. 'Testing,' said Tuppe. 'One two. One two.'

His words were broadcast over a surprisingly large number of streets. But then, it *was* so late, *and* so quiet, and everything.

One two. One two, they went. Echoing about the fish-scale slates and the Gothic Revival ridge tiles. Rattling the richly ornamented terracotta chimney pots, twanging the satellite dishes and screwing up the reception for late-night viewers of the Italian porn channel. *One two. One two*.

Tuppe gave Cornelius the thumbs up. 'Blow,' said he.

And Cornelius blew. He wasn't much of a musician. Anything of a musician in fact. So he gave it a bit of the old 'free form'.

'Holy God!' Folk leapt from their beds. 'What the bloody Hell was that?' they exclaimed, in voices of rightful indignation.

Cornelius, Anna and Tuppe peered out through the windscreen at the overgrown wall. Tuppe scratched at his little head.

Cornelius scratched his cap.

'It didn't work.' Tuppe looked up at his friend. 'Blow it again.'

Again. Again. Again. In a quarter-mile radius lights were flicking on and dogs beginning to howl.

Cornelius gave the ocarina another big big blow.

And portals opened aplenty. Portals of the front door persuasion. And folk issued into the streets. They wore dressing-gowns and pyjamas. Some carried sticks. All were shouting.

Beyond the overgrown wall, in a quietly patrolling police car, Sergeant Sturdy said, 'Follow that noise!'

Inspectre Hovis perused the luminous dial of his half-hunter. Enough was enough. All the lights were now out in number twenty-seven Moby Dick Terrace. Mulligan must surely have turned in for the night. There was nothing to be gained by sitting about here any longer. It was just a dead end.

'Verily verily, thus and so.' The downcast detective wound up his window, gathered his wits and girded his loins.

And then he drove away, in a red rankle and a grey Morris Minor.

As the streets were so quiet and so clear of traffic, he didn't bother to check his rear-view mirror. Not that he would have seen much if he had. The car that slid silently after him wasn't showing any lights. And it was a very small car. No more than about one foot in length. But it didn't have any trouble keeping up. No trouble at all.

Mulligan's Ices stood with its headlights out and its microphone switched to the 'off' position. Its three occupants were crouched on the floor. They had their hands clamped over their ears.

Because it had grown somewhat noisy of late. What with all the yelling and the shouting and the pandemonium of fists beating on the sides of the van, and everything. It was quite evident that the good burghers of Hammersmith did not take too kindly to being roused from their beds by late-night serenades on the reinvented ocarina.

Those of the cul-de-sac had soon spied out the source of their disturbance and were now venting their collective spleen upon it.

As his forehead bumped up and down on the floor, Cornelius Murphy felt that perhaps he had been just a trifle hasty in dismissing Anna's objection to his plan, without hearing it first. The spleen-venters were just beginning a concerted rocking of the van, with a view to overturning it, when the police car arrived on the scene.

Inspectre Hovis lived in reduced circumstances in a large Georgian house on Kew Green. So reduced had these circumstances become over the years that the great detective had found himself having to let out room after room of the ancestral home, in order to support its upkeep. And he now occupied but a single garret room, whose only window, as cruel fate would have it, looked out across the Thames to Brentford.

Hovis finally found a parking space, three streets from home, and climbed wearily from the Morris Minor. He left the car keys adangling in the dash. One thing he definitely meant to do, first thing in the morning, was to demand the return of his temporarily relocated police-issue Daimler.

The Inspectre turned up his tweedy collar to the cold of the night, gripped the pommel of his cane and struck out for home. He didn't notice the tiny car, parked just across the street. Nor did he see the curious transformation which it now underwent. The

tiny car bulged, distorted and grew into a great
manlike shape. The effect was not at all unlike those
created by the now legendary *Industrial Light and Magic*
for *Terminator 2*. But, as those in the know, know,
ILM create their effects mainly by using Soft Image
and Parallax Matador software, running on Silicon
Graphics Iris 4D workstations. Digital matting and
the parallel processing of live action and computer-
generated elements, by scanning everything into
large-scale framestores. This wasn't anything like that.
This was much better.

But, as the Inspectre wasn't looking in that direction, he missed it.

' 'Ello 'ello 'ello. What's all this then?' Police Sergeant
Sturdy stroked his military moustachios as he spoke
the traditional greeting and approached the mêlée.
Constable Ken sat fidgeting in the car. He was acting
under direct orders from his superior officer. 'Shut
up. Stay put. Do not radio for assistance and keep
your sticky fingers off the shooter.'

'All right, all right,' continued Ron, as he elbowed
his way into chaos. 'Unhand that ice-cream van, or
I'll run the lot of you in.'

Suddenly aware that there was a police presence
in their midst, the pyjama'd protesters ceased their
rancour and began to shuffle uncomfortably in their
carpet slippers.

'Right,' said Ron, 'now, who is the ringleader of
this riotous assembly?'

'Do what?' A lady in a straw hat and a gingham
housecoat stepped forward to confront the policeman.

'Who is responsible for this unlawful gathering?'

'I don't know what you're talking about,' said the lady in the straw hat. 'We were just queuing up for ice-creams.'

'Really?' Ron tucked his thumbs into his waistcoat pockets and rocked back on his heels in a manner much favoured by PC Dixon of Dock Green. 'Queuing for ice-creams.'

'That's right,' agreed the lady's neighbours, bobbing their heads up and down.

'A drink on a stick please,' said someone.

'Two choc ices and a King Cone,' said another.

'All right,' said Ron. 'Don't wind me up. I'm sure none of you solid citizens really want to be dragged away to the cells in your jim-jams. Away to your homes now and we'll say no more about it.'

And that was about all he needed to say. The crowd melted and was gone. Front doors closing without a single slam.

Sergeant Sturdy returned to the police car. 'There,' he told the youthful pimply one. 'That is what we call doing it the old-fashioned way. Now. Get out the shooter and we'll have a word with the driver of the ice-cream van.'

It was big and bad and ghastly green all over.

And well-muscled every inch from head to toe.

And it curled its evil lip.

And its tail began to whip.

You could tell it wasn't very nice to know.

But you couldn't tell exactly *what* it was. Not without the handbook. And the handbook was kept under lock and key. In a filing cabinet, in one of the Forbidden Zones.

And whatever it was, it was now coming after Inspectre Hovis.

The great detective felt it coming before he turned and saw it. Not that he was the seventh son of a seventh son, or anything like that. He was the only son of a belted earl. But he knew bad poetry all right. Oblivious to alliteration and pseudo-Shakespearianisms he might be, but not to unwarranted dollops of duff verse, bunged in out of the blue and creeping up behind him.

Hovis faced the thing as it approached him. It was grinning from ear to ear, exposing a double rank of lime-green teeth.

'Have a care,' counselled the detective, gripping his cane between both hands.

'Hands above your head and come out quietly,' called Sergeant Sturdy. 'Hold the gun up straight now, Constable.'

'Gun?' Cornelius groaned.

'We're in trouble now,' whispered Tuppe.

'Sad,' said Anna. 'Very sad.'

'Shall I put a couple of rounds through the side to shift some ass?' asked Constable Ken.

'No need to be hasty, lad.'

Cornelius rose to face his fate. Anna pulled him back. 'Let me handle this.'

'Certainly not. This is my responsibility. I got you into this mess, after all.'

'And I shall get us out, trust me.'

Cornelius looked at Tuppe.

And Tuppe looked at Cornelius.

'Trust her,' they both said.

Anna stood up. Straightened her hair and smiled from the serving window. 'Sorry about the delay,' she said. 'Who wanted the King Cone?'

'What do you want?' Inspectre Hovis stood his ground, as the joyless green giant moved closer, its reflected image swelling in the detective's mirrored pince-nez.

The creature stopped, but yards away. Still grinning, it shone like a sprout by the light of the moon.

'What order of being art thou?' enquired the Inspectre, who numbered necromancy and conjuration amongst his many interests.

The creature ran a forked tongue, green it was, about lips of a likewise hue. 'Of the order of Trismegistus,' it replied in a deep dark rumbling tone.

'Then have a care, odious one. My cane is thrice blessed.'

'Thrice what?'

'Thrice blessed. By the word of the Tetragrammaton. By the twenty-third Aethyr of the Enochian call. And by the Hindoo Howdo Hoodoo Voodoo Man of George Formby.'

The creature cocked its head on one side. 'You cannot be serious,' it said.

'Try me.' Hovis stepped back and traced a pentagram in the air with the tip of his cane.

'Get out of here. George Formby?'

'A great wizard.' Hovis made mystical passes

70

with his cane, to and fro, and mimed the playing of a ukulele. 'The Lancashire Thaumaturge. Be
warned.'

'You're pulling my plonker.' The creature took a
step forward.

Hovis took another step back. 'What do you want?'
he asked once more.

'The diamonds.'

'Aha! The Godolphins. I have them here.' Hovis
patted a pocket. 'Take them if you will.'

'I will.' The beast stormed forward.

'You bloody well won't.' Inspectre Hovis twisted
the silver pommel of his cane and drew out a shining
blade.

'Come taste my steel,' said he.

Car twenty-three backed out of the cul-de-sac and
drove away.

'I don't believe that.' Cornelius climbed to his feet.
'I just do not believe you did that.'

'She sold them ice-cream,' said Tuppe.

'And I politely answered all their questions. And I
apologized for any inconvenience I might have caused
them. And I didn't charge them for the chocolate
flakes.'

'Huh,' went Tuppe.

'And what is "huh" supposed to mean?'

'It's not the way *we* would have done it.'

'And just how would *you* have done it?'

'Tell her, Cornelius.'

'Well . . .' said the tall boy. 'I . . .'

'He'd have leapt into the driving seat and swerved

71

around and sideswiped the police car and . . .' Tuppe made screeching noises.

'And probably got us all killed.'

'It would have been more exciting than selling them ice-creams,' Tuppe complained.

'Have you quite finished?' Anna asked.

'No,' said Tuppe.

'Yes,' said Cornelius. 'He's quite finished.'

'I have not.'

'You have.'

'Huh!' said Tuppe.

'Listen,' said Anna. 'You're going about this all the wrong way. You haven't planned ahead.' She sat down on the floor of the van. 'You have the ocarina. But you don't know which notes to play.'

'The new ones,' said Cornelius.

'But you don't know what order to play them in. You surely didn't think you could just belt out any random bunch of notes and expect one of these portals of yours to swing right open?'

'I did,' said Tuppe.

'*You* would,' said Anna.

'Hold on,' said Cornelius. 'What you are saying is that the new notes must be played in a precise sequence?'

'Like knowing the right combination to open a safe, yes.'

'It makes sense. It does make sense, doesn't it, Tuppe?'

'S'pose so.' Tuppe made a huffy face.

Cornelius took out the reinvented ocarina and handed it to Anna. 'Go on then,' he said.

'Yeah,' said Tuppe. 'Go on then.'

Anna examined the instrument. 'You are quite sure you drilled the holes in the right places?' she asked in a cool voice.

'Absolutely certain. I told you, the holes correspond to points on the map that Tuppe and I stopped at during our epic journey.'

'Then they would be your best bet.'

'What do you mean? We should go back to all the places?'

'No.' Anna shook her beautiful head. Her mother had told her that all men were basically stupid. She would one day pass this wisdom on to daughters of her own. 'Play the notes in the same order as you visited the places. That would be my plan.'

Cornelius adjusted his cap, opened his mouth to speak, but couldn't think of anything to say.

'You can remember the order?' Anna asked.

'Yes,' said Cornelius. 'I mean, no. But I have the map here.' He dragged the crumpled item from his pocket and spread it out on the dashboard.

'Then', Anna handed back the ocarina, 'why don't you have a little practice and when you feel confident, we'll give it a quick burst through the loudspeaker and see what happens.'

'And if nothing does?' Tuppe asked.

'If nothing does, it will mean one of two things. Either I'm wrong, or you are.'

'I'm not wrong,' said Cornelius Murphy.

'Then go for it.'

'OK, but we will do it this way: Tuppe will play the ocarina, I will sit at the wheel, with the engine

73

running, ready to make a swift getaway if needs be. And you will keep a look out. How does that sound?'

'Sounds good to me.' Tuppe scrambled up on to the dashboard and perused the map. Anna turned her back upon him and gazed out of the rear window. Cornelius passed the small man the ocarina.

'Right,' said Tuppe. 'I think I can get my fingers round it. Here we go.' He put the ocarina to his lips and he blew.

Now, there is music, and then there is music. But a tune is a tune is a tune. It can be 'The Birdy Song', or 'Big Eyed Beans from Venus'. Or even that brown thing that lies underneath the grand piano (Beethoven's last movement). But you can always get, as they say, a handle on it somewhere. There is always something you can recognize. Some note, or tone, or scale. No matter how discordant, or off the wall, you can always recognize *something*.

But not this time. Not with these notes. Now played in their correct order, they simply bore no resemblance whatsoever to any other notes yet known. They inhabited a realm of sound as yet uncharted by the human ear.

The effect they had upon the occupants of the stolen ice-cream van was, to say the least, varied.

Anna was enraptured. Her mouth fell open and her breath hovered in her lungs. Shivers ran up and down her spine and all around many other places besides. She suddenly felt as horny as hell.

Cornelius didn't. He felt anything but. The notes put his teeth on edge and had his bladder reaching critical mass.

74

And as for Tuppe.

'Help!' screamed the small one, as he swept from his perch on the dashboard, to become plastered against the roof of the van. Here he floundered around, dropping the ocarina and whatever tenuous hold he ever had on reality. 'Get me down! Get me down!'

Cornelius leapt immediately to his friend's aid. He clawed at Tuppe. Tried to prise him down. But the player of the reinvented ocarina was now stuck fast.

'Do something Cornelius,' he howled. 'I'm getting crunched here.'

'Anna, help us.'

Anna stood, gazing into space and wearing a foolish grin.

'Anna, help. Help Tuppe, come on.'

Anna blinked. 'That was wonderful. Do it again.' She turned and gaped up at Tuppe. 'Shiva's sheep!'

'Come on, hurry. I can't get him down.'

'Hurry,' gasped Tuppe.

'Magic,' gasped Anna.

'Come on. Help me.'

Anna sprang forward and began to tug the Tuppe. 'Magic.'

Tuppe was growing red in the face. 'I can't breathe. I can't breathe.'

'We'll get you down.' Cornelius wrestled with the small fellow's shoulders. Anna swung from his feet. But he wouldn't be shifted. Not one jot. One iota. Not one nothing. He was stuck, like Beethoven's last movement to a blanket.

And his eyes were starting to bulge from his face. And his face was starting to turn blue.

'Cornelius, he's dying. He's dying. Do something.'

Do something? Cornelius put his brain into gear.

Inspectre Hovis put his legs in gear. Although, surprisingly, nothing had been heard of him for the last twenty-three minutes, he'd been keeping himself busy.

Running mostly. There'd been quite a lot of running. But not very much in the way of heroic swordplay. Not any heroic swordplay at all, in fact. Which probably accounts for the singular lack of exciting intercuts in the narrative.

Or possibly a paragraph got left out somewhere. That sometimes happens.

But, whatever the case, he was back now. And he was somewhat up against it.

Inspectre Hovis jumped nimbly onto the bonnet of a parked Ford Fiesta, as a great deal of green muscularity caught him up.

'Are you going to give me a taste of that steel, or what?' asked the limey leviathan.

'Have at you then.' Hovis took up the classic fencer's position. Left elbow on the fence post, cup of tea in the right hand and fag hanging out of the mouth. And, 'I'm sorry, madam, but if the wind blew it down, that's no fault of mine. And if you want us to put it up again, we'll have to charge you full price again. And cash up front, or we don't lift a mallet.'

The creature looked at Hovis. 'Is that a misprint, or what?'

'Have at you then.' Hovis took up the classic fencer's *pose*. Knees slightly bent. Left arm back and crooked at the elbow. Left hand adangling. Sword-stick held firmly in the right hand, parallel to the ground and level with the tip of the nose.

Traditionally, fencers hold their foils in the left hand, to avoid possible injury to the right. Hovis didn't.

'Have at you.' A swish and a flash of steel. And the creature now longed for the return of his nose.

'Yours I believe.' Hovis proffered the severed conk, shish kebabed on the tip of his blade.

'*My dose!*' The creature snatched it back and refastened it to his face. You couldn't see the join. 'Now gimme those diamonds.'

'*En garde.*' Hovis skipped onto the roof of the Ford Fiesta, cleaving silvery arcs in the air.

'Your flies are undone,' said the creature.

'Pardon me.' Hovis hastened to adjust his dress.

A big green fist hit him right in the teeth.

And something hit Cornelius Murphy. Right in the brain.

'The ocarina.' He threw himself to the floor and scrabbled about in search of it.

'Forget the ocarina.' Anna clung to Tuppe. 'He can't breath any more.'

'But I ćan.' Cornelius snatched up the ocarina, put it to his lips and blew.

*   *   *

The great green thingy dragged Inspectre Hovis to the pavement and began to knock seven bells of Beethoven out of him.

And Cornelius Murphy played the reinvented ocarina.

6

A summer storm had risen from the south and the rain was starting to fall. It sang like frying bacon on the roof of the ice-cream van and laughed in the gutters, like a drain. It battered down upon the bandaged head of Cornelius Murphy, without grace or good humour. The tall boy stood, wringing his cap between his hands and staring down at the body of his dearest friend.

'Is he alive?'

Tuppe lay on his back like a broken doll. Anna was giving him mouth-to-mouth resuscitation. He wasn't moving. She looked up at Cornelius. Her face was white and streaked with tears. 'I don't know. I'll keep trying.'

She bent back over the supine one. Pinched his tiny nose and applied her lips to his.

Then she jumped back with a cry and struck Tuppe a mighty blow across the left cheek area. 'You little sod!'

'Ouch!' Tuppe rubbed his cheek. 'That smarts.'

'Tuppe, you're alive.' Cornelius flung his cap into the sodden sky and knelt to embrace the revenant.

'Alive and licking.' Anna spat. 'Your beastly friend just stuck his tongue down my throat.'

'I feel greatly reinvigorated.' Tuppe grinned

shamelessly. 'But I do appear to be getting somewhat wet.'

Inspectre Hovis was getting very wet indeed.

He was lying on his back in the middle of Kew Green, wearing nothing but his monogrammed underwear and his handmade socks.

Very wet indeed. That's what *he* was getting.

All about and around and around and about lay the shredded remains of his once immaculate suit. Torn to buggeration. The Godolphin diamonds were no longer on the person of the man from Scotland Yard.

Hovis awoke with a start. He gagged and spat. He gasped and swore. He tried to rise but fell back. He groaned. He groped at his head. He drew himself up a few inches and then collapsed again. But this time to the accompaniment of a great and terrible scream. It began life as a ghastly groan. But he'd already done one of those and there was nothing particularly distinguished in the repetition. But then this groan rose in pitch. Up through the octaves it went, taking them all in and passing them by. Finally to end as a shriek of such an ultrasonic persuasion that few were even the dogs of Kew, the king's included, that woke to its soul-splitting intensity.

And was this for the ruination of his suit? Oh no.

Then for the shame at the beating he'd taken? Not that.

Then, the loss of the Godolphin diamonds? Nope.

What then? What? What? What?

'Twas for the blade of his silver pommelled sword-stick. That's what. And specifically its present location. The blade rose Excaliburesque, its pommel proud to the sky, its tip buried into Mother Earth. But, 'twixt pommel and tip, the blade passed directly through the crotch of the Inspectre's underpants.

'OH MY GOD!' Hovis raised himself upon his elbows and stared in terror at the shining steel. He was pinned to the ground, pinned like a moth on a specimen board.

But how was he pinned?

Pinned by the privy member, that's how.

Another unholy wail escaped the dire detective's lips. Pinned by the pranger! Horror born of horror, born of nightmare, son of dread. And great grandaddy to the worst of all imaginings.

Hovis threw back his head and howled.

The wind also howled and the thunder roared. Inside the ice-cream van, Anna fumed, Cornelius schemed and Tuppe asked, 'How did you get me down off the ceiling?'

'You've Anna to thank for that.'

'He has?' Anna asked.

'Magic.' Cornelius straightened his now sodden cap and returned it to his head. 'The notes you played, Tuppe, to open the portals. They might open the portals, but whoever plays them is going to end up in orbit.'

'Nifty bit of defence.' Tuppe shifted his shoulders about. He ached plentifully. 'There's no under-estimating these fellows, is there? So what did you do?'

'I played the notes in reverse order. That voided

the spell and you floated down. Well, fell down. We nearly caught you.'

'Well thanks a lot. I really mean it. Where does that leave us now, by the way?'

'Sitting pretty.' Cornelius Murphy grinned for all he was worth. 'Because *I* now have a plan.'

Inspectre Hovis wasn't grinning. And he didn't have a plan. But he did cease the howling. He had no wish to be found in this condition by anyone, St John Ambulance, anyone.

He was going to have to get himself out of this.

Drenched to the skin, he lay and shivered. He was a dead man. He knew it. Cut off in his prime. Emasculated. It was the monastery for him. Saint Sacco Benedetto's.

Inspectre Hovis tried to marshal his thoughts. But marshalled they would not be. They ran riot. They roared about the many things he had never done and now would never do. They kept roaring around certain lady newsreaders, and porny video viewings with the lads from vice squad. And in his delirium they roared around lady newsreaders in porny videos and him in porny videos with lady newsreaders and him at home with a lady news-reader, watching himself onscreen in a porny video with . . .

And then.

And then.

Hovis jerked up his head and gaped in the direction of his loins.

There were now two swords Excalibur. One rising

82

from the outside of his pants. And a new one, rising to join it from within.

'O joy!' Hovis threw up his hands to the rain. The blade had missed him. His pranger was un-pranged. 'O joy. O bliss. For this deliverance, much thanks, O Lord.' The intact Inspectre cupped his hands in prayer. 'And now, where did that bastard go with those diamonds?'

At a little after one, the storm blew over and the stars returned to the night sky.

In the ice-cream van Cornelius asked, 'Are we all set?'

'I'm set,' said Tuppe.

'I'm not altogether set,' said Anna. 'Would you kindly run through this plan of yours, just one more time?'

'Certainly.' Cornelius sat at the driving wheel. 'Tuppe, as you can see, is now securely belted into the passenger seat. I will switch on the speaker system. Tuppe will play the magic notes. Throughout this musical interlude, you and I will have our fingers firmly plugged into our ears. When the portal opens, I switch off the speaker, Tuppe plays the notes in reverse order to void the spell on himself. If the portal is big enough, I back the van in. If not, we rush it on foot. Grab whatever looks worth grabbing then make our departure. That will be quite enough for one night.'

'I like it.' Tuppe nodded enthusiastically. 'I like it very much.'

Anna didn't like it. She shook her head.

83

'Would you prefer that I dropped you home before we start?'

'No way.' Anna folded her arms. 'I'm in this now, no matter what.'

'Good, then shall we do it?'

'Let's do it.' Tuppe raised a small thumb in large support.

'Right.' Cornelius keyed the van's ignition and brrrrm'd the engine. 'Ready, Tuppe?'

'Ten four.' The small fellow tightened his seat belt.

Cornelius switched on the speaker system. 'Then blow,' he whispered.

And Tuppe blew. The magical notes breathed out into the otherwise still night air, piercing the firmament. Severing that oh-so-slim and fragile little thread, which tethers us all to what we know as 'reality'.

Tuppe nodded to Cornelius. The tall boy took his fingers from his ears and switched off the speaker. Tuppe hastily replayed the notes in reverse order, ceased to strain at his seat belt and slumped down. 'Did it work?' he enquired.

Anna peered out through the rear window. 'Holy shit!' said she.

'That would be a yes, I think.' Cornelius scrambled back to join her. Tuppe did likewise.

Something was happening. And it was something awful strange. The ancient ivy-hung wall was vibrating. Rattling all about. There came a hissing and a grinding, as of steam being released and vast cog wheels engaging. And then a section of the

84

wall literally plunged into the ground. Dropping away to reveal the yawning maw of proverb. The gateway, or one of them at least, into a world beyond.

Three faces gazed into it from the rear window. They wore expressions of considerable awe.

The long high one on the left said, 'I think we've cracked it.'

The low and cherubic one on the right nodded in agreement.

And the very beautiful one in the middle said, 'Let's grab that booty.'

The hideous green muscular thingy stood on Kew Bridge. It was smoking one of Inspectre Hovis's handmade cigarettes and wearing his regimental necktie. It was looking pretty pleased with itself. And feeling somewhat euphoric, these were rather special cigarettes, after all. It grinned, farted and tossed the little bag of diamonds up and down on the palm of its left claw. Another job jobbed. And gone midnight, that was time and a half. It would put in for its expenses with Mr Kobold as soon as it got back. All that was wanting now was the black cab that was supposed to pick the big green thingy up. Where was that Mulligan?

Fast asleep in his bed, that's where Mulligan was. And down in his wretched kitchen, the little red plastic telephone stood on the table. The receiver was off the hook.

*   *   *

And now upon Kew Bridge stepped unshod feet. A dripping wreck of a man hefted his swordstick in a muddy mit.

'Right, you bastard,' whispered Inspectre Hovis. 'You bally bastard. Enjoy your smoke. A few more puffs and you're all mine.'

'In and out,' said the tall boy at the wheel. 'Let's go.'

'Let's go.' Anna and Tuppe clung to what they could as Cornelius put the van into reverse. The wheels span on the wet road and Mulligan's Ices slewed through the open portal.

From one world to another.

And then it came a-shuddering to a halt. And then three people looked out from it. Somewhat uncertain of what they should actually do next.

'Lordy Lordy Lordy,' whistled Tuppe.

'And then some.' Cornelius tried to take it in. It took a fair amount of taking. They were now parked inside a vast Victorian warehouse. It spread away, acres of it, towards towering walls and rising iron-work. The roof was lost in shadow. What light there was came from no identifiable source.

The warehouse was here. But it couldn't be. They all knew it couldn't. They had driven through a gap in a wall, which led, according to the A-Z, and all reason, surely to the road which lay on the other side. But it didn't.

'It's incredible,' said Cornelius.

'It's impossible,' said Tuppe.

'It's empty!' said Anna.

And it was.

'Let's go see.' Cornelius swung open the driver's door and climbed down from the van. He sniffed the air. It was dead. Dry. Nothing lived in this place. Nothing. The tall boy shuddered. There was something deeply unsettling about this huge and empty hall.

Tuppe shinned down and dropped to the floor. 'Cornelius.'

'Yes, Tuppe?'

'I don't think we're in Kansas any more.'

'That's very sad,' said Anna, following him down.

'Well I thought it was quite funny actually. I've been saving it up.'

'I liked it,' said Cornelius.

'Thank you, my friend.'

'Don't mention it.'

'So where is all the booty?' Anna asked. 'Don't get me wrong, this is very impressive. But other than for opening it up as a Rave Venue, it sucks.'

'Perhaps it's just an entrance,' Tuppe suggested.

Cornelius searched the horizons. 'I don't see any other doors.'

'Perhaps someone got here before us. Cleaned the place out.'

Cornelius shrugged. 'Let's take a look around. We might find something.'

'You take a look.' Anna folded her arms once more, in a manner which the epic duo were beginning to find mildly annoying.

'Please yourself.' Cornelius struck off across the

deserted floor. 'I'll see what I can . . . Oh shit!' He
began to hop around on his left leg, clinging to his
right knee.

'Is that supposed to be funny?' Anna asked. 'Because, if it is, it isn't.'

'I bumped into something.' Cornelius hopped to
and fro. 'Something . . . invisible.'

'Whoa,' went Tuppe. 'Invisible.'

'Don't take the piss. I did. I really did.' Cornelius
ceased his foolish hopping and kicked out, favouring
the left foot.

'I think he means it,' said Anna.

Tuppe chewed at his lip. 'Did you ever see
Predator?' he whispered.

'Yeah,' said Anna. 'Wasn't that the one where the
alien had this electronic camouflage that could bend
light? Make itself invisible?'

'That's the boy. And it ripped out people's spines
and took their skulls for trophies.'

A dull clang echoed about the walls of the warehouse.

'And Cornelius has just kicked it in the codpiece.'
Tuppe hid his face. 'Tell me when it's all over, I don't
want to watch.'

'Gotcha,' called Cornelius.

'Gotcha?' Tuppe asked.

'Over here, come on.'

Tuppe shrugged and hastened over to Cornelius.
Anna was there before him. 'What have you got?'

'Grazed knee.' Cornelius raised a trouser to display
the wounded appendage.

'You've got really skinny legs,' Anna told him.

'I've got really short legs,' said Tuppe. 'They only just reach the ground. What *have* you found, Cornelius?'

'There's something here. Something big.' Cornelius lowered his trouser leg and felt about before him. 'Here. Feel. Put your hands out.'

'I'm not keen, did you ever see—?'

'Come on. Feel it.'

Tuppe looked at Anna.

And Anna looked at Tuppe. They exchanged shrugs. Then they stretched out their hands. Then they both went, 'Ooh.'

'Something big,' said Cornelius.

'Covered by fabric,' said Anna.

'Canvas,' said Tuppe.

They traced their hands along, around and about it.

'It's quite long,' said Anna.

'But not too high,' said Cornelius. 'I can feel the top of it.'

'And I can see its wheels,' declared Tuppe.

'Its wheels?' Cornelius turned around in small circles. 'Where are you, Tuppe? You've vanished.'

'I'm here.'

'You're not.'

'I am. I'm underneath. It's a car. Covered by some kind of tarpaulin. You can see it from under here. Pull it off.'

Cornelius gripped a handful of invisible tarpaulin and began to tug. The thing came away, weightlessly.

The visual effect was quite stunning. Far better, in fact, than anything you could do with the old Soft Image and Parallax Matador software, even if run on Silicon Graphics Iris 4D workstations, digitally matched and scanned into a large scale framestore. Of course you really had to be there to fully appreciate it. In the full 3D and everything.

Anna's eyes widened as the mantle of invisibility fell away.

'It's . . . it's . . .'

'Beautiful,' said Cornelius Murphy. 'Beautiful.'

And it was. Cornelius had seen cars and he had seen cars. Many cars. His adoptive daddy had wangled it for him to test drive some of the very best. But he'd never seen anything quite like this. The car was evidently of pre-war design, but with many features that looked distinctly modern. And it was silver. All over. Silver. Not as in silver paint. But as in silver. Polished, burnished silver. It was long and broad-bodied, yet the lines were sleek and aerodynamic. Flared fenders that swept into the shell without visible join. High bumpers and trailing fins.

'What make of car is it?' Anna jigged from one foot to the other.

'I'm not sure.' Cornelius paced slowly about the marvellous automobile, peering in at the windows, lightly brushing the polished bodywork with his sensitive fingers, holding down his cap and shaking his head all the while.

Tuppe climbed to his feet and joined the tall boy in his perambulations.

'Is it real?' was his question.

Cornelius shrugged.

'It looks fresh off the production line. But it's not, is it?'

'I don't think so.' Cornelius reached out and tried a door handle. The door clicked open. Cornelius lowered his face and took a little sniff. Showroom fresh. He pulled the door wide open and prepared to climb into the car.

'Careful, Cornelius. You never know.'

'Don't be fearful.' Cornelius settled into the driving seat. It was very comfortable. Green leather upholstery squeaked in a posh, exclusive manner. The steering wheel was of shining golden wood. Cornelius ran his hands about it. Savouring the feel. He studied the dashboard. The milometer displayed a row of seven stylized zeros.

'It's never been driven.'

'Let's have a look.' Anna flung open the passenger door and dropped down next to Cornelius. 'It's booty, isn't it? What do you think it's worth?'

'A very great deal. Especially if it is what I think it is.' Cornelius opened the glove compartment and scooped out a sheaf of papers. 'And I think it *is*.'

'What?' Anna bobbed up and down in her seat.

Cornelius leafed through the papers. 'Oh yes,' said he. 'Oh yes.'

'Come on, tell me.'

'Anna, this is the *MacGregor Mathers*.'

'Oh,' said Anna.

'Not *Chitty Chitty Bang Bang* then?' Tuppe scrambled into the car and perched himself on Anna's knee.

'Not. This is the *MacGregor Mathers*, you must have heard of it.'

Tuppe looked at Anna.

91

And Anna looked at Tuppe.

And they both said, 'No.'

'If you're going to sit on my knee, then keep your hands to yourself,' said Anna.

'We give up,' said Tuppe.

Cornelius smiled. 'Then I shall tell you a little story. Are you sitting comfortably?'

'*I* am,' said Tuppe.

'Then I shall begin. Back in the nineteen thirties a rumour circulated in America. It concerned a Scottish inventor supposedly called MacGregor Mathers, that he had invented a car engine that ran on tap water.'

'Oh I've heard that one,' Tuppe put in. 'He tried to get it patented, but everyone laughed at him. Then he demonstrated it to Henry Ford, or some bigwig, got tricked out of it and vanished into obscurity. Ford, being in cahoots with the petrol industry, burned the plans. It's an FOAF.'

'A what?' Anna asked.

'A friend-of-a-friend story. An urban myth. Like the dyslexic devil worshipper who sold his soul to Santa.'

'That's not an FOAF,' Anna replied. 'That's just a duff gag.'

'Have you both quite finished?' Cornelius asked.

'I have,' said Tuppe.

'Then allow me to continue. MacGregor Mathers did not exactly vanish into obscurity. He returned to England where he found a wealthy backer. A member of the British aristocracy. Mathers rebuilt his engine and demonstrated it before a group of scientists. The engine ran like a dream. A consortium was formed in secret and the prototype car was built.'

'And?' Tuppe waggled his bum.

'Careful,' said Anna. 'And?'

'And it would seem that we are sitting in it.' Cornelius made a flourishing gesture. Spilling papers to the floor.

'Er no,' Tuppe put up his hand to speak. 'There would appear to be a bit more between then and now.'

'The prototype was built, as I said. Put on a lorry to be transported to Brooklands for a test drive. But the lorry never got there. There was this big storm. Just like tonight. They say the driver got lost, or something.'

'Or something.' Tuppe raised an eyebrow. 'What about MacGregor Mathers?'

'Vanished once more into obscurity,' Anna suggested.

'Or sold his soul to Santa and is now living at the North Pole,' Tuppe tittered.

'No.' Cornelius gathered up the papers and shuffled them between his fingers. 'He vanished all right. Vanished off the face of the earth. But not into obscurity. You see MacGregor Mathers wasn't his real name. It was an alias. His real name is right here on the car's documents. This car was invented by my father. Hugo Rune.'

7

Coincidence? Synchronicity? The unplucked nasal hair of destiny?

'The way I see it,' said Cornelius Murphy, 'this is now *my* car.'

'Oh it's definitely you.' Tuppe was all smiles. 'Understated elegance. Classic refinement. Top of the range.'

Anna opened her mouth to voice her opinions, but Cornelius went on. 'I think we should take it out for a spin.'

'What?' Anna now found her moment. 'If this car has been standing here for the last sixty years, you don't really expect it to work, do you?'

'Of course it will work.' Cornelius made little pointing motions towards the ignition key that dangled from the dashboard. 'Brrrm brrrm,' said he.

'Get real.' Anna found she couldn't fold her arms, so she duffed Tuppe on the head for good measure.

'Ouch,' said Tuppe. 'Trust him,' he said also.

'Right then. Hold on to your hats.' The ignition key was an elegant thing in itself. Silver and shaped as a dolphin. Cornelius gave it a bit of a turn. Something made a bit of a click. But that was about all. That was completely all, in fact.

'Well?' asked Anna.

'Engine's a bit cold probably.'

'A bit cold? If this thing really runs on water, which I seriously doubt, the water will all have evaporated decades ago. This is very sad.'

'Take no notice.' Tuppe mimed encouraging key twists. 'Give it another go.'

'I will.' Cornelius gave it another go. Not a whisper. 'Needs a bit of choke perhaps.' He tweaked several enigmatic organ-stop sort of arrangements on the dashboard. 'Brrrm brrrm,' he said once more, as he once more turned the key.

'I felt something.' Tuppe bobbed up and down. 'I felt something.'

'Feel it again and you're a dead boy.' Anna bopped him on the ear.

'Do it again, Cornelius.' And Cornelius did it again. And this time, a shiver ran through the silver car. A swift vibration. And then a purr and a whisper and a long low note.

Gurgling noises issued from the bonnet region. Cornelius massaged the accelerator pedal. The gurgling increased to become a throbbing rush. 'There we go,' said the tall boy, fingers dancing on the dashboard. 'Like a dream.'

'A wet dream?' Anna suggested.

Cornelius raised the eyebrow of admonishment, pressed forward the gearstick of hope, and let out the clutch of, well, just the clutch, really.

The dream car moved forward without a shake, a rattle, or a roll. Magic.

Cornelius steered it around Mulligan's ice-cream van, through the portal and out into the night. As

95

they left the cul-de-sac, Tuppe even managed to locate the switch for the headlights.

Anna glanced back over her shoulder. 'What about the portal, Cornelius? Shouldn't we have tried to close it, or something?'

'Certainly not. Tuppe and I are sworn to expose the blighters in the Forbidden Zones. We won't be closing any doors after us. We'll be leaving them open, for all the world to see.'

'Fair enough. This car drives beautifully, doesn't it?'

'Certainly does.'

And it certainly did. They cruised through the backstreets and off towards the main road. As they approached this, they were forced to slow down. A car ahead was waiting to turn right. Its indicator was jammed on. The driver did not appear to be in any hurry.

Cornelius pulled up behind him. 'Go on then,' he muttered. 'There's nothing coming. Get a move on.'

The car didn't move.

'Meep your horn,' said Tuppe.

'I don't think it would be wise to draw too much attention to ourselves right now. Not in this car. Perhaps he's just stalled or something. We'll give him a moment.'

They gave him a moment. And several more.

'What's up with him?' Cornelius wound down the window and stuck his head out.

'Meep your horn.'

'No. Not yet. Not . . .' Cornelius sniffed the air. He sniffed again. 'That's odd.'

'What can you smell?'

'Nothing.'

'*Nothing* is odd?' Anna shook her head.

'For me, yes. Wait here.' Cornelius got out of the car and gently closed the door. 'I'll just take a look.'

Anna and Tuppe watched him. They saw him sneak up to the car in front, peep in at the driver's window, jerk back, stoop to retrieve his cap from the road, peep once more into the car, then open the door and reach in.

And then they saw him pull out his hand at considerable speed, slam shut the door and lurch back towards them.

Cornelius flung himself into his seat. Breathing heavily.

'What's wrong?' Anna gaped at the boy with the grey face and the popping eyes. 'What is it?'

'There's a dead man driving that car,' said Cornelius Murphy.

'A dead man?'

'A dead man. Sitting there, staring straight ahead. He must just have died. He's still warm.'

'It's not Kevin Costner, by any chance, is it?'

'No, Anna, it is not.'

'Pity for him then. Because I'm not giving anyone else the kiss of life tonight.'

'We should do something,' said Tuppe. 'Not that I know exactly what.'

'Phone for an ambulance.' Cornelius put the car into gear. 'Make an anonymous call. Whatever happened here is nothing to do with us. I'll drive round him and we'll find a phone box. OK?'

'OK,' said Tuppe.

Cornelius steered carefully around the stopped car. As they passed it by, Anna and Tuppe made furtive peepings. The driver sat like a dummy, staring straight ahead.

'How very horrid.' Tuppe made a sour face. 'Drive on quickly, please.'

Cornelius did so. A hundred yards up the main road they came to the general post office. Three telephone boxes stood before it.

'Wait here.' Cornelius parked the car, got out and ran over to make the call. He lifted the receiver in the first box, waited, shook it against his ear, waited once more and then cursed briefly. The phone was dead.

Cornelius tried the next one. And the next. Then he returned to the car and leaned in at the window. 'Out of order.'

'All three?' Anna asked.

'All three. Lines are dead. Nothing.'

Cornelius looked up and down the road. It was deserted. Not a soul in sight. He sniffed the air once more. And then he shivered.

'What is it?' Tuppe got a worried look on.

'I can't smell anything. Not anything at all. I can smell us. But nothing out here. Something's very wrong.'

'Get back in the car, Cornelius. Drive us home.'

'Yes indeed.'

Cornelius drove on. There was a haunting stillness to the night. As if the very life had been sucked right out of it. The three travellers felt uncomfortable, oppressed. They didn't speak.

They were nearing the Chiswick roundabout when they saw the bus. It was the late-night single-decker from Richmond. It was coming towards them. Or rather, it wasn't. The bus had stopped a few yards before a request stop, where an old man stood with his arm outstretched. The old man was standing very still. Very still indeed.

Cornelius pulled up alongside the non-oncoming bus and stared up into the driver's cab.

'Not another stiff?' Tuppe hid his face in Anna's T-shirt.

'I don't like the look of this.' Cornelius gave his bottom lip a bit of pensive chewing. 'You two wait here. I'll take a look.'

'No,' said Anna. 'Why don't you wait here, and I'll take a look?'

'Why don't you both take a look, while I wait here?' Tuppe suggested.

Cornelius couldn't get the bus door open, but, as he crept along the side, he could see all of the passengers.

There were just the four of them. A lady in a straw hat, reading a paperback. A black guy in a leather jacket, half risen from his seat. Two yobbos in shell suits, lounging by the door. All were still. Frozen, like characters in a waxwork tableau.

'Hello.' Cornelius drummed on the window. 'Can anyone hear me in there? Hello. Hello.'

'Cornelius,' Anna called, 'come over here and check this out.'

The tall boy joined her at the request stop. She was examining the old fellow. 'Is he dead then?'

'I suppose he must be. His heart's not beating and he doesn't have a pulse. But he's still warm. Feel his face.'

'I'd rather not, thank you.'

Anna hugged her elbows. 'Cornelius, something terrible's happened here. Something really terrible. Do you know what I'm thinking?'

'No,' said Cornelius. 'I don't.'

'I'm thinking, is it all over? Did some plague, or something, sweep across London while we were inside that warehouse? Cornelius, I'm thinking, are we the last people alive?'

The tall boy gave a shudder, which he tried very hard to disguise as a shrug. 'Let's go.'

'Where to? To your house? Should we go there, do you think?'

'No, I don't think we'll do that.'

'Where then?'

'We'll drive around,' said Cornelius. 'Have a look. See what we can see. Yes?'

'Yes. All right.'

He chanced an arm about her shoulder as they walked back to the car. She didn't seem to mind. Or perhaps she just didn't notice.

'What's going on?' Tuppe asked, as Anna shifted him once more onto her knee.

'I don't know.' Cornelius dropped into his seat. 'I really don't know.'

'But they're all dead?'

'Seems so. But I just don't get it. Dead people do not stand at bus stops with their hands stuck out.'

'They do in the kind of movies I watch.' The small

100

fellow fluttered his fingers. 'Then, when you're least expecting it, they pounce! And they suck your brains out of your nostrils. Did you ever see *Night of the Living Dead*?'

Anna looked at Cornelius.

And Cornelius looked at Anna.

'Don't be silly,' said the tall boy, putting his foot hard down.

They drove through Brentford. It looked a picture beneath the full moon. Miami? Vermont? The Taj Mahal? Forget 'em. Brentford by moonlight. You want romantic? You got romantic.

But somehow not tonight. The big moon hung above the silent borough, ghost-white in the cloud-clear sky. And halfway up the Ealing Road the travellers came upon two fellows.

They were frozen in attitudes of drunken cama-raderie. Arms about each other's shoulders. Captured in mid stagger, a few yards from the door of The Flying Swan.

'Do you know what I'm thinking?' Tuppe asked.

'Very possibly, but go on anyway.'

'I'm thinking, perhaps it's the end of the world.'

'No,' Cornelius assured him. 'The end of the world is all fire and brimstone.'

'Well, so the Bible says. But what if that's a misprint or something? What if the end is just, the end? Everything simply stops, like a clock, runs down and stops.'

'Like a clock?'

'Or a movie. The big freeze frame. End picture, roll credits. Produced by, directed by, from an original idea by God. Fade out.'

101

'No.' Cornelius tried to make his 'no' sound convincing. But it lacked a certain something. 'It can't be that. What about us, then?'

'The exception that proves the rule. Or . . .' Tuppe paused.

'Or what?'

'Nothing. Absolutely nothing.'

'Out with it, Tuppe.'

'Well.' Tuppe scratched his tiny chin. 'Suppose this is some unwritten version of the Biblical End. The end of a particular cycle. The beginning of another. Now, if this was the case and God, in all his infinite wisdom, wanted there to be a new cycle, then He'd need, you know . . .'

'I don't know,' said Cornelius. 'What would God in his infinite wisdom need?'

'He'd need a new Adam and a new Eve,' said Anna.

'Exactly,' said Tuppe.

'*What?*' Cornelius stood on the brake.

Tuppe slumped back, holding his head. 'Easy on the emergency stops. I nearly went through the windscreen.'

'What are you saying, Tuppe?'

'Calm down, Cornelius. Think about it. It makes sense, doesn't it? The stuff of epics thing. I mean, how epic can you get? Fathering the new humanity.'

'Me?' A bit of a smile came to the tall boy's mouth. 'Father of the new humanity? I could go for that.'

'You?' Tuppe fell back with more than a smile. 'I wasn't thinking of you. I was thinking of *me.*'

102

8

It hadn't been Mickey's day at all. The police finally arrived at Minn's Music Mine, about two hours after he'd called to report the 'robbery'. By which time Mickey, whose powers of recuperation were the stuff of local legend, had sobered up sufficiently to realize the deep brown stuff he was getting himself into.

There were just the two policemen. One was a pimply youth, who spoke in a curious, unidentifiable accent. The other, a solid-looking body with a military moustache and a steely gaze. His name was Sergeant Ron Sturdy.

Mickey recognized the pimply youth at once. He was a dedicated purchaser of plectrums. Sergeant Sturdy recognized Mickey Minns.

'Surely I used to be your probation officer,' he said.

The scene-of-crime investigations didn't take too long. Sergeant Sturdy despatched his junior associate to make inquiries next door at Mr Patel's. 'Just mention my name and take a statement.'

'You got it, Sarge.'

For the next five minutes Sergeant Sturdy said nothing. He stood and twirled the ends of his pussy-tickler, smiling occasionally at the fretting, sweating Minns.

When the long five minutes were up, the lad

returned, sucking a *Snickers*. 'Patel sang like a Bronx canary,' he informed his superior officer.

'Read from your book, son.'

'Yes, sir.' Constable Ken turned back the cover of his regulation police-issue notebook and read from it.

'Big fat fellow he was (Mickey pulled in his stomach), but he had a mask on, so I didn't see his face (Mickey let out his stomach). Van was Ford Transit. Painting on sides of flowers and love and peace. Very rusty old van. No tax disc, by the way.'

'Anything else?' Ron asked.

'Yes, sir.' Constable Ken continued reading. 'Van had *Minn's Music Mine* printed in big letters on back. It Mr Minns' van. It Mr Minns in mask loading van with guitars. Mr Minns not paid paper bill for six months. Mr Minns hire out *Donkey Capers* porn video from me and not return it. Mr Minns very bad man. Mr Minns—'

'Thank you, Constable,' said Sergeant Sturdy. 'I think we get the picture.'

Mickey opened his mouth to protest his innocence. But he was bang to rights and he knew it. His best chance was a complete confession, accompanied by a plea of mitigating circumstances. The old *crambe repetita*, in fact.

And so he began. He wasn't a well man, he told the police officers. He'd never been the same since he'd done that three-month acid trip with Syd Barrett back in the Sixties. The chemicals were still in his bloodstream and only large libations of alcohol neutralized them and kept him on an even keel. And

104

it was all his wife's idea anyway. And she wasn't a well woman. She beat him up a lot. Not that she could help herself. She'd never been the same since she was bopped on the head by a police truncheon during a peaceful protest about the war in Vietnam. And business had been so bad lately, what with the recession. And there was the unpaid paper bill and the road tax for the van and the hole in the ozone layer and everything.

Sergeant Sturdy offered a sympathetic ear to Mickey's tale of woe. But when he felt that this ear had been bent quite enough, he raised a hard and horny hand.

'Put the cuffs away,' he told Constable Ken, who now had Mickey up against the wall with his legs spread and was giving the shopkeeper an intimate body search. 'And wait in the car.'

'Aw, but, Sarge—'

'Just do it.'

Constable Ken slouched from the shop, muttering in a mid-Atlantic manner. Sergeant Sturdy shook his head sadly. 'This is a sorry state of affairs,' said he. 'Get up off the floor and stop crying, Minns,' he continued.

Mickey had not been dragged away to the station. But he had been given a very stern talking to. Crime, Sergeant Sturdy told him, was best left to the professionals. The Robert Maxwells and the Carlos the Jackals of this world. Not to balding ex-musos with beer bellies and bad breath.

Society would be a better place if folk simply stuck to what they did best. Every man and every woman is a star, the policeman explained, shining in the firmament of their own individuality. Know thyself and to thyself be true.

Mickey nodded thoughtfully and wondered whether the sergeant had ever spent any time round at Syd's place in the Sixties.

The stern talking to concluded with the instruction that Minns should never again stray from the path of righteousness and, that as a penance for his transgression, he should personally offer a month's free guitar tuition to Sergeant Ron's son Colin.

'He needs a really decent guitar to thrash about on, he's a clumsy boy, but means well. Give him a go of your Les Paul Sunburst.'

Mickey's wife was on the phone, booking a suntan session and a bikini wax, when her hubby returned home with the bad news that all the guitars had to go back to the shop. She'd beaten him up.

Mickey had limped off in search of a beer. He'd found one at The Flying Swan and located and disposed of a good many more before Neville, the part-time barman, called for the towels up and brought his knobkerrie into play.

Mickey then limped next door to Archie Karachi's Star of Bombay Curry Garden for the traditional post-pub after-burner. It is an interesting fact, that, just as the Queen believes that all the world outside Buckingham Palace smells of fresh paint and new carpet, so, all Indian waiters believe that every Englishman is a foul-mouthed drunken fascist. It's a weird and wonderful world we live in, and as Hugo Rune once wrote, 'It has never ceased to fascinate

106

me, that no matter where I travel, nor in what far-flung reach of civilization I unroll my sleeping-bag, no matter how educated or primitive the people, how rich or how poor, how spiritually enlightened or how entrenched in fundamentalist dogma, one thing remains forever the same. And that is the smell in the gents' toilet.'

When Mickey had finally worn out his welcome at Archie's (which was three pints of *Cobra* downed and still unable to decide upon a starter), he was politely ejected into the street. Which left him with the very real problem of where to go next. Home for another thrashing? Mickey wasn't keen. Round to some friend's place, for a big spliff and an all-night chin-wag? Seemed sound. But for the fact that he had exhausted all such hospitality many years back. No, there was no choice involved. At two in the morning, Jack Lane's Four Horsemen was the only place in town.

Of all the pubs in Brentford, The Four Horsemen held the distinction of being the only one that did not recognize any licensing hours. As Jack Lane had now passed his one hundredth year, the local constabulary turned a blind eye to the fact that he rarely opened his doors until all the other pubs closed theirs. It was a tradition, or an old charter, or something. And it was the only place the officers of the force could grab a decent pint when they came off late shift.

Two of them were doing so even as Mickey walked in. And one of these looked up to greet him.

'Evening, Mickey,' said reliable Ron Sturdy. 'Your round I think.'

It was precisely three minutes past two, when Anna Gotting, Cornelius Murphy and Tuppe entered The Four Horsemen.

'Oh no,' Anna caught her breath. 'It's Mickey.'

'And the two policemen.' Cornelius stepped across the silent bar. Various patrons were posed in pubbers' positions. One making a throw at the darts board. Another in the act of ordering a drink. More, conversing about tables. A single fellow heading for the gents, which smelt, no doubt, identical to any other in the world. Old Jack held a glass beneath the whiskey optic. Ron Sturdy had his mouth open and his right hand on Mickey's shoulder. All shared one thing in common, however. A certain quietude. All were utterly still. None appeared to be breathing.

'We shouldn't hang around here too long,' said Tuppe. 'There is the fathering of the new order to be got under way. This I consider to be a matter of high priority, praise the Lord. Mine's a Jim Beam, if you're in the chair, Cornelius.'

'And mine's a very large vodka,' sighed Anna. 'Poor Mickey. I really quite fancied him.'

'Now that *is* sad.' Tuppe scaled a barstool.

Cornelius made his way behind the bar and took down a bottle of Tsar Nick, The Emperor of Vodkas, from the shelf.

'I can't hold with any of this,' he said as he rummaged for a glass. 'There is no way the entire world can come to an end the moment we turn our backs for a few minutes. It just can't be.'

'Looks very much as though it is,' said Tuppe.

'But it just can't. I'll bet they're still all warm. Give them a feel.'

'I certainly will not.' Tuppe shook his little head. 'I have not ruled out the possibility of contagion. You touched the fellow in the car, didn't you?'

'I touched the bloke at the bus stop.' Anna began to wipe her hand nervously on her T-shirt.

'That doesn't matter.' Tuppe tipped her the wink. 'As the mother of the new order, you will have a natural immunity. Shame about Cornelius. How does he look to you?'

'I look fine and I feel fine, thank you, Tuppe.' Cornelius popped the cork from the vodka bottle and made an attempt to pour out a large measure. But with no success.

'Something's wrong here,' he said, shaking the bottle about and peering into its neck. 'The drink won't pour. It's solid.'

'Whoa!' went Tuppe.

'What whoa?' Cornelius made with the vigorous bottle shakings.

'New order.' Tuppe folded his arms. 'No alcohol in the new order. God won't allow it. My case is proven I so believe.'

'Nonsense. It's just gone off, or something.'

'Or something. Try another then, O doubting Thomas.'

'I will.' Cornelius took down a bottle of *Lagavulin*. It wouldn't pour. Nor would the *Dalwhinnie*. Nor the *Johnnie Walker Black Label*. Nor even the *Bell's Extra Special*.

'Don't forget the *Jim Beam*,' called Tuppe.

Cornelius tried the *Jim Beam*. Pour it would not.

'Want to try your hand at the pumps?'

'No. No I . . .' Cornelius hesitated. His eye had become drawn to a most extraordinary phenomenon. And it centred about the right hand of Mickey Minns. This hand hovered, immobile, a few inches above an ashtray on the bar counter. It was arrested in the very act of flicking ash from a cigarette. And it was this ash that caught the attention of the tall boy. The ash and the way it hung motionless in the air, halfway between cigarette and ashbowl. Cornelius stared at it in awe. And as he did so, a great and terrible truth came to him. An Ultimate Truth, as his daddy might have described it.

'Oh shit,' said Cornelius. 'Oh shit, shit, shit.'

'What is all this shitting?' Tuppe asked. 'Are you auditioning for the part of serpent in this new Eden, or what?'

'No.' The eyes of Cornelius Murphy took it all in. All of it. He pointed with a quivery finger. 'Behold the dart,' said he.

Anna and Tuppe turned to behold. The dart hovered in the air, a mere six inches from the double top.

'Cor,' whistled Tuppe. 'That's clever. How does it do that?'

'It doesn't. It just seems to.'

'Very erudite, Cornelius. It doesn't, it just seems to. Would you care to enlarge on that at all?'

'It's us.' Cornelius chewed upon his knuckle. 'It's not them. There's nothing wrong with these people. It's us that's all wrong.'

110

'Still not following you, I'm afraid.'

'I am,' Anna smoothed back her hair. 'Think about Rune's car. Sixty-odd years old, but it smells brand new and it starts first time. It's the Zones. Time must be different in there. We went in and we came out and now we're—'

'What?' Tuppe shook his head to and fro. 'We're what?'

'We're different. We're moving much too fast. The car is still new because sixty years in there equals about one minute out here. These people aren't really standing still, nor is the dart. We're moving so fast that we can't perceive their movement. We're in a different time frame. That's why the phones wouldn't work, the bottles won't pour. Why we can't feel any heartbeats.'

'This is deep,' said Tuppe. 'Very deep.'

'This is bad,' said Cornelius. 'Very, very bad.'

'Bad for me,' said Tuppe mournfully. 'But not so bad for you, I'm thinking.'

'Why do you say that?'

'Oh come on, Cornelius. This is perfect for you surely. Use your loaf. If we're really moving thousands of times faster than everyone else on earth, think what you can do. Before one second of real time has passed, you could open up every Forbidden Zone in London, pull out all the booty, liberate your real daddy, print out the truth on broadsheets and stick one through the letter-box of every influential bod for miles around. And all before anyone can blink an eyelid. You win. You've solved it.'

'And if all that were so, how is it bad for you?'

111

'I don't get to be the father of the new order any more.'

'You never were,' said Anna. 'But you're right on this, isn't he, Cornelius?'

'No,' Cornelius held down his cap and shook his bandaged head. 'Sadly not. Because for one thing we won't be able to get back into the Zones.'

'Why not? You still have the reinvented ocarina. And we know that it works.'

'It works when you play it at a normal speed. But at the speed we're moving? Forget it. We may be invisible to the naked eye, but we are also inaudible to any ear you like. It won't work. We're done for. Before that dart hits the dartboard, we will probably have died of old age.'

'Depressing thought, isn't it?' said a voice from the door.

It was the voice of Arthur Kobold.

9

'Well look who it is,' said Cornelius Murphy. 'It's Mr Kobold. Say hello to Mr Kobold, Tuppe.'

'No thanks.' Tuppe had no wish to speak to Mr Kobold. And nor did Anna. She kept very still indeed, hoping not to be noticed. This was not the right place to be, and it was certainly not the right time. All she now wanted was out.

Arthur beamed at the tall boy and took a pace forward. He was dressed, as ever, in his Victorian morning suit. High starched 'throttler' with silk cravat. Diamond stud. Gold watch fob gleaming. Hair combed up above his round flat face. Bigger side whiskers than ever. He was prim and portly. Round and romantic. He was not a nice fellow to know.

'I'll take the ocarina,' said he. 'Very enterprising of you, that. I will also take the route map and Rune's A-Z.'

'I think not,' Cornelius replied.

'And the keys to the water car. We wouldn't want that thing falling into the wrong hands. Can't have mankind getting above itself, can we?'

'Can't we?' Cornelius held the bottle of *Jim Beam* behind his back. His fingers tightened about its neck.

'I wouldn't throw that if I were you,' said Arthur. 'Just hand over all the goodies and go home to bed.

When you wake up in the morning, all this will be a bad dream. Not that you'll remember much of it. We'll see to that.'

'You see to everything, don't you?'

'Everything important. We let mankind deal with the trivialities. But we control the higher issues.'

'Why?' Cornelius asked. 'Tell me why.'

'All right.' Arthur stepped up to the bar and placed his bottom on the stool next to Anna. 'Bottle,' said he.

Cornelius passed him the bottle.

Arthur poured a measure of its contents, without difficulty, into the empty glass. 'It's an us and them situation,' he explained. 'Or a me and you. You represent mankind, and I, let us say, another people. The good folk, you might call us.

'We are known in the highlands as the *Daoine Sidhe*. The Welsh call us the *Tylwyth Teg*. The Irish, *Tuatha De Danann*, or *Sleagh Maith*. But it all means the same.'

'What *does* it mean?' Cornelius asked.

'It means fairy,' said Tuppe, in a leaden tone. 'He's a frigging fairy.'

'Please, please.' Arthur sipped from his glass and raised his drinkless hand. 'That is a term we prefer not to use nowadays. Too many unsavoury connotations. But it does get the job done nicely. Say you believe in an invisible god who built the world from scratch in six days and most people will think you quite normal. Suggest that this god might have built more than one world, and that some of the denizens of another planet he's knocked up might be visiting

114

here in a UFO, and most people will think you moderately normal, but a bit eccentric. But mention a belief in fairies and they'll have you carted off to the funny farm.'

'But that's what you are, a fairy?'

'I'm a Kobold,' said Arthur Kobold, finishing his drink and pouring a refill. 'A fairy, if you like. Or don't like, going by the look on your face. It's all down to evolution, I suppose. Separate races evolving separately. But at the same time. You in your way and we in ours. Your lot somewhat overran us. We had to take shelter. But just because there's more of you, it doesn't follow that you know what's best. There are more ants in the world than men, but they don't run the show.'

'But you do?'

'We do our best. And we do it in good heart. We aren't vindictive. We have a sense of humour. Noted for it. The situation you now find yourself in is not without a certain measure of high farce, you must agree. If you could adopt a detached attitude, you would no doubt see the joke.'

'You tricked us. And you owe me money.'

'I'll pay you what you earned. And a good deal more. But you must promise not to bother us any further. We mean you no harm. We are firm but we are fair. We just maintain the *status quo*. Try and prevent your lot from buggering up the planet completely.'

'Then you're not making much of a job of it,' said Tuppe.

Arthur ceased to smile. 'We're doing a lot better

115

than you know. If it wasn't for us, your lot would have blown each other to oblivion long ago. Not that that would have been much of a loss to the universe. Self-destructive parasitic vermin so you all are.'

'I say!' Cornelius took a righteous step forward.

Arthur Kobold took a righteous step back. 'Violent by nature,' he declared. 'That's why you have to be managed. Kept under control.'

'And put down if we get out of hand?'

'When we deem it necessary, yes. A little plague here, a little war there, a famine round the corner. A bit of seasonal culling never does the livestock any harm.'

'*Livestock?*' Cornelius was appalled. 'Is that all we are to you, livestock?'

'And *vermin*,' said Tuppe. 'Don't forget vermin.'

'We endure you.' Arthur sipped at his drink. 'If I had my way I'd stamp the lot of you out. And I could do it too. Make a proper job of it. But *I* don't run the show. I am but a humble minion.'

'Who *does* run the show?' Tuppe asked.

'The guvnor of course.'

'And who's that? Oberon, king of the fairies?'

Arthur Kobold laughed. It was not the sound of fairy bells. 'Not him. But you *really* wouldn't want to know who.'

'*I* would.' Cornelius ground his teeth.

'No, no, no. That would spoil the joke. And such a good joke it is too. Now come along, I've wasted too much breath on you already.'

'Where is Hugo Rune?' Cornelius asked.

'Not him again.'

'Him again.'

'That man is a thorn in our flesh.'

'*Is?*' Cornelius managed a small smile. 'Not *was?*'

'Is, was, it's neither here nor there. Now hurry up. We have spoken enough. The ocarina, if you please, the route map and the A–Z. I will put you back into your own time and you can wake up in the morning with a nice fat bank balance. What more could you ask for?'

'Much more than that.' Anna turned on her bar stool and struck Arthur Kobold a devastating blow to the chin.

It was a masterstroke.

And the fairy fella fell.

10

It was still three minutes past two. And it looked like being that way for some time yet to come.

Cornelius, Tuppe, Anna and Arthur Kobold were now in Jack Murphy's garden shed. Cornelius was in a state of near to absolute fury.

'Bastard!' he cried, as he paced where he could in the crowded outhouse. 'Bastard. Bastard. Bastard.'

The reason for this uncharacteristically uncouth language was quite specific and it did not concern certain remarks about 'vermin' and 'livestock'. It concerned a certain silver car. And the loss thereof. Because, when Tuppe, Anna and Cornelius had carried the unconscious Mr Kobold from The Four Horsemen, the car was gone. Someone, or some *thing*, had stolen it.

'Bastard!' shouted Cornelius Murphy.

Tuppe upended a pail of water above the head of Arthur Kobold.

'I bet that would have woken him, if it had come out.' The small fellow peered up into the upturned pail.

'Smack him about a bit,' said Cornelius.

'With pleasure,' Tuppe hastened to oblige.

'Let me,' said Anna. 'My hands are bigger.'

'What, what and when?' Arthur Kobold came alive. 'Stop hitting me.'

'Where is my car?' Cornelius demanded.

'I haven't got it.'

'But I bet you know a man who has. The AA fairy, was it?'

'I don't know. I was supposed to collect it. You've got the key. Keep this mad woman off me.'

'You're in big trouble,' Cornelius told the protester. 'Big trouble.'

'You'd better let me go, if you know what's good for you. Untie me this instant. Notice I didn't say this *minute*. Little bit of humour there, to lighten the situation.'

Cornelius took up the electric drill. 'I don't want to waste any more time at all on you,' he said. 'So you will now tell me everything I wish to know. Or I will drill out your eyeballs.'

'Heav-ey!' said Tuppe. 'That's perhaps a little drastic, isn't it?'

'Not at all. It's being firm, but fair. Arthur understands that. Sacrificing an individual for the common good. He'd do the same, if the situation was reversed.'

'I'm sure I wouldn't.' Arthur Kobold squirmed uncomfortably.

'Well *I'm* sure you would. So speak up or get your medicine. It's nothing personal.'

'*Hasta la vista*, baby,' said Tuppe.

'Oh come off it,' Arthur strained at his bonds. 'Let me go. The drill doesn't have a plug on it anyway.'

'That's OK. The shed doesn't have a power point.'

'Eh?'

'I was meaning to ask about that.' Tuppe gave his head a scratch.

'Let me go, you . . .'

'I think he's going to use the "V" word again,' said Tuppe.

'Let *me*.' Anna took the drill from Cornelius. 'This needs a woman's touch. You two step outside for a moment. Notice I didn't say *minute* there, Mr Kobold. But it shouldn't take too long. It's knowing just where to stick the drill that matters.'

Arthur made one of those big Adam's apple gulp-jobs. 'Now just you see here—'

'We'll be outside if you need us then,' said Cornelius.

'I think I'll put my fingers in my ears,' said Tuppe. 'What with all the screaming and everything.'

'No. Er . . . no.' Arthur smiled hideously. 'There is no need for any unpleasantness. I will be glad to tell you anything you wish to know.'

'Then where's my car?'

'I don't know that.'

'We'll be outside if you need us, Anna.'

'No, don't go.' Arthur's bottom lip got all a-quiver. 'I do know something.'

'Mr Kobold, you know *everything* I wish to know. And you *will* tell me.'

'I will. Oh yes.'

'Oh yes, you will.' Cornelius smiled at Anna. 'You can wear my daddy's gardening apron if you want. Shame to get blood all over your T-shirt.'

'I know where Hugo Rune is,' gushed Arthur Kobold.

*   *   *

It was still three minutes past two. But at least it wasn't raining. 'We will have to walk,' said Arthur Kobold. 'Although I could call you a cab.'

'You could,' Cornelius agreed. 'But it's a very old gag.'

'Eh?' said Tuppe.

'No,' said Arthur. 'Call us call a cab, to save the walk.'

Cornelius shook his head carefully. 'The walk will do us good.'

'I'd prefer the cab,' said Tuppe.

'Not *his* cab, you wouldn't.'

'Quite so, Cornelius. Which way then, Mr Kobold?'

'This way.' Arthur Kobold set off. His hands were tied at his sides. A rope had been secured around his neck. Anna held the end of this. Tightly.

'It's just the other side of Kew Bridge,' said Arthur Kobold.

It's a good ten-minute walk from Moby Dick Terrace to Kew Bridge. And it was nearly four minutes past two by the time they got there. Nearly, but not quite.

Halfway over the bridge they came upon a scene of no small singularity. A large green muscular thingy leaned upon the parapet. It was captured in the act of drawing on a handmade cigarette and wore a blissful look upon its gruesome visage.

A few short feet behind it another figure was posed. This one was attired in mud-bespattered underlinen.

121

Clasped in hands, held high above a face that wore an anything but blissful expression, was a shining blade. The second figure was frozen in the act of plunging down this blade into the large and vulnerable backside of the first.

'Oh dear,' said Arthur Kobold. 'That's not supposed to happen. Would you mind if I just made one or two adjustments?'

Cornelius smiled grimly. 'That would hardly be sporting.'

'But he's going to . . . Owww!' Arthur Kobold leapt into the air.

'So sorry.' Anna examined the tip of the power drill.

'Keep that woman off me.'

'Get moving,' said Cornelius Murphy.

They stood before the house of Hovis.

'This is it,' said Arthur. 'You can untie me now.'

'I think not.' Cornelius looked up at the great dark house. It was a fine enough building. Constructed to one of Sir John Soane's neo-classical designs. Demonstrating his predilection for horizontal skylines and love of an aurora in the tympanum of the central pediment. This latter being a well-placed detail, which, although small, conferred a certain distinction to the elevation.

'And Hugo Rune is here?'

'Bottom bell,' said Arthur. 'The one marked A. THOTH.'

'A Thoth?' Cornelius asked.

'Well, you didn't expect it to read H. Rune?'

'Oh, I don't know. But then, I don't really expect H. Rune to be in there.'

'But he is. Go on, press the button.'

Cornelius stretched forward a long slim finger, but he could not quite bring himself to press the button. Somewhere inside his head, the needle of suspicion fluttered into the red zone.

'Perhaps it would be better if you pressed it, Mr Kobold.'

'With pleasure. Untie my hands.'

'Use your nose.'

'Oh really!'

Anna made little drilling noises with her mouth.

Arthur craned his nose towards the bell push.

'Er, just a moment.' Tuppe put up his hand to speak. 'Before anyone presses anything, there's just a couple of small points I'd like cleared up.'

'Speak on, my friend,' said Cornelius.

'Well,' Tuppe began, 'I have been following all this quite carefully. And if Hugo Rune really is in there, how is he going to open the door? I mean, if we're in a different time frame from everyone else on earth, we will be invisible to him and he'll just be a statue to us. Oh, and the bell-push won't ring the bell, will it? Remember the telephones and the bottles that won't pour and everything?'

'Ah,' said Cornelius. 'Good points. What do you think, Mr Kobold, good points?'

'Very good points.' Arthur Kobold made an uneasy face. This being a face which now displayed signs of unease to an even greater degree than the one which he was previously wearing. Which had already had a great amount of unease on it. So to speak. 'Ideas anyone?'

'I have one,' said Anna.

'I thought you might,' said Arthur Kobold. 'Does it involve you sticking that drill up my bottom again?'

'No. It involves you voiding the spell.'

'Void the spell?' Arthur took a step backwards. But just the one. Anna held him tightly by the halter rope. 'I have no idea what you mean, young woman.'

'Oh, I think you do.' Anna looped the rope around her hand and gave it a significant jerk. 'This different time frame business sucks. And do you want me to tell you why?'

Cornelius looked at Tuppe.

And Tuppe looked at Cornelius.

'Yes please,' they said.

'Then I will. I don't pretend to understand how "magic" works. Before tonight, I would have doubted that it worked at all. But I do understand some things about the laws of motion. So tell me this, if we're all moving faster than a speeding bullet, how come we aren't experiencing friction from the surrounding air? If we were moving that fast under normal circumstances, we'd be glowing white hot by now, having first had the flesh stripped straight off our bones, of course. But we're not, Mr Kobold, are we?'

'Ah,' said Arthur. 'It would appear not. Although I am experiencing a degree of sweatiness at the present time.'

'So,' Anna continued, 'it is my supposition that we

124

are held within some kind of protective cocoon. A magical cocoon.'

'She's good for a girl, isn't she?' said Tuppe to Cornelius.

Anna turned a glare towards the small fellow. 'You will get a smack', said she, 'if you make any more remarks like that.'

'Sorry,' said Tuppe.

'I should think so too. Now, if you and Cornelius would care to bend Mr Kobold over, I will drill all the necessary details out of him.'

'No no no.' Arthur edged his back to the wall. 'No need for any of that. It is a spell, yes. But it's not my spell. It belongs to the guvnor. It's his special birthday spell. I'm not supposed to use it.'

'Then why did you?'

'Because you stole the guvnor's favourite car. The alarm went off in my office. It seemed the best thing to do at the time. We couldn't have anyone seeing that car. The guvnor was asleep, so I used his spell. Why couldn't you have stolen one of the other cars? There's hundreds of them in there to choose from.'

'Hundreds?' Cornelius made with the open mouth.

'Oh dear,' said Arthur Kobold. 'You didn't see all the rest then?'

'Void the spell,' said Anna. 'And do it now.'

'I can't. It's more than my job's worth. The spell is only to be used once a year, on the guvnor's birthday. And only by him. You'll just have to get used to life in the fast lane, I'm afraid.'

'The bastard,' said Tuppe. 'He never had any intention of returning us to our normal time.'

'Down with his pants,' said Anna. 'I've had quite enough.'

'No,' wailed Arthur. 'No, no, no.'

'Then void the spell. This is the last time of asking.'

'All right. All right. But you'll have to untie my hands.'

'I'll be right behind you.' Anna gestured with the drill. 'One dodgy move and it's the steel suppository for you.'

'No dodgy moves. I swear.'

'Right then. Cornelius, untie his hands.'

'Certainly.' Cornelius loosened the ropes. 'There now,' he said. 'Do your thing.'

'Hm.' Arthur pressed his fingers to his temples and began to rock gently on his heels. And then he uttered the magic words. They appeared to be the standard bogus-latin gobbledegook that you get in the movies. But, then, this wasn't the movies. This was real life. Oh yes.

There was a crash, a bang, a wallop and the sound of water going the wrong way down the plughole. And then.

Cornelius felt the breeze on his face. And a million smells rushed into his nostrils. He opened his eyes, because evidently he must have closed them, and he saw that the world was right once more.

Well, almost right. Anna was there. And Tuppe was there.

But Mr Kobold wasn't there. And neither were the ocarina, the route map or Rune's annotated A-Z.

11

'Have at you, varlet!' The hands of Hovis drove down the steel, thrice blessed. Right up to the pommel in the big green beast's backside.

The creature spat reefer, mingled with profanity, and screamed. Inspectre Hovis turned his blade. 'You have my diamonds, I believe,' said he, administering another vicious twist.

'Ooooooooooooooooooooooooooooooh!' went the creature.

And then, BANG!

It was a particularly messy kind of a BANG! Inspectre Hovis was showered with odorous ooze. He toppled backwards as the fetor engulfed him.

When he was able to rise, which he did to the accompaniment of much coughing, spluttering and gagging generally, he became aware of two things. The creature had gone. But so too had the diamonds.

'It would seem that we have egg on our faces,' said Cornelius Murphy.

'And jam.' Tuppe licked his lips. 'Strawberry jam.'

'The bastard!' Anna threw her hands in the air. 'Look at me. Look at me.'

Now, a tall, seventeen-year-old woman can look

good in most things. Dressed even in a plastic bin-liner, she can seem like heaven. But carrying off that covered-in-banana-custard-from-head-to-toe look, that's asking a lot. And certainly more than Anna Gotting was prepared to be asked.

'Look at my T-shirt! That was signed by the lead singer! Look at my hair! Oh my God!' She turned upon Cornelius with the fury that hell hath none of. 'This is all your fault, you bloody clown!'

'My fault?' Cornelius wiped egg from his face. 'I don't think that's altogether fair.'

'*Fair? Fair?*' Anna made claws. Bright yellow ones.

'Well,' said Cornelius, 'I was for pressing the bell-button. I was quite prepared to overlook the obvious fact that we were defying the laws of motion. At least until I'd got to meet Hugo Rune. I would have broached the subject then, of course.'

'What? What?' Anna plucked at her T-shirt.

'Er, excuse me.' Tuppe raised his hand once more. 'Perhaps we might push the bell-button now. I mean, if Hugo Rune is in there, maybe he'd let us use his bathroom.'

'You press it.' Anna's voice rose to perilous heights. 'Push the bell, bang the bloody knocker. Do what you damn well please. But I've had enough. You can stick your Forbidden Zones. Stick your fairies. Stick their magic spells. Stick Hugo Rune and his wonderful water car, which you lost! Stick it all and stick yourselves. You are a fool, Cornelius. And you, Tuppe, you're quite unspeakable.'

'Does this mean that sexual intercourse is out, then?' the small fellow enquired. 'Ouch!' he continued, as a sticky yellow fist caught him squarely in the face.

'And stick your stupid old jokes. I'm finished. Goodbye.' And with that she turned about and stormed away across Kew Green. Not quite as pretty as a picture.

The two lads watched her go.

'You might have handled that a mite better,' said Cornelius, when she was finally out of sight.

Tuppe rubbed his chin. 'Good riddance,' said he.

'Good riddance? What do you mean?'

'Well.' Tuppe's tiny face puckered and his bottom lip got a definite quiver on. 'She spoiled things, Cornelius. It was much better when it was just the two of us. The Epic Duo, eh?'

'But we weren't very epic. We've lost everything this time.'

Tuppe began to blubber. 'You'll figure it out, I know you will. And we always get girls along the way. You don't need her hanging around all the time.'

'She did come up with some rather good ideas.'

'You come up with ideas all the time.' Tuppe sniffled and snuffled. Cornelius offered him the use of his hankie, a nice oversized red gingham one.

'Have a blow.'

'Thanks.' Tuppe made great foghorn noises into the handkerchief.

'I'm sorry,' he said.

'It's OK. We'll get by.'

'Of course we will. You and me, eh?'

'You and me.'

Tuppe made another mighty blow into the handkerchief before offering it back. 'Thanks.'

Cornelius considered the sodden germ-carrier. 'Keep it,' he said. 'A present.'

'Thanks very much.' Tuppe stuffed the thing down the front of his dungarees. 'So what do we do now?' he asked with considerable bright and breeziness. 'Ring the bell? See if your real daddy is at home to callers?'

'No. I don't think so. It occurs to me now that the name Thoth rings a bit of a bell itself. As in the Egyptian god Thoth.'

'And is that bad?'

'It could be when you translate the name into Greek. That would make it Hermes. Hermes Trismegistus to be precise.'

'Oh shit.' Tuppe took a step back from the front door. 'As in *Train of Trismegistus*?'

'That would be the one.'

'Best not ring for service, then?'

'Best not. Let's go home and get some sleep. We've screwed up quite enough for one night.'

'Another day, another ocarina, is that what you're saying?'

'Something of that nature, yes.'

'Then might I trouble you to give me a piggyback? My legs are all walked out.'

'That', said Cornelius Murphy, smiling like a good'n, 'would be my pleasure.'

Inspectre Hovis had quite forgotten the meaning of the word 'pleasure'. He now sat in the gutter, cleaning the blade of his swordstick on a discarded Kentucky Fried Chicken box. A young woman all covered in custard had just passed him by. The two of them had clashed terribly, colourwise, and she had looked him up and down and denounced him as a pervert. The Inspectre shook his head. It was an un-funny old world and no mistake.

Hovis shook green slime from his fingers and climbed to his feet. He was rightly perplexed.

It is a fact, well known to those who know it well, that all policemen above the rank of sergeant are not only Freemasons, but Jesuits. The reason for this is quite obvious when you think about it. The coming of the Millennium and the inevitable appearance of The Antichrist.

The exact dates and details of these earth-shattering events are known only to a chosen few. The Pope, his wife and their son Colin. Just how the pontiff came by this privileged information is a bit of a mystery. Some say that the dates and details were edited out of the New Testament, during its translation from the original Greek, in the year 999. Others, and this seems very much more likely, that the Pope is on first-name terms with the Almighty, who regularly drops in for a cappuccino and a 'feet-up' in front of the telly, to watch the Italian football.

But, be all this as it may, the Church of Rome, seeking as ever to better the lot of the common man, has, over the years, taken certain steps to prepare itself for the big showdown.

Making sure that the police forces of the world are in its back pocket being just one of them.

Inspectre Hovis had mused upon the foregoing many times since his compulsory initiation into the Jesuit brotherhood. But he hadn't believed one word of any of it.

But all this business tonight had him rightly perplexed.

The Inspectre sheathed his now once-more-immaculate blade and flexed his shoulders. He had best be away home before somebody reported him to the police.

He didn't see the silver car until it was almost upon him.

It came without much sound, but at considerable speed. As it mounted the pavement the Inspectre and the driver stared for the briefest of moments into each other's eyes. And then the great detective leapt for his life. Over the parapet of the bridge and down into the icy depths of the River Thames.

Cornelius gaped in horror. He'd seen the whole thing. And now the silver car was heading straight in his direction.

'Oh bugger!' The tall boy turned and took flight, clutching the now slumbering Tuppe about his shoulders. The silver car whistled after him.

Cornelius did not run down the middle of the road, as they do in the movies. He knew better than that. He made for the trees of Kew Green.

The silver car bumped up on to the turf, gouging great ruts out of the grass. A strongly worded letter, from the local residents' committee to the Home Secretary, would be penned the following day, regarding these ruts. Although they would be some-what far down the list of complaints, as a lot worse was to follow this night.

Cornelius dodged in and out of the oak trees, seeking a low bough to swing up on. But all had been clipped against such possible outrage.

'Bugger,' puffed the runner.

The silver car swerved after him in hot pursuit.

'Wake up, Tuppe. We're in big trouble.'

'Zzzzzzzzzzzzzz,' went Tuppe.

The church on Kew Green is a historic affair. Designed by Sir Christopher Wren, it presents a wealth of period detail to the lover of ecclesiastical architecture. The transcept to the north is of particular interest, with its fan vaulting and distinctive gilded funerary escutcheons.

Thomas Gainsborough lies buried in the church-yard and the walls enclosing this were built high against the 'resurrection' men. They remain high to this day. They may be scaled, using considerable care, but as to 'leaping them in a single bound'? No way.

Cornelius suddenly found himself pressed up against the south-facing wall, with nowhere left to run. The silver car moved forward, catching him to perfection in its headlights.

The tall boy straightened the sleeper on his shoulders and raised a hand to stir him from his rest. But then he thought better of it. If they were both to die here, smashed up against a graveyard wall, perhaps it was kinder that Tuppe didn't know about it. He could apologize later. In heaven.

The silver car ploughed forward and Cornelius stood his ground.

It pulled up not three yards away and stood, its engine throbbing.

Cornelius shielded his eyes to the glare, clung to Tuppe with one hand and made a fist with the other.

'I'm ready,' said he.

The passenger door swung slowly open, and a voice called out the now legendary words, 'Come with me if you want to live.'

Cornelius squinted into the headlights' beam. 'Mr Schwarzenegger, is that you?'

'Don't be a silly arse,' the voice replied. 'Get into the car. *They* are close behind.'

And close behind *they* were. Across the green four sets of headlights swept into view. They sliced between the trees and across the grass. *They* were very close behind.

Without further words spoken, Cornelius dragged Tuppe from his shoulders, cradled him in his arms and ducked for the silver car.

The driver put the vehicle into reverse and spun the wheel around.

'It might be appropriate, at this time, that you position your head firmly between your knees. Sudden impact is a predictable circumstance.'

'Shiva's sheep!' Cornelius clutched Tuppe to his bosom and ducked his head. The driver tore the car about and bore towards his pursuers. He struck the first a glancing blow which sent the tall boy sprawling to the floor.

'Wake up, Tuppe,' said he.

134

But Tuppe snored on.

'I'll show these fellows I mean business,' said the driver.

'Hold on,' Cornelius clawed at the dashboard. 'What's happening?'

'We are under attack from the forces of darkness. You would do well to maintain the "crash position". Further concussions are reliably forecast.' The driver did a nifty handbrake turn and side-swiped an on-coming vehicle, rolling it into a tree, where it did the right thing and burst into flame.

'A satisfactory result,' said the driver. 'I recall a time in Shanghai. Lord Lucan and I were engaged in a rickshaw race. Fifty-guinea wager. His lordship had the temerity to have his coolie elbow mine from the thoroughfare, in just such a fashion. Mind you, I evened the score on that occasion. Took out my pistol and shot the pair of them dead.'

'Oh great,' thought Cornelius to himself. 'I've hitched a ride with a psycho.'

'I heard that,' said the driver. 'Thoughts have wings. And yours flutter against my ears, even in the pitch of battle. Keep your head down please.'

He screeched to a halt. A car, rushing up from behind, ploughed into the rear with spectacular effect.

The driver laughed uproariously. 'That stopped the blighter in his tracks, what? Two down and two to go. Shall we make a chase of it?'

'Anything you say, friend.'

'Friend me no friends. No friends have I.'

'Whatever you say.' Cornelius chanced a glance up from the foetal position he had assumed on the floor.

135

He observed a stretch of Fair Isle sock. A goodly spread of Boleskine tweed. Much waistcoat, with a golden fobchain. Considerable silk cravat. And then a wealth of chins.

'My name is Hugo Rune,' the driver said. 'But you may call me guru.'

12

The guvnor's court was grand and Gothic. Ancient and imposing. And craving of description in the medieval manner.

Broad were the flagstones that paved its ample floor and worn were they as glass beneath the tread of shoeless feet. Royal tabards, cloth of gold, adorned its sombre walls. And on these tabards beasts and weird devices were displayed. Wrought thereupon in such a distant age, that nought remained of meaning but their majesty withal.

The guvnor himself was also old. And though his subjects, far and near, did celebrate his birthdays with appropriate occasion, none was there to accurately count the candles for his cake.

The guvnor was also fat. Prodigious were his limbs and great the girth of him each way about. His middle regions pressed they hugely at a belt as broad as three hands' span and of such length that, stood upon its end, the tallest of the court could not stretch up to reach its buckle.

And of his boots? His tall black boots? Such was the bigness of these boots that, it was said by those who knew these matters and reported them with truth, the whole tanned hides of bullocks, two in number, had been employed, without much waste, their cobbling to complete.

And bearded also was the guvnor, very much indeed. And oh the beard of him, pure white, a pillow's fill. A pillow? Nay, a duvet. Several duvets, and a pouffe.

And of the robes of him? Speak of his robes? Of regal red were they, what other colour should a sovereign clothe? And trimmed with ermine, to a niceness, pleasing to behold. Unless thou art an ermine, naturally.

The guvnor was also drunk this night. And in his cups waxed anything but merry.

'Kobold!' cried the guvnor, and his subject answered, 'Sire?'

'Arthur,' said the king. 'Where have you been?'

'I just popped out,' said Arthur, with his shoes off and his knees bent in a bow, 'my Lord.'

'Out? Where out? And why?'

'On business, sire. As ever in the service of your realm.'

'I see.' The king leaned forward in his throne. And such a throne was his. So girt and splendid that no words might vaguely touch its grandeur or convey its glory, no. So shan't.

'It has reached my royal lughole', said the king, 'that there has been a spot of bother.'

'Nothing I can't handle, sire.'

'That's good to hear. To hear that's good. Most truly.'

'Good,' said Arthur. 'Truly good. Then I shall take my leave. Good night.'

'Not quite good night I feel.' The king raised up

a hand. And what a hand it was. Bedecked with rings as splendid as the throne above. If not more so.

'My liege?'

'My car!'

'Ah, that.'

'Ah that indeed. My favourite car. My special car. Where might it be?'

'I fear', said Arthur, wringing out his hands, 'that it has been appropriated.'

'As in *stolen*, you mean?'

'Regrettably yes, sire. The lad Murphy, whom I recently employed to recover certain documents which threatened our security, he gained access to your private car park. Drove off in the motor.'

'Then get after him.'

'I did, sire.'

'And?' The king sighed hugely (and such a sigh was his, etc.).

'There was some unpleasantness. And whilst I was otherwise engaged, the car was stolen once more. By another party.'

'And this occurred whilst you were using *my* birthday spell?'

'Ah,' said Arthur, wringing away like a mangle. 'You heard about that, then?'

'I am the King!'

'And such a king are you,' said Arthur. 'August, proud and true. And of a wisdom sound and fair and—'

'Drop it, Kobold. We tired of the medieval twaddle.'

'Sorry, sire.' Arthur hung his head.

139

'You used my special spell without permission.'

'In order to recover your car, sire.'

'Which you did *not* do.'

'No, sire. But am doing now.'

'Oh yes?'

'Oh yes, sire. I despatched four of your bodyguards to drive around the area in search. They called in a few minutes ago to say that they had located your car and were in pursuit. So all is really well and good. Good night.'

'*Well and good?*' The king rocked forward in his throne and threw his great arms wide. 'You despatched four of *my* bodyguards? My great, thick, clumsy, gormless bodyguards?'

'Yes, sire.'

'To *drive* around the area, did you say?'

'Yes, sire.'

'In what, Kobold? In what are they driving?'

'Well. I told them to go down to your car park and take whatever they thought would get the job done.'

The king fell back. His mouth wide open in his horror. '*My* bodyguards? Given free rein with *my* motor cars? Have you lost all your senses? Are you bereft, Kobold? How could you think of such a thing? What made you do it? What?'

'Well, sire,' Arthur Kobold chewed upon his knuckles, 'you see, it's not just the matter of your favourite car. It's the matter of who stole it from Murphy.'

The king groaned. 'Go on,' said he. 'Tell me the worst. If worse there can possibly be.'

'I'm afraid there can. Far worse. You see, when

140

Murphy stole the car from your car park, it wasn't entirely empty. I have every reason to believe that one of our "guests" had hidden himself inside the car. A certain category-AAA "guest".'

'A prisoner has escaped? I mean, "a *guest* has chosen to leave us?" Which one? Not Elvis?'

'Elvis?' Arthur Kobold asked. 'We don't have Elvis staying with us, do we?'

'Ah . . . er . . . mm. Of course not, Kobold. Whatever put that into your mind?'

'You just said—'

'No I didn't. You must have imagined it. There is only one King. And I'm he. So speak up, damn you. Who's nicked my car?'

'H . . . H . . . H . . .'

'Out with it, Kobold.'

'H . . . H . . .'

'Spit it out. Or truly will you know my wrath.'

'Hugo Rune,' said Arthur Kobold. 'Can I go now, sire, I need the toilet.'

Hugo Rune put his foot to the floor and the silver car streaked over Kew Bridge towards Brentford.

'As a rule I rarely drive,' he told Cornelius. 'There are two kinds of people in this world: those who sit behind a wheel and drive, and those who sit behind *them* and tell them where to drive. I am of the latter persuasion.'

'You are my father,' said Cornelius.

'Mayhap. However, put aside all thoughts of falling on my neck with kisses. Our lives are still in some peril.'

A gorgeous long-bodied landaulet, which would have found a pride of place in the collection of Lord Monty, drew level with them. Its driver, a hideous great green thingy, yelled something gross in their direction.

'One moment's pause, before you yet again enjoy the pleasure of my conversation.' Rune drew down hard on the steering wheel, caught the landaulet a thunderous blow and sent it spinning from the road. Cornelius peeped over his shoulder to make what he would of the explosion. Thoughts of the evil Campbell returned to his mind, and the devastation *he* had wrought upon a score of police cars. Like father like son.

'Only one remaining now,' said Hugo Rune.

'If you hang a right after the traffic lights, we can easily lose him in the backstreets and hide out at my house.'

'What an absurd suggestion. We shall go directly to my manse.'

'Whatever you prefer then. Kindly lead the way.'

'Now that', said Hugo Rune, 'is what I do the best.'

They lost the final car, a rare, if not unique example of the Cord, when Rune nudged it off the road into the newly reglazed front window of Polgar's Pet Shop.

From then on the drive became more sedate. They left the suburbs of the metropolis behind and travelled north. And Rune discoursed upon a great diversity of subjects. Cornelius spoke little and though a

142

thousand questions crowded in his head, he couldn't get a word in edgeways on. And so, at last, he fell asleep.

He awoke to find the sun upon his face and Rune's words once more in his ear.

'And that is how', said Rune, 'the scoundrel Einstein stole my notes and walked off with the Nobel Prize.'

'Outrageous,' said Cornelius. 'Are we there?'

'Behold the manse.'

The car was parked upon a sweeping drive of Chichester stone.

Before it rose an ancient country pile, *circa* 1690. It was fashioned from the granite of the region, mellowed to a golden hue. The house had a hipped roof, pediment and cornice, which combined with the classic façade, so favoured in the period by Inigo Jones. There remained the Gothic touch in the mullion and transom windows. And near the angles, pilasters took the place of the usual rusticated quoins.

Rune left the car and stretched his limbs before the house. Cornelius urged Tuppe into wakefulness.

'Don't shake me all about,' said the small bloke. 'I've been awake all the time. God, your knees are bony.'

'Awake all the time, eh? Then I suppose you know where we are.'

'No,' said Tuppe. 'I'm quite lost.'

Cornelius viewed Hugo Rune through the windscreen. 'And what do you make of him?'

'He's looking well on it,' said Tuppe. 'Doesn't seem to have aged a day since that picture was taken.'

143

'The one we found in Victor Zenobia's trunk?'

'Do you still have it?'

'Of course.' Cornelius wormed the crumpled relic from his pocket. There was Rune, surrounded by his acolytes, on his birthday, more than half a century before. And no, he hadn't aged one day, one jot, or one iota. Nor had the suit he wore, the same nineteen thirties Boleskine tweed plus-fours number by all the looks of it.

Cornelius looked up from the Rune of yesterday to see the Rune of today waving him to follow.

'Shall we join him?' asked Cornelius.

'Do you smell breakfast cooking?'

Cornelius wound down the window and flexed his sensitive nostrils. 'And then some,' he replied.

13

The hall was 'baronial', with a hammerbeam roof. The design of this roof, however, differed from most other hammerbeam roofs, in that it carried the great arch-brace through the hammerbeams and hammer-posts, instead of under the point of junction of the hammerbeam and hammer-post. Thereby balancing the vertical and oblique thrusts so perfectly as to permit a large span. As an additional vanity, spandrels between the king post and the braces had been filled with cusping.

A long oak table, groaning with a veritable banquet, stood at the centre of this hall. And Hugo Rune spread out a great arm and said, 'Behold the beano.'

Cornelius had never seen such food, nor smelled such smells. The mingling fragrances rising from the exotic fare, as such it was, comprising dishes and delights to baffle the most seasoned gourmet, made music in his nose.

'Seat yourselves.' Rune took his place at the head of the table. 'And feast.'

Cornelius looked at Tuppe.

And Tuppe looked at Cornelius.

And they both sat down and feasted.

It took more than an hour for the three of them

to get through it all. But they did. The spread was reduced to a desolation suggestive of a soldier ant march past.

Rune licked clean his plate, released the lower button of his waistcoat and belched mightily. 'Adequate,' said he.

Tuppe grinned through a layer of chocolate cake.

And Cornelius said, 'Incredible.'

'Fair to middling.' Rune dabbed his mouth with a napkin. 'Shall we partake of cigars, before we gravitate to the main course?'

'Main course?' Cornelius made with the popping eyes.

'Unless you'd care for a little more starter.'

'No, I'm fine, thank you.'

Tuppe licked his fingers and thumbs. 'He likes his nosebag, does your daddy.'

'I'll take a cigar please,' said Cornelius. 'I think that we have much to speak of.'

'Correct in essence, but not in specific detail. *I* have much to speak of and *you* have much to listen to.' Rune plucked a long green cigar from a bound brass case and poked it into his mouth. He turned the case towards Cornelius.

'Thank you.' The tall boy took out a cigar, put it to his nose and breathed in its glory.

'Argentine,' Rune bit the end from his cigar and spat it the length of the room. 'Rolled upon the thigh of a dusky maiden. It recalls to me a time I spent in that fair land. I had been invited to stay with the president, old Juan Peron and his passionate wife, Eva. The president wished to purchase the patent for a bullet-proof garment I had recently perfected. Have you ever heard of the Three-fold Law of Return?'

Cornelius nodded and so did Tuppe. But as Rune didn't trouble to look in their direction, he continued without pause.

'The Three-fold Law of Return is an occult law, whereby a magickal current, raised by an inadequate magician to attack some enemy, reflects, with a triple force, back upon him. And serves the bugger right. Incompetence in the Arts Magickal deserves no better reward. My bullet-proof garment, *Rune's Patent Protector*, functioned upon this principle. It reflected the assassin's bullet straight back at him with a triple force. Most effective.

'Unfortunately, I was unable to capitalize on this particular invention. There was some unpleasantness.'

'You mean it didn't work,' said Tuppe.

'Of course it worked. *I* invented it. The unpleasantness to which I allude was of a personal nature. The president took exception to the relationship I had formed with his wife.'

'What?' Tuppe fell back in his chair. 'You don't mean he caught you shagging her?'

'Tuppe, really!' Cornelius took his cigar and stuck it into the small fellow's mouth.

Rune fluttered his fat fingers. 'Shagging is not the word I favour to describe an intimate congress between two kindred spirits. Although it was the one Peron used when he burst into his bedchamber to find his wife and me "taking tea with the parson".'

'Stone me,' said Cornelius. 'What happened then?'

'The tardy fellow put me before the firing squad.

"Any final request?" he asked. "Only that your men aim for my heart," said I, "for it has been my undoing." Happily they did. Twelve shots rang out. Twelve men fell dead. *Rune's Patent Protector*, tried and tested. I left the country with my head held high and my reputation intact.'

'And the bullet-proof vest?' Cornelius asked.

'Vanished into obscurity?' Tuppe suggested.

'Hardly that.' Rune sucked upon his cigar. It took flame, which was a neat enough trick, but no great shakes. 'Peron hung on to that. He intended to equip his entire armed force with it. And no doubt did. Woe betide any nation that dares to wage war upon Argentina.'

Tuppe opened his mouth to speak, but chose to suck upon his cigar instead. His didn't light.

'Where *have* you been for the last eighteen years?' Cornelius asked.

'Held prisoner within the Forbidden Zones. Waiting for you to release me. And last night you did.'

'I don't think I did.' Cornelius scratched his cap. 'I'm sure I would remember a thing like that.'

'You drove me out.' Rune puffed upon his cigar. 'In my own car.'

Tuppe affected an expression of supreme enlightenment. 'You were hiding in the boot.'

'I certainly *was not*! Rune does not lurk in car boots like a spare wheel. *I* was sitting in the rear seat.'

'There was no-one in the rear seat,' said Cornelius.

'Oh yes there was.'

'Oh no there wasn't.'

148

'He's *behind* you,' called Tuppe in a pantomime voice.

Rune delved into a waistcoat pocket, brought out something unseeable, stretched it between his hands and promptly vanished from sight.

'The mantle of invisibility,' said the voice of Rune. 'I always carry a piece for my private use. After all, I invented it.'

There was a slight swish and Rune reappeared. 'Convinced?' he enquired.

'Convinced,' said Cornelius. 'But how did you know we'd find our way into that particular zone, at that particular time? And choose to drive out that particular car?'

'I made certain calculations. You need not concern yourself with these. But suffice it to say, I merely sat in the car and awaited your arrival.'

'Well,' said Cornelius, 'I hope I didn't keep you waiting long.'

'Not long,' said Hugo Rune. 'Just the eighteen years.'

Polly put the Portakabin kettle on. 'Rough night?' she asked.

'*Rough night?*' Inspectre Hovis emptied the contents of his nose into a monogrammed handkerchief. 'Something inhuman attacked me last night. Some bally great green ghastliness. If I hadn't kept my nerve and employed my steel, there is no telling how things might have ended. A lesser man would surely have perished.'

Polly turned up her eyes. 'Really?' she said.

'Really. But that's not the half of it. Having defeated this supernatural adversary, I was then forced to leap from Kew Bridge, in order to avoid being run down by a bally joyrider. Do you know what it's like at the bottom of the Thames?'

'Mostly clay, I suppose. Hydrated aluminium silicate, quartz and organic fragments, sedimentary rocks and other deposits. A certain amount of alluvial matter . . .'

Hovis ground his teeth and pocketed his hankie. 'Thank you,' said he. 'I experienced it at firsthand. If I didn't hold an Olympic Silver for the high dive and the Athenaeum Club record for remaining face down in a punchbowl of *Pol Roget*, there is no telling how things might have ended.'

'A lesser man would surely have perished,' said Polly, fighting hard to keep a straight face.

'Without doubt. But that's not the half of it. Having dragged my frozen body from the icy waters, I attempt to make my way home. And what do I find?'

Polly shrugged.

'I find that Kew Green has become a war zone. Upturned cars blazing away. The fire brigade out in force and our lads preparing to baton charge the local residents' committee. And if that's not enough.'

'Go on,' said Polly.

'I then realize that I have lost my front-door key.'

Polly chewed upon her bottom lip.

'But that's not the half of it. As I am attempting to gain entry to my own premises, through a side window I know to be open, a young constable leaps out with a pistol in his hand and orders me to "get up against the wall and spread'm, buddy".'

Polly turned her face away and fought against hilarity.

'Constable Kenneth bloody Loathsome. I shall do for that blighter. And I will do for the joyrider also. I caught a glimpse of his great grinning mug. And I never forget a face, especially when it's one I have on file.' Hovis scribbled a name on a piece of regulation police-issue notepaper and handed it to Polly. 'Pull this gentleman's file for me, if you can manage it without hysteria.'

'Yes, sir,' said Polly.

'But now I think a cup of *Lapsang* would not go amiss. I feel as if I have been through some baptism of fire. And after the horrors and indignities that have been heaped upon me, I truly believe that nothing this day can throw in my direction could faze me one little bit.'

'That is pleasing to hear', said Polly, warming the pot up, 'because I've just remembered, Chief Inspector Lytton wanted to see you in his office. Urgently. Ten minutes ago.'

Cornelius, Tuppe and Hugo Rune sat puffing on their green cheroots.

'I will tell you a little story,' said Hugo Rune, 'to fascinate and entertain you before the arrival of the main course.'

'Goodo,' whispered Tuppe to Cornelius.

'Sssh,' said the tall boy.

And Rune began. 'There was a young fellow called Breeze—'

'Whose dongler hung down to his knees?' Tuppe asked. 'I think I know this one.'

'Silence!' The mage snapped his fingers and Tuppe collapsed in his chair, flapping at his face.

Cornelius leapt to his friend's assistance. 'What have you done to him?'

'Just quietened him down for a few moments.'

'If you've hurt him . . .' Cornelius fought to pull Tuppe's hands away from his face. Tuppe looked up at him with frightened eyes and gestured frantically. He no longer had a mouth.

Cornelius glared back at Hugo Rune. 'That is an evil trick.'

'It is no trick, I assure you.' The voice belonged to Tuppe. And it came from Tuppe's mouth. A mouth that now occupied the centre of Hugo Rune's forehead.

'Put it back,' growled Cornelius.

'As you will.' Rune wiped his hand across his forehead and fluttered his fingers once more in the air. Tuppe's mouth returned to its place of origin. 'Bastard,' it said.

'Keep it closed from now on,' Rune advised, 'or I will transport it to a part of your body that will ensure you never again dine out in public.'

'Best do as he says,' said Cornelius.

Tuppe coughed smoke. 'I've swallowed my cigar,' said he.

Cornelius passed him a glass of water.

'Now,' said Rune. 'There was a young fellow called Breeze.' He paused.

'Kindly continue,' said Cornelius. 'It's fascinating so far.'

'This Breeze', said Rune, 'was a common thief. A housebreaker. He stole without conscience, because, having never owned a house, or items precious to himself, he did not understand their importance to others. The common mind can understand nothing but the commonplace. You understand?' Rune tapped ash from his cigar on to the table and drew circles in it. 'I will not tire you with a catalogue of Breeze's crimes. As he lacked conscience, they were naturally vindictive. His enterprise brought misery to many.

'Now, there lived near Breeze an ancient fellow. Bent of back and ragged in the day-wear department. He inhabited a house, once grand, but now as bent and ragged as its owner.

'Breeze became convinced that this ancient was possessed of great wealth. And Breeze considered him a fruit, ripe for the picking. And so, one night, he took up his jemmy and his flashlight and gained unlawful entry to the premises.

'He moved from room to darkened room, but nothing could he find. The house was empty of all furniture, the floors laid bare, the walls, of pictures, unreplete. All that there was in that house was a great and terrible silence.

'But Breeze crept on through it, opening doors before him, until, at last, he came upon a central chamber. He entered this and *Bang*!'

Rune brought his great fist down upon the table and the hall plunged into darkness.

'Help,' wailed Tuppe.

'Bang,' said Rune in the darkness. 'His flashlight had gone out and he was all alone in the utter blackness of the grave. And then . . .' Rune clapped his hands together and the light returned. Exactly where from was anyone's guess. From the same place it disappeared to, probably.

'Get off me, Tuppe.' Cornelius prised the small fellow from his lap and dumped him back on to his chair. 'Behave yourself.'

'Sorry.'

'The room filled with light,' said Hugo Rune. 'And there stood the ancient. He was smiling. Like this.' Rune made a hideous grin.

'I need the toilet,' whispered Tuppe.

'Cross your legs,' Rune ordered.

Tuppe crossed his legs.

'Smiling,' Rune continued. 'He beckoned to Breeze. "I believe you have come to see this," he said, indicating something which stood upon a pedestal, covered with a silken cloth. "My treasure."

'The ancient removed the cloth and Breeze drew near to see the wonder revealed. It was a perfect miniature of the room in which he now stood, precise in every detail. But it was more than just some architect's model. This was something altogether unique.

'As Breeze stared down into the model, his eyes fell upon two small figures, standing within it. One was old and ragged. And the other was himself.

154

Breeze leaned nearer, that he might study this marvel. And, as he did so, the tiny facsimile of himself did likewise. It was somehow animated.

'Breeze took a step backwards and his tiny facsimile did likewise. He raised his arm and it raised its arm. "What you see, Mr Breeze," the ancient explained, "is a microcosm. It is a reflection. Take this." He handed Breeze a magnifying glass. "Study the precision."

'Breeze took the lens and peered at the model. He saw himself, in each and every detail. The image now held a magnifying glass and was studying an even smaller model room. Which, of course, contained another copy of himself, studying another tiny room. And so on and so on and so on. It was a treasure indeed.

'The ancient spoke once more. "As above, so below," he said. "Microcosm and macrocosm. It has been my life's work to create it. It is my life. Will you take this from me, Mr Breeze, as you have taken so many things from so many people?"

'Breeze eyed the ancient and he eyed the model room. Within it his *doppelgänger* did likewise. And then Breeze struck.' Rune smote the table once more to the terror of Tuppe. 'He struck and he struck and he struck. With his jemmy, he struck down the creator of the marvel. Struck him down and killed him. Dead.'

'Golly,' said Tuppe.

'Quite so. The treasure was now his. Breeze feasted his eyes upon it. It was all his. This wonder beyond price. But it did not please him. Even now that he possessed it. It did not make him happy. And why?'

'Because it now contained the image of himself standing over his murder victim?' Cornelius asked.

'Quite so,' cried Rune. 'There it was, you see. The damning evidence. The thing of infinite beauty, now soiled. So what should he do? Smash it to smithereens? Too drastic. Destroy the damning evidence? That was it. Reach into the model, pluck up the figure of himself and snap it between his fingers. The work of a moment. As above, so below.

'And that's exactly what he did. He delved into the model, fascinated to see that his little duplicate did likewise. And he squeezed it to a lifeless pulp.

'It was the last thing he ever did. The police came across his body some days later. Lying there in that central chamber. The coroner's report stated that it was almost as if some great hand had descended from above and crushed him to a lifeless pulp.'

Tuppe fought with his crossed legs. 'You mean . . .'

'As above, so below,' said Rune. 'And as below, so above. For ever and ever, in each direction, up and down, and around and about. My uncle told me the story. And I tell you.'

'Is it meant to be allegorical?' Cornelius asked.

'No. It's meant to be true.'

'Ah,' said Cornelius.

'You don't believe it, then?' Rune looked surprised.

'I didn't say that. It's just, well—'

'Well what?'

'Well, what happened to the model and the body of the old man?'

Tuppe was about to suggest that they might well have vanished into obscurity, but he thought better of it.

'I embellished the story slightly,' said Rune, 'to make it more interesting. The ancient did not actually die. He lived on for some years afterward.'

'Before vanishing with his table into obscurity?' asked Cornelius. Tuppe hid his face.

'Before bequeathing the table to my uncle,' said Rune. 'Who in turn bequeathed it to me. It is there, standing in the corner. Would you care to have a look at it?'

14

As the Inspectre's security key, which gained him access to the express lift, was now at the bottom of the Thames, amongst the hydrated aluminium silicate, quartz, organic fragments, sedimentary rocks and other deposits (not to mention a certain amount of alluvial matter) Hovis was forced to take the stairs.

Had he not held the Argyle and Southern Highlanders Hill Yomp trophy for a full three years, there is no telling how things might have ended. A lesser man would certainly have perished.

Inspectre Hovis straightened his spare regimental necktie, slicked back a brilliantined forelock, squared the immaculate shoulders of his other suit and stood to attention before the door which had so recently been his.

His name was no longer upon it. A large new brass plate engraved with the words: CHIEF INSPECTOR LYTTON. KNOCK AND WAIT. was firmly screwed in its place. It looked anything but temporary. Knock and wait! Hovis swung open the door and marched straight in.

And he was not pleased at what he saw. Chief Inspector Brian Lytton had made himself very much at home. All trace of Hovis, other than for his precious Louis XV ormolu-mounted, kingswood and parquetry kneehole desk, the gift of a grateful monarch, had been wiped away. The walls were now painted a frightful puce. Horrid computer things flanked them and the carpet was definitely of a man-made fibre. A large framed print of white horses coming out of the sea hung near the window.

Excruciating! Inspectre Hovis viewed it all with distaste.

Especially the man behind the desk. Chief Inspector Lytton was short, stout and baby-faced, with that fresh scrubbed look. He had little piggy eyes. His suit was double-breasted.

He sat behind the royal desk, drinking from a paper cup. An Olympic logo of cup stains bastardized the priceless surface.

'I didn't hear you knock,' he said.

'I did,' Hovis replied. 'Several times.'

'I really must get a bell installed then. The door is quite thick and I fear it presents difficulties for those enfeebled officers of advancing years, who no longer retain the strength in their right arms.'

Hovis moved his mouth, as if in speech, but uttered no words.

'Sorry?' said Lytton. 'I didn't catch that.'

'I said, you'd better get a great big bell,' Hovis shouted. 'In case you have a problem hearing it. What with the traffic noise, and everything,' he added politely.

'Ah yes. Indeed. Sit down then, Hovis. Take a pew.'

Hovis sat down.

'Settling into the Portakabin all right?'

'No,' said Hovis. 'It is completely inadequate for my needs. I will certainly need to return to this office, if I am to successfully instigate the secret taskforce operation that I was discussing last night with the chief of police.' He paused to evaluate the effect of this outrageous lie.

'I shall await my briefing from him then,' said Lytton. 'I happen to be dining with him tonight.'

Beneath the wrong side of his desk, Inspectre Hovis clenched and unclenched his fists.

'Now let us talk of other matters.' The chief inspector set down his paper cup. 'Sherringford, might I call you Sherringford?'

'Of course, *Brian*.'

'So glad. Now, it behoves me to tell you that, as you may have noticed, the department is currently going through major restructuring. It is all down to government funding, or the lack of. The recession. Cut backs. Things of that nature. Someone has to go. That is the nub of it.'

'We will be sorry to lose you,' said Hovis.

'*Me?* Oh very droll. You will have your little joke.' Hovis smiled. Lytton did not.

'Weight-pulling, that's the thing. Some of us are doing it. Others not. Crime figures. Clear-up rates. Books to be balanced. Not my province really. The big boys upstairs. Administration. What do they know about grass-roots detection? Huh?'

'Nothing.' Hovis shook his head. 'Nothing at all.'

'Nothing at all. You're so right. But they do have the say-so. Isn't it always the way?'

'Always,' said Inspectre Hovis.

'So there you are.'

'Where?' asked Hovis. 'Where am I?'

'Out,' said the chief inspector. 'Out on your ear, I'm afraid. Redundant. Taking an early retirement. That's where.'

'What?' went Hovis. 'What? What? What?'

'Knew you'd take it like a man. Told them upstairs. Begged them to reconsider, of course. But they were adamant. Still, look on the bright side. Give you a chance to spend more time with your wife and family.'

'I do not have a wife and family.' Hovis gripped the arms of his chair and began to rock in a distinctly manic fashion.

'No wife and family? Then you should get one, my dear fellow. I've two girls myself, eight and ten. That's a photo of them over there on the wall. On the ponies.'

'No!' said Hovis. 'No! No! No!'

'Bit of a shock, eh? Thought it might be. Given your life to the force. Feel like you've been kicked in the teeth. Worthless. Thrown on the scrapheap. My heart goes out to you. And if you ever need a reference, don't hesitate to write.'

'I!' went Hovis. 'I . . . I . . . I . . .'

'No need to thank me. But cut along now. And don't forget to hand in your warrant card. End of the week, eh? Sorry to have to rush you, but we need the Portakabin. Temporary ladies' loo apparently. What a world we live in, eh?'

Hovis rose from his chair. He would make it look

161

like an accident, or suicide. The chief inspector, stricken with remorse, threw himself from the window.

Chief Inspector Lytton took a regulation police-issue revolver from his top drawer and pointed it at his murderer-to-be.

'Don't even think about it,' he said. 'Now piss off out of my office, before I call a policeman.'

'Behold the marvel,' said Hugo Rune, tearing aside the silken cloth.

'I can't behold from down here,' Tuppe complained. 'Give us a lift up, Cornelius.'

'My pleasure.' Cornelius hoisted Tuppe into the viewing position.

'Crikey,' went the small one. 'Now *that* is a neat trick.'

'Isn't it though.' Rune fluttered his pudgy fingers. Tuppe flinched accordingly. 'Do you now understand the beauty of the thing?'

'It's here,' said Cornelius, gazing with considerable awe. 'It's a miniature of *this* room. And of us. I thought you said it was a copy of that ancient fellow's chamber.'

'A microcosm,' Rune explained. 'The device is built into the table top. Take the table where you will. Uncover it, and there displayed will be a microcosm of the immediate surroundings.'

'It's very clever. How does it work?'

'Have you ever heard of the transperambulation of pseudo-cosmic anti-matter?'

'Not as such.'

'Best not to concern yourself then. It works. It is a thing of wonder.'

'And it scares the shit out of me,' said Tuppe. 'Am I really that small?'

'You're as big as you feel,' said Cornelius. 'How *do* you feel, by the way?'

'About ready for the main course now.'

'Well,' Cornelius put down the Tuppe. 'Thank you for showing it to us, Mr Rune.'

'Forget the Mr Rune, my boy. You may call me—'

'Daddy?'

'No, it's still *guru*,' said Hugo Rune. 'And so you see the beauty of my plan.'

'What plan is this?' Cornelius looked baffled.

'My plan to bring down the denizens of the Forbidden Zones.'

'Ah, that plan.' Cornelius nodded gently. He felt sure that he was much taller than Hugo Rune. But somehow he always seemed to be looking up at him.

'Let us discuss it over the main course,' said Rune. 'Come on, Shorty.'

'Please do not call my friend Shorty,' said Cornelius.

'I wasn't talking to your friend,' said Hugo Rune. 'I was talking to *you*.'

Inspectre Hovis returned to the Portakabin. Polly recognized his distinctive door-slamming and did not look up from her work.

'Would you like me to put the kettle on again?' she asked.

Hovis did not reply.

163

'I located that file you wanted. It is a big fat one.'
Polly rose to hand it over. And found herself staring
into a face which seemed to have aged by at least ten
years in less than half an hour.

'Sit down.' Polly reached forward and took Hovis
by the arm. 'You look dreadful. It's probably a
reaction to that Thames water. Sit down and I'll call
for a doctor.'

Hovis allowed himself to be helped into the Portakabin's only chair. It occurred to him, as Polly fussed
about, that he could not recall when he last felt a
woman's touch upon him.

A dismal groan escaped from his lips.

'Just take it easy,' said Polly. 'I'll get help.'

'I don't need any help,' the Inspectre told her.
'There is nothing physically wrong with me. It is just
that I have received some tragic news.'

'Not a death in your family?'

'No. I said *tragic* news.'

'Eh?'

'You had best take the rest of the day off, Polly.
Or the week, if you please. You must find yourself
another position. I will furnish you with superb
references.'

'You're sacking me? What have I done?'

'Not I,' Hovis crossed his heart. 'Brian "the bastard"
Lytton. He has cut me back. I am redundant.'

'He can't do that,' Polly protested. 'I've read up
on your cases. You've solved more crimes than
anyone else in the history of the force.'

'I am touched that you should show such an
interest,' said Hovis, who truly was.

164

'But all in Brentford,' said Polly. 'How come you solved every crime in Brentford?'

Hovis hung his head.

'But he *can't* sack you. He just can't.'

'He can and he has. Early retirement.'

'Then we'll fight him. You must have many connections. Many friends in high places. *Life has no blessing like a prudent friend*, to quote from Euripides.'

'I have no friends,' said Hovis.

'What, none at all?'

'None at all. I have no connections. Everybody hates me.'

'Everybody?'

'Everybody.'

'Oh,' said Polly. 'That makes me feel a lot better. I thought it was only me. Hating you, that is.'

'It's an image thing. All we really great detectives have it. The eccentric mannerism, the funny voice, the strange moustache, the pipe, the tin leg, the penchant for tiny woodland creatures.'

'Ugh,' said Polly.

'Mine is being hated by everybody.'

'Oh, I understand. You're a sort of anti-hero.'

'No,' said Hovis. 'I'm just a nasty bastard.'

'You're not so bad.' Polly would have placed a consoling hand upon the immaculate, if now somewhat drooping, shoulder of the great detective, had not the very thought sickened her to the stomach. 'You really aren't that bad. Really. Certainly you're arrogant, conceited, short-tempered, misogynistic, boorish and boring. No offence meant.'

'None taken, I assure you.'

165

'But you are a brilliant detective. And so you must not be sacked. What do you intend to do?'

'Pack up and go home, I suppose. Sell my memoirs to a Sunday tabloid. Maybe get a spot on *Crimewatch*.'

'But what about The Crime of the Century? This destiny you told me you had to fulfil? *No man or woman born, coward or brave, can shun his destiny* – Homer.'

'I have been given until the weekend to put my affairs in order.'

'*A week in politics can be a long time*, to quote—'

'Quote me no further quotes,' said Hovis, 'please.'

Polly made fists at the ceiling. 'I don't want to be made redundant. It sucks on the dole. Surely we can think of something. There has to be something.'

'I did have one idea,' said Hovis thoughtfully. 'It's an old trick, but it might just work.'

'Tell me. Tell me.'

'You must swear to keep it secret.'

'I swear.' Polly licked her finger and made motions above the bosom area. 'Cross my heart and hope to die.'

'We could discredit Lytton.'

'Now that *is* a brilliant idea. What should we do?'

Inspectre Hovis leaned back in his chair and stared into space.

'Catch him in a compromising situation. In the arms of some harlot. Burst in, camera in hand. *Flagrante delicto*. The deed is done. I think that would do the trick.'

'And serve the bugger right too. Jumped–up little shit.'

'Quite so. Right then. I'll pop out to Boots and

get some film for the old box Brownie. You go up to his office, whip off all your clothes and prostrate yourself across the desk. Shall we synchronize watches?'

Polly looked at Hovis.

And Hovis looked at Polly.

'Go and suck,' said Polly Gotting. 'I'm off to the Job Centre.'

Unseen hands had replenished the great table and another course lay ready for the digging into.

Rune dug in. And he spoke as he did so. 'We must wipe out the beings in the Forbidden Zones,' quoth he. 'Wipe them out while there are still a few of us left.'

'I don't think I quite follow that.' Cornelius heaped goodies on to his latest plate.

'Mankind declines,' said Rune solemnly. 'We grow fewer every day.'

'I would hate to be the one to contradict you, er, guru. But the population of the world is, as ever, on the increase.'

'It is nothing of the sort. Those within the zones grow in number. We decline. Once we were many, but we grow fewer by the year.'

'And might I ask how you come to this conclusion?'

'Simple mathematics. Allow me to explain.' Rune thrust his thumbs into his waistcoat pockets and regarded his audience.

'How many are there of you, personally?' he asked Cornelius.

167

'Me personally? One, I suppose.'

'Correct, one. And how many parents do you have?'

'Two,' said Cornelius. 'Everybody has two. A mother and a father.'

'Correct again. Two. And how many grand-parents?'

'Four,' said Cornelius.

'And great-grandparents?'

'Eight.'

'And great-great-grandparents?'

'Sixteen.'

'And great-great-great-grandparents?'

'Thirty-two.'

'And so it goes on. Every generation you go back, you double it. By the time you go back a mere twenty-three generations, you have a figure in excess of four million people. Every one of which was necessary if you were ever to be born at all. The further you go back, the greater the number of people.'

'There has to be something wrong with that,' said Tuppe, giving his head a serious scratch. 'But for the life of me, I can't think what.'

'There cannot be anything wrong with it,' declared Rune. 'Work it out on a pocket calculator if you don't believe me. You cannot disprove an Ultimate Truth.'

Tuppe began to count on his fingers.

Cornelius asked, 'Where is this getting us?'

'We must wage war upon the Forbidden Zones now.' Rune struck the table another mighty blow.

168

'We must purge the planet of this unseen pestilence. This cankerous bubo, this septic pus-filled—'

'I think we get the picture,' said Cornelius Murphy. 'We're all for that. Tuppe and I have sworn ourselves to this very end. It's just that we haven't made much of a success of it, so far.'

'But that is because you lacked the wisdom and guidance of Hugo Rune.'

'Ah,' said Cornelius. 'You think that was it then?'

Rune nodded. 'Indubitably. Under my benevolent leadership, we will stamp out these "fairies", devils, more like. Throw off the shackles that constrain mankind. Raise high the battle standard of Ultimate Truth.'

'Do you have a plan?' Cornelius asked.

'Plan? Do *I* have a plan? *I* have a stratagem.'

'Tell us, guru,' said the Tuppe.

Cornelius raised an eyebrow to the small fellow.

'It is a two-part stratagem,' said Rune. 'Part one is concerned with drawing the world's attention to the existence of the Forbidden Zones, I will speak of that in good time. Part two deals with the extermination of those inside these zones. And this is where the ragged ancient's magical table comes into play. Allow me to explain. I have spent many years inside the zones. I am *au fait* with their layout. There exists a great hall, the hall of the king. And when part one of the plan has been put into operation, and there is much confusion within the zones, it is to this great hall that the so-called fairy folk will rush. And suppose that one of us is there. And the magical table is there with them. Use your imagination, gentlemen.'

Tuppe grinned and pictured himself reaching down into the miniature facsimile of this great hall to place his thumb upon the head of Mr Arthur Kobold.

'*Hasta la vista*, baby,' said the Tuppe.

Chief Inspector Lytton peered down through the venetian blinds. He watched Polly leave the Portakabin and storm across the car park.

'And that,' said Lytton, 'would appear to be that.'

The telephone began to ring and so he picked it up. 'Lytton.'

'Everything sorted?' asked a voice.

'He's clearing out his desk.'

'Good work. You've done very well. I think you can expect another promotion within the year.'

'Thank you very much,' said Brian Lytton.

'Don't mention it,' replied the voice of Arthur Kobold. 'We look after our own.'

15

Mickey Minns awoke to find himself staring at a strange ceiling. The experience, in itself, was not altogether strange. It had happened many times before. But it caught him temporarily off guard. Minns hastily shut his eyes and made a serious attempt at a mental rerun of last night's closing moments. Glimpses came to him. Buying drinks for policemen. A bottle of *Jim Beam* that literally materialized beside him. Jack Lane clouting him with a walking-stick. And that was about all really.

Mickey groaned. Perhaps there'd been some unpleasantness. Perhaps he was in the nick. He opened his left eye and took in the ceiling. Georgian blue. Mickey set free a small sigh of relief. Not the ceiling of a police cell then. Police cell ceilings were invariably white. Stark and intimidatingly so.

Where then? The hospital? No, hospital ceilings are generally green. Hospitals were always painted green in the old days. Something to do with all the blood. And how when you stare at red for a long time and then look away, you see green. Colour opposites, or some such thing. So they painted the walls green, which was the opposite of red, and when you looked up from the blood, you didn't see green and throw up everywhere. Or was it a tradition, or an old charter? Or something? And did they still paint hospitals green anyway? Mickey seemed to think that they didn't.

And so he opened both eyes. Thinking about hospitals always depressed him. He'd been pumped out too many times, and had too many eager-faced young interns going on at him about his liver.

Georgian blue. It was definitely Georgian blue. He'd once owned a guitar that colour which had belonged to Jimi Hendrix. But the thing was bewitched and used to feed back in the middle of the night, when it wasn't even plugged in. Mickey had sold it on to a coven in Acton.

Georgian blue. Who did he know that had a ceiling painted Georgian blue?

And silk pillows? Mickey dug his fingers into them. He wasn't lying on the floor! He was lying in somebody's bed!

There came to Mickey's ear the whisper of silk sheets. And to his senses, the realization that he was not alone in this bed.

Mickey turned his head to the side.

'Shiva's sheep!' He was blinking at a head-load of golden hair. And now at the face of Anna Gotting.

'Good morning, Mickey,' said Anna, yawning and stretching, luxuriously, with naked arms. 'I'd bet you'd like some coffee.'

'I . . .' Mickey rammed a knuckle into his mouth. 'I . . .'

'You were wonderful,' sighed Anna. 'Where did you learn all those moves? I've never "taken tea with the parson" before. Incredible.'

'I . . .' Mickey fought with his brain. Come on, you bastard, he told it. Remember. Please remember. He jerked upright and began to belabour his skull with his fists. 'Remember, or I'll smash you to pieces!'

'Stop it,' Anna leapt to restrain him. She didn't have any clothes on.

'Naked!' Mickey doubled the assault on his head.

'Stop it. You didn't do anything. I was just winding you up.'

'What?' Mickey's fists hovered in the air. 'What?'

'I was walking home and I found you asleep in a phone box. I dragged you back here and put you to bed.'

'Oh,' said Mickey.

'Oh,' said Anna.

'Oh shit!' Mickey struck his head once more.

'Stop hitting yourself.'

'I'm sorry.' Minns fell back on the pillow and draped a forearm over his face. Not too far to obscure his view of Anna's nakedness, but just far enough so she couldn't see him looking.

As the silken sheet covering Mickey's mid-section began to rise, Anna said, 'Forget it, Mickey. I'll get you some coffee.'

She flipped out of the bed, into a peach-coloured towelling robe and was gone from the room.

Inspectre Sherringford Hovis sat all alone in the Portakabin. And he was actually smiling. He rubbed his palms together and considered the big fat file which lay upon the desk. The file of Hugo Artemis Solon Saturnicus Reginald Arthur Rune.

'I think I can state, without fear of contradiction,' said Hovis with a chuckle, 'that I have definitely seen the last of that appalling young woman. Which leaves me two full days, all alone and undisturbed, to solve The Crime of the Century.'

Now, a lesser man, having suffered as Hovis had suffered, under sentence of redundancy, and faced with the prospect of trying to solve a crime which had yet to be committed, might well have given up the ghost and tossed himself off some high building.

But not Inspectre Hovis. Soon to become Lord Hovis of Kew. No tosser he! The future peer of the realm tapped a smiling mug shot of Hugo Rune with the fingertip of accusation.

'You, my fine fellow,' he said to it. 'You, the face at the wheel of the speeding silver car. I know you, don't I? And I know that car. My extensive knowledge of automotive arcana tells me that was nothing less than the now legendary MacGregor Mathers Water Car. I spy a pretty pattern here, and no mistake. A train from nowhere. Diamonds from nowhere. A green demon from God knows where. And the return of Hugo Rune. Add to this two burnt-out cars, of rare vintage and unknown origin, on Kew Green and two more in the surrounding area.'

Hovis took up the mug shot and studied the broad and grinning face. 'The great unsolveds,' said he. 'And the greatest yet to come. But not unsolved this time. Oh no, sir. Not this time. You are the man I seek, sir. And you are the man I'll find. You're out there somewhere, hatching some diabolical scheme,

I can feel it in my water. I will have you, Hugo Rune. You see if I don't.'

If the ears of Rune were burning, the Master showed no sign. He placed his great hands on the table and heaved his not inconsiderable bulk from his chair. 'We are going to best and beat these buggers,' he declared. 'Wipe them out. Delete them. But, as I have said, most eloquently, before, it is not sufficient that we do it in private. Retribution must be seen to be done. The whole world must watch us when we do it.'

'The whole world?' Tuppe whistled.

'The whole world.' Rune pushed his chair aside and began a ponderous pacing. 'We must expose the villains. Expose what they have done to mankind. Reveal the truth. The Ultimate Truth. That they have manipulated us throughout the centuries. All the world must know. And all the world must watch.' He ceased his pacing and made that 'picture this' gesture that people sometimes make. 'In order that the world might watch, the world must be given something that it wants to watch. Something really well worth watching.'

Tuppe nodded enthusiastically. 'What?' he asked.

'A crime,' said Rune. 'A great crime. Committed live before the watching world. A crime of such magnitude and audaciousness, that it will be considered The Crime of the Century. This crime will arouse the passions of the world. This crime is part one of my stratagem.'

'Golly,' said Tuppe.

'Picture this,' said Rune, referring back to a gesture he'd prepared earlier. 'The great crime is committed. The world looks on. The authorities are baffled. The police are baffled. Everyone is baffled. And then one man steps forward. "I can solve this crime," he says. "I can lead you to the door, to the many doors in fact, where the criminals lurk." '

'The entrances to the Forbidden Zones,' said Tuppe.

'The very same. To all of them in London. Every one. At the same time. Imagine it. All those armed policemen. All those Special Forces blokes in the body armour. All those fine young soldiers. All that weaponry.'

Cornelius thought he could imagine it only too well. And he did not like this imagining one little bit. 'This one man who steps forward to solve the crime. That would be you, I suppose.'

'None other,' said Rune.

'And the crime itself. That would be committed by . . . ?'

'Yourself and your companion. Under my instruction, naturally.'

'Naturally. But about this crime. This Crime of the Century that will have the world sitting on the edge of its collective seat. What will this crime be, exactly?'

'The kidnapping of Her Majesty the Queen,' said Hugo Rune. 'On prime-time TV.'

Colin Collins was sitting all alone in his little glass booth at the Job Centre when Polly Gotting walked in. He was dreaming about trains.

His full name was Colin does-anybody-want-to-fish-this-bugger-out-then? Collins. Which was all to do with the vicar dropping him into the font during the christening.

Now, this would have been nothing more than a tired old gag, if it hadn't been for the fact that the vicar did it on purpose.

At the time, the cleric's extraordinary behaviour bewildered the little congregation of family and friends. But as the years dragged by and Colin dragged himself towards the estate of manhood, all those who had attended the christening considered that, perhaps, it might have been better if 'the bugger' had not been fished out at all.

It wasn't that Colin was evil. That would have been considered acceptable in a family that proudly numbered amongst its ancestry three iconoclasts, two serial killers and a horse mutilator.

It was that Colin was dull. Dull! That's what he was. Soul-destroyingly, mind-numbingly dull. His father, Colin Collins Senior, was dull. But his was an everyday, easygoing sort of dullness. And all those who knew the Collins family considered Collins Senior the very acme of wit and personality, when placed against his son.

Now it is a well-known fact amongst those who know it well, that the world is full of Colins. They are everywhere, though, as a rule, you don't notice them. There's one in every class. Study any old school photograph, you'll see him. Middle row, easy to miss and no-one can remember his name. It's Colin.

And when they leave school, these Colins, they go
to work for the DHSS.

Here they sit, wearing *those* glasses, *those* shirts, *those*
ties, *those* cardigans, *those* open-toed sandals and *those*
grey socks.

And they dream about trains.

Other than for Polly, the Job Shop, as it had been
humorously renamed, by a man called Colin, was a
veritable Mother Hubbard's cupboard, when it came
to seekers after employment. This was probably
because there weren't any jobs for sale.

Polly surveyed the uncompromising row of little
glass-fronted booths. All appeared unmanned. She
strode up to the first and rapped on the glass. 'Shop,'
she called.

Colin stopped dreaming about trains. 'How can I
help you?' he asked.

Polly glanced in the direction of the voice. It came
from the next booth. 'Sorry,' she said, 'I didn't see
you there.'

'Do you want a green form?' Colin asked.

'What shade of green is it?'

'This shade.' Colin held up the green form.

'Not really,' said Polly.

Colin's eyes began to glaze over.

'I want a job.'

'You'll have to fill in a green form then.'

'But I already filled one in.'

'Well, give it to me and I'll get it stamped.'

'You already have it.'

'Do I?' Colin scratched his head. He had dandruff.
'I don't think I do.'

'Well, somebody does. I filled it in the last time I was here.'

'When was that?'

'About four weeks ago.'

'I wasn't here then.' Colin straightened the row of Biros in the top pocket of his cardigan. 'I was doing in-house training.'

'*Learning makes a man fit company for himself.* As Young once wrote.'

'I'm sorry?'

'Never mind. Would you like to go and get my green form from your files?'

'Oh, all right.' Colin rose from his chair.

'Wouldn't you like to know my name first? It might help.'

'I know your name. It's Polly Gotting.'

'How do you know that?'

'You used to be in my class at school.'

'Did I?'

'Yes. I sat next to you.'

'Oh yes, of course.' Polly tried to make it sound convincing. 'It's Dermot, isn't it?'

'It's Colin,' said Colin.

'Oh yes. Colin. That's it.'

'I'll get your green form then.'

'Thank you, Colin.'

'Oh, it's not Colin any more,' said Colin, drawing Polly's attention to the smart name badge he wore. 'It's *Mister* Collins now.'

It was a very big filing cabinet. And G can take a bit of finding. Especially if you're dreaming about trains.

'I'll have to hurry you now,' said Mr Collins, when he finally returned. 'It's half-day closing.'

'Is that my green form?'

'Yes. It all seems to be in order. What did you say your query was?'

'I don't have a query. I want a job.'

'But you have a job. And a good one too. With a pension.'

'I just got made redundant.'

'Redundant is a red form,' said Mr Collins.

'I just want another job. What do you have?'

Mr Collins studied Polly's green form. 'Polyhymnia Gotting. Polyhymnia?'

'The muse of singing and sacred dance. It's Greek.'

'It is to me.' Colin had a go at a smile. But he just couldn't pull it off. 'You passed all your exams,' he said. 'All of them.'

'That's what they were there for. To be passed.'

'I didn't pass any of mine.'

'Perhaps you weren't clever enough. No offence meant.'

'None taken. But it can't be anything to do with being clever.'

'It can't?'

'No. Because I'm clever enough to be in full-time employment, and you're not.'

Polly was clever enough to keep her temper. 'Do you have any jobs on offer?'

'Not for you.'

'Why not for me?'

'Because you are over-qualified.'

'What does that do?' Polly pointed to a gleaming

new computer terminal that stood on Mr Collins's desktop.

'That', said Colin proudly, 'is an on-line computer. It gives an hour-to-hour update of all new job opportunities. You punch in the qualifications of the applicant and the computer matches them to any available employment and prints out the reply. It's brand new. It only arrived half an hour ago.'

'Why not punch in my qualifications and see what happens?'

'I'd love to. But I can't.'

'Why not?'

'Because it's half-day closing. And we just closed.'

Polly would dearly have loved to drag Mr Collins from his little glass-fronted booth and punish him severely. But instead she smiled.

'It looks incredibly complicated,' she said.

'It is. Very.'

'I can understand you being wary about operating it.'

'Who said I was wary?'

'Careful then. It must be a bit of a responsibility. I know, if I were in your, er, sandals, I wouldn't fancy trying it out without my supervisor present.'

'I am fully capable of using it. I did it at in-house training.'

'Of course you did. But I can understand you being nervous.'

'I'm not nervous.'

'It probably doesn't work anyway.'

'Of course it works.'

'Sure it does. I bet.'

181

'It does work and I'm not nervous about using it.'

'I'll come back tomorrow and speak to your supervisor,' said Polly. 'I expect she's a woman. She'll have the bottle to try it out. Always best to go straight to the top. Cut out the unambitious technophobes who don't want the glory of being the first to make a placement with such hi-tech equipment. *Men have sight; women insight* – to quote Victor Hugo. So long, Colin.' Polly turned upon her heel.

Mr Collins dithered. He hadn't understood half she'd said. But he got the general gist. 'Just you come back here,' he said.

Polly watched him as he worried at the computer keyboard. Her mother had told her, as she had told her sister Anna, that all men were basically stupid. And she, like her sister, would pass this information on to daughters of her own one day.

'Eureka!' said Colin suddenly.

'Eureka?'

'*Eureka*. It was an LNER passenger train. Classic 4-6-2 arrangement. Four-wheel bogie in front, six coupled driving wheels and a pair of trailing wheels. Eureka.'

'It's Greek to me.'

'It's a perfect match.' Mr Collins was looking quite excited. 'On the computer. The job just came up this very minute. And your qualifications match it exactly.'

Coincidence? Synchronicity? The steam-driven bogie truck of destiny?

'It's at Buckingham Palace,' said Colin. 'Personal assistant to His Royal Highness Prince Charles.'

The bogie truck has it!

182

16

Hugo Rune had gone off to the toilet.

Having witnessed him single-handedly complete the breakfast that had become elevenses, then lunch, Tuppe and Cornelius were hardly surprised.

'I've never seen anyone eat like that before,' said Tuppe. 'Not even when I was travelling with the circus. Are we really going to kidnap the Queen, by the way?'

'No,' said Cornelius, 'we are not. We are going to get out of here, and fast.'

'Before pudding?'

'At once. I don't know whether that man is really my daddy. But I know one thing, he's barking mad.'

'You noticed that too?'

'He's a monomaniac. Let's get.'

'Do you think he'll let us get? He's a bit nifty with the old magickal passes.'

'Just leave the talking to me.'

Rune returned from the bog. 'Have you noticed', he asked, 'how, no matter where you go in this world, the smell in the gents is always the same?'

Cornelius put up his hand to speak.

'You have my attention.' Rune settled back into his chair.

'Tuppe and I have been discussing your stratagem.'

'And naturally you find no fault in it.'

'Naturally. But it occurred to me, as one who has studied *The Book of Ultimate Truths*, that you are not without friends amongst the royal household. That you used to be, in fact, a regular guest at the palace.'

'There are few in high office with whom I am not on intimate terms.'

'That's what we thought. So wouldn't it be better if you took care of the actual kidnapping part, yourself?'

Rune nodded thoughtfully. 'No,' he said.

'No?'

'No. It just wouldn't do. It is a long time since I have seen the Queen, but she would recognize me at once.'

'You could wear a mask,' Tuppe suggested. 'And a cloak, if wanted.'

'No,' said Rune. 'It simply wouldn't wash. The whole point of this brilliantly conceived two-part stratagem, is to stir up the world and stir up the fairy folk, have the whole world look on, get the blighters into their great hall and squash the lot of them in the magic table. I will have much to organize. You must see that the Queen is in the great hall when the popping off begins.'

'Why must *she* be there?'

'Because she's one of *them*, of course.'

'One of *them*?'

'One of the fairy folk. She isn't just our queen. She's their queen as well.'

'You are saying that the Queen of England is not a real human being?'

184

'I never thought she was,' Tuppe said. 'After all, she doesn't go to the toilet.'

'Of course she goes to the toilet.' Cornelius sssshed Tuppe.

'Well, I've never seen her.'

'No, no, no.' Cornelius took off his cap and flapped it all about. 'This is complete and utter madness. Eighteen years in the Forbidden Zones has addled your brain.'

Rune rose once more to his feet and cast his chair aside. 'I am Rune!' he cried, his voice echoing amongst the hammerbeams. 'I am the Logos of the Aeon. The greatest thinker of this or any age. I am Babylon. Alpha and Omega. Rune, do you hear? I think, therefore *I'm* right!'

'And I am Cornelius Murphy,' said the tall boy, with a fearlessness that surprised even himself. 'And *I* am the Stuff of Epics. I am not your cat's-paw, nor your acolyte. I will not call you guru and fall at your feet. Your stratagems bring insanity to an art form. I will have none of them.'

Tuppe cowered in his seat. 'Hang on to your mouth,' he whispered.

'We have enjoyed your hospitality,' Cornelius went on, 'but not your company. You are clearly unscrupulous and prepared to further your own ends, at no matter what cost to others. I swore to reveal the truth about the beings in the Forbidden Zones for the good of all mankind.'

'And liberate some of the stolen booty for the good of us,' Tuppe put in.

'Yes, well, that too. Arthur Kobold owes us plenty.

But, I will not aid you in some bid of your own for world domination. Nor will I be a party to mass murder. If you are my real father, then I disown you. I vowed to release you from the zones and this I did, however unknowingly. But that is an end to it. It ends here. You and I have nothing more to say.

'Come, Tuppe, we're leaving.'

Tuppe looked up at his friend. The small fellow's mouth hung hugely open.

Hugo Rune's mouth was also open. And, for possibly the first time in all his life, he was speechless.

'You might have handled that a mite better,' said Tuppe.

He and Cornelius had now reached the end of the drive and stood in the bright sunlight, facing an open road. 'Asked him for some bus fares, or something.'

'The man is a stone bonker.' Cornelius stuck his hands in his trouser pockets and idly kicked stones about.

Tuppe shrugged. 'So what are we going to do now?'

'Thumb a lift?' Cornelius squinted along the country road.

'To where?' Tuppe followed his squint.

'Who cares?'

'Who cares? Whatever do you mean?'

'I mean I've had enough. I quit.'

'But you can't quit. You're the Stuff of Epics.'

'I'm having a bit of a problem with that right now.'

'Rune really got under your skin, didn't he?'

186

'And then some. Kidnap the Queen. What sort of plan is that?'

'An epic one?'

'No.' Cornelius shuffled his feet. 'It's madness.'

'So what about *them*?'

'What about them?'

'Well, we have to wipe them out, don't we?'

'Wipe them out? Think what you're saying, Tuppe. If they are some parallel race, good, bad or indifferent, do you really think genocide is a healthy option? I'll agree that Kobold needs wiping out. But what if he's got a wife and kids? Wipe them out? Get real.'

'Get real? Oh that's very good. We're talking about wiping out wicked fairies, and you tell me to get real.'

Cornelius shrugged.

'So you're just going to forget it then? Forget how they screw up mankind's progress. How *they* decide what's good for us to know and what isn't.'

'Well there's always someone doing that. Perhaps they do the job as well as any.'

'I can't believe I'm hearing this. "Livestock", Kobold called us, "Vermin".'

'Listen, Tuppe, when Rune was ranting on back there about retribution, it all came to me in the proverbial flash. We can't expose *them*. It would be disastrous. Think what *they* might have in there. Kobold said that mankind would have blown itself up long ago, if it hadn't been for him and his kind. Maybe they've got plans for superbombs? What? Imagine stuff like that all suddenly falling into government hands. And what about the people? When the people find out that their actions have been governed by some secret society in their very midst fingers will be pointed. Folk will say, "That's why so-and-so got so successful, he must have been in league with *them*." Society, as we know it, will grind to a halt.'

Tuppe screwed up his face. 'What you are saying is, when it comes right down to it, *they* are best left alone.'

'Something like that.'

'It all seems to have become very complicated,' said Tuppe. 'And not a lot of laughs. All right. Maybe it would be a bad idea to expose Kobold's mob to society. But they should still be stopped. Think of all the good stuff they must have stolen. What about Rune's car? A thing like that could make the world a better place.'

'It could if it really worked.'

'But it does work. You've driven it.'

'I thought you said you were awake during our journey here from Brentford.'

'I might have nodded off once or twice.'

'Me too. But I woke up on two occasions. When he stopped to fill up with Four Star.'

'The scoundrel. The man is a fraud.'

'The car is a fraud. That's for certain.'

'And what about the magic table? I saw that, with the little us in it.'

'Yeah. I saw it too. But whether I believe it. That's another matter.'

'Well, well, well.' Tuppe made with the bright and breeziness. 'That seems to be it all sorted. Rune is a stone bonker intent on genocide. His car is a fraud.

188

We don't know about the table, but we think James Randi could rubbish it, given a couple of minutes. The lads in the Forbidden Zones are not altogether to be wished, but they're probably the better of two evils, so leave them to get on with it. It's all so simple really, I don't know why I didn't think of it.'

'I expect you would have, eventually.'

'And so we just forget all about it, thumb a lift and seek our fortunes elsewhere?'

'You have a better idea?'

'Quite a few, as it happens. We should go back to the house, tell all this to Rune. He may be a stone bonker, but he's also a powerful magician, you saw what he did to my mouth. You have to reason with him, Cornelius.'

'It's not my responsibility.'

'Oh, responsibilities, is it? Well *you* drove the car. *You* set him free. What if he was better penned up in the zones? What if *they* kept him there because of how dangerous he is? Did you think of that?'

'Not until now. Did you?'

'Not until now, no. We'd best go back.'

'We can't go back.'

'Of course we can. You can reason with him. He let us go without changing us into white mice. He likes you.'

'We can't go back. See for yourself.'

Cornelius gestured back towards the house. To where the house had been, but wasn't any more. There was just an overgrown plot of land, with an estate agent's sign up. MILCOM MOLOCH ESTATES. DEVELOPMENT SITE FOR SALE.

Tuppe turned a bitter eye from the site and back to his friend. 'You knew that was going to happen, didn't you?'

'I began to suspect something a couple of minutes ago. When I realized how hungry I still was.'

Tuppe rubbed his stomach. 'Me too. And after we ate all that—'

'Did we?'

'Aw shoot!' Tuppe turned in a small circle. 'The car's gone and everything. This is well beyond me.'

'And me also. Shall we thumb for a lift?'

'Any particular direction you favour?'

'None whatever. You stand this side of the road and I will stand on the other. We'll let fate decide.'

Tuppe looked at Cornelius.

And Cornelius looked at Tuppe.

'Let's do it,' said the small fellow.

17

The bus was a single-decker British Leyland, *circa* 1958. To say that it had seen better days would not altogether be telling the whole truth. Unless you considered plying a regular and turgid trade between Hounslow bus station and the Staines depot for twenty-three long and thankless years to be your definition of 'better days'.

Not so the bus. For it, the better days were now. Because this was a liberated bus. A bus now free of its yoke. Gone were the rows of dreary seats. Gone the dull green paintwork. Gone the sweaty driver's bum upon its forward throne. And gone, all gone, its number.

I am not a number. I am a free bus!

The free bus was now a bus apart. It had been lovingly repainted in many a rainbow hue. It housed two young families. And it was driven by a lady with a perfumed posterior. It was a happy bus.

It pulled up without even a squeak, although its brakes had long gone off to kingdom come. A young chap with curly black hair and a smiley face, swung open its doors. 'Want a lift?' he asked.

'Yes please,' said Cornelius Murphy.

'And your mate?'

'Please also.' Tuppe scampered across the road and clambered after Cornelius.

'Magic bus,' said the small one, taking it all in. 'You're not Ken Kesey, by any chance?'

'Bollocks,' said the young chap.

'Excuse me. No offence meant.'

'None taken. That's my name. Bollocks.'

'Is that Mr Bollocks, or Bollocks something?'

'It's bollocks to everything.' The young chap smiled hugely. 'Shut the door and make yourselves at home.'

'Thanks, we will.' Cornelius ducked his head, they made buses smaller in those days. And he shut the door. 'Where are you heading?'

'To wherever the good times are.'

'That's where we'd like to go,' said Tuppe.

'Then you're in good company.'

'Yes.' Cornelius gave the interior of the bus a thoughtful sensory scan. Bright-eyed children grinned at him from a hammock strung crossways between the windows. A guitar was being played with skill and a girl was singing. And delicious smells wafted from the cooking area. It was all rather blissful.

'Very good company indeed,' said Cornelius Murphy.

The lady at the wheel put the happy bus into gear and it rolled onwards.

'Want some eats?' asked Bollocks.

Tuppe looked at Cornelius.

And Cornelius looked at Tuppe.

'Yes please,' they said.

*   *   *

They dined on pulses and brown rice and fresh vegetables and strawberries and cream.

'OK?' Bollocks asked.

'Not half.' Tuppe loosened a button on his dungarees. 'Not half, thank you very much.'

'You guys employed?'

'Ah now.' Cornelius took off his cap and stroked his bandages. 'We were, sort of. But it didn't work out.'

'What happened to your head?'

'We ran into a spot of trouble,' Tuppe explained. 'Cornelius got some of his hair pulled out. It wasn't very nice.'

Bollocks nodded. 'Cornelius. That's your name, then?'

'Oh, I'm sorry,' said the tall boy. 'We haven't introduced ourselves. I'm Cornelius Murphy and this is Tuppe.'

'Tuppe?' asked Bollocks.

'It's short for Tupperware. Not a lot of people know that.'

'It comes as a revelation to me,' said Cornelius.

'I was going to save it for some special moment. But, sod it.'

'Bollocks to it,' said their host.

'Absolutely.'

'What about you?' Cornelius asked. 'I guess that's your lady at the wheel. And the two marvellous kids in the hammock are yours. And then there's the other family. Although the adults aren't sleeping together at the moment. Something to do with him getting stoned and falling into a slurry pit, I shouldn't wonder.'

193

Bollocks viewed Cornelius with alarm. 'How?'

'His nose.' Tuppe tapped the small one of his own. 'He has a gift. He can smell who's who. Who belongs to who. Stuff like that.'

'Can you smell trouble?' Bollocks asked.

'Oh yes. I can smell that all right.'

'Smell it now?'

The tall boy sniffed. 'No. But I can smell the dope in your left top pocket though. Lebanese Scarlet. Any chance of an after-dinner spliff?'

Bollocks collapsed into a pile of gaily coloured cushions and laughed like the drain of now legend.

The happy bus rolled onward. Spliffs were shared and Bollocks made all the introductions. There was his wife, Louise. Flaxen hair, Pre-Raphaelite features, coffee lace and ankle bracelets. Bone. Big Bone, slurry pit survivor. Tattooed in moments of madness and built like a brick shit-house. His untattooed wife Candy, brown eyes to drown in, a degree in astro-physics and the kindest hands in Christendom.

And then there were the children. Five in all, they seemed like ten. And laughed a lot. Everybody laughed a lot.

Cornelius sat amongst the cushions. 'How did you get all this together?' he asked Bollocks.

The smiley fellow smiled. 'Necessity,' he said. 'Which, like Frank Zappa, is the mother of invention. No jobs, no hope and a bus all rusting away in a scrapyard. We found each other and the bus found us. And that's how it is now. The bus and us.'

'How do you get by?'

'There's the dole cheques and diesel is cheaper than rent. Where are you guys from?'

'We're from Brentford,' said Cornelius.

'Brentford?' Bollocks fell into laughter once more. 'You have to be kidding.'

'I wouldn't lie about a thing like that. What's so funny about Brentford anyway?'

'Nothing's funny about it. But that's where we're heading. To Brentford!'

Prince Charles sat in his private office at Buckingham Palace. The mid-afternoon sun shone in at his window and the drone of the London traffic went on and on and on.

But the prince didn't hear it. Because the prince was dreaming about trains.

He spent most of his time nowadays, dreaming about trains. Not that he didn't have other things to do. There was never any shortage of mail to be opened, read through and answered. And being, as the Press now called him, the People's Prince, he did it all himself. And he did have a very great deal of this mail piled up on his desk before him right now. But he didn't feel in the mood to answer it. Most of the envelopes smelt strongly of perfume, and contained, as ever, offers of marriage.

Prince Charles sighed. In his mind's eye he saw the Duchy of Cornwall. Not as it was, but how it could be. Would be, when he became King. Translated into a great steam network, with a full-size reproduction of the 1920s marshalling yards of Crewe, superimposed across five hundred acres of 'set-aside', he'd personally 'set-aside' for the purpose. And he saw himself, all spruced up in a natty black uniform, striped waistcoat and cap, checking his regulation GWR-issue pocket watch up on high in the signal box. Skilfully manipulating the levers, as the mighty King Class locos rolled onto the turntables, took on water and blew their whistles.

The prince had long ago realized that the only way forward was backwards. If mankind was to survive, it must throw off the shackles of technology and return to traditional values. A fair day's work for a fair day's pay. A proper class system. And steam trains that ran on time. And a steam train named after himself! The *Good King Charles*.

He knew exactly the kind he wanted too. The American 1940s *Big Boy*. Biggest steam locomotives the world had ever seen, the *Big Boys*. Eight front-driving wheels fixed, another eight swivelled, front and rear bogies. 4-8-8-4 wheel arrangement. They ate up twenty-three tonnes of coal every hour. Wonderful.

He could really be the People's Prince in one of those. They could pull over seventy coaches. He could do out the carriages, load up his art collection and the best of his furniture, get the phone laid on, television, guest sleeping cars, sell up all his palaces and country piles to house the homeless, then travel the country. Royalty on the rails. The monarchy on the move.

'Toot toot tooooooooooooooo,' went the prince. 'Woo woo woooooooooooooooo.'

Ring ring ring, went his telephone. Ring ring ring.

The People's Prince picked up the receiver. 'One speaking,' said he.

'Yo, Babylon,' came the hearty Rastafarian tones of his new equerry, former Brentford used-car dealer Leo Felix. "Ow's it 'angin'?"

'Er, yo bro',' answered the prince. 'How's it hanging, yourself?'

'Like one of your granny's bloodstock. Blood clot. Dere's a chick 'ere, say she come about de job of secret-Harry, or som'tin. You say you doin' all de interviewin' yo'sel'. Shall I an' I send 'er in?'

'Ah yes. If you and you would be so kind.' Prince Charles replaced the telephone, straightened his tie and his double-breaster and stroked a few hairs over his bald spot. A knocking came at his chamber door and the prince rose slightly and said, 'Come.'

Polly Gotting opened the door and entered the office. Her long golden hair was tied back in a severe bun. She wore a white linen blouse, a calf-length skirt of appropriately royal blue, dark stockings and a pair of sensible shoes she'd borrowed from her mum. 'Should I curtsey?' she asked.

'Umm. No . . . I . . .' Prince Charles gazed upon Polly Gotting. She was very possibly the most beautiful girl he'd ever seen in his life. And he'd seen some. The sunlight played upon her hair and formed a glittering corona all around and about. She veritably radiated.

'Would you like some tea?' asked the heir to the throne.

'Do you want me to put the kettle on?'

'Oh no. Of course not. Please sit down. Please.'

He indicated a chair and Polly sat down upon it. The prince lifted the telephone to order tea. But then thought better of it. The last time Leo had made him tea, the prince found he couldn't walk straight after the second cup. 'Perhaps later.' Charles folded his fingers before him on the desk and smiled at the stunning seventeen year old. He suddenly felt a bit lost for something to say, which was not really like him, as a rule.

Polly smiled back. She was fascinated. This man was a piece of living history, and she was sitting all alone in a room with him, sharing moments of his time, somehow possessing a fraction of history, just for a few short minutes. But really for ever. It was a curious sensation. And she felt suddenly stuck for words herself. Which was not really like *her*, as a rule.

'Do you like steam trains?' Prince Charles asked.

Polly considered the question and the eager look on the prince's face. 'Yes,' she said. 'Very much indeed. Only this morning I was talking to a friend about *The Eureka*. LNER passenger express. Classic 4-6-2 wheel arrangement. Four-wheel bogie in front, six coupled driving wheels and a pair of trailing wheels. Perhaps you know of it.'

'I do,' said the prince. 'I mean, *one* does. Oh yes.'

Polly smiled some more.

Prince Charles took out his fountain pen. 'One must take up references,' he said in a manner which he hoped would imply an interest in such things. 'Who have you been with?'

'Been with?' Polly asked.

'Worked for,' said the prince.

'The police force. I was made redundant.'

'Oh dear,' said the prince. 'Have they closed down the police force?'

'Just my bit of it. If you want to take up a reference, you must speak to Inspectre Hovis, at Scotland Yard.'

'Sherringford Hovis?' Prince Charles put his fountain pen back in his pocket.

'Do you know him, then?'

'One should say so. He sorted out a spot of bother concerning one of the brothers, a homeopathist named Chunky and a Dormobile named Desire. Sound chap.'

'He's been made redundant also.'

'That's a pity. He was up for a knighthood. Have to cancel that if he's been given the old heave-ho.'

Serves the nasty bastard right, thought Polly. 'That's a shame,' she said. 'He was a fine policeman.'

'Yes,' agreed the prince. 'He was. Can you start at once?'

'You haven't told me what you want me to do yet.'

Prince Charles considered the beauty sitting before him. I want you to bear my children and share my throne, he thought.

'I want you to be my personal assistant,' he said.

'And would this involve tea making?'

'No, not really.'

'Then I would be pleased to accept, sir.'

Back on the magic bus, and some little while earlier, Cornelius groaned dismally.

199

'Why are you heading for Brentford?' Tuppe asked Bollocks.

'We're going to the festival.'

Tuppe scratched his head. 'There isn't any festival in Brentford. There was a bit of a do the night before last. We were there.'

'Good was it?'

'Not good. That's where Cornelius got his hair . . . you know . . .'

'This is a rock music festival.' Bollocks mimed a heavy guitar. 'Starts on Friday night. There's this big hill. You must know it.'

'Star Hill.' Cornelius groaned anew.

'It's a sacred site, but not one the cops know about. Gandhi's Hairdryer are going to play there. A freebie for the travellers.'

'A freebie for the travellers?' Tuppe whistled. Having grown up amongst fairground folk and lived his short life in a caravan, which, since his daddy's retirement, was hauled from the common land at the foot of Star Hill at least once a month at the behest of the Star Hill Preservation Society, a group of well-to-do worthies whose properties backed on to the golf course, the small fellow felt a certain warm glow inside at the prospect of a wagon train of travellers turning up on their doorsteps for a rock festival. That would go down a real treat.

'How many of you blokes will be going to this gig, then?' he asked.

'All, I think,' said Bollocks.

Tuppe rubbed his hands together in glee. 'Should be a gig to remember,' said he.

* * *

Anna Gotting was playing guitar at Minn's Music Mine. Mickey was on the telephone talking excitedly. The matter of Anna leaving the shop unattended the previous afternoon had, by mutual consent, been forgotten. Although Anna could hardly forget Cornelius Murphy and all that she had been through with him. But she intended to try.

Mickey put down the phone. 'That was Cardinal Cox,' he said brightly.

'Of Sonic Energy Authority? They're really good.'

'That's him. The Authority are playing support to Gandhi's Hairdryer, on the UK leg of their world tour.'

'Nice one.'

'And then some. The Authority's bus just blew up on the M25. The Cardinal wants to hire all my old WEM Vendettas and amps for the gig on Friday.'

'Best get cash upfront, then. You know what they're like.'

'I am a professional,' said Mickey Minns, hoisting up his jeans and tucking in his stomach. 'How would you like to be a roadie at the gig?'

'What, with The Hairdryer? Not half. When is it? Where?'

'They're playing a freebie on Star Hill. Friday night. Should be a gig to remember.'

And Mickey was certainly right about that too. It would be a gig that everyone would long remember.

And then some.

201

18

The day moved on from afternoon to evening, touched midnight and vanished, never to return. The happy bus was parked in the middle of a crop circle, in the middle of a cornfield, in the middle of nowhere. The children were all asleep. The adults were all over the place. Bone had wandered off, in search of something or other. Louise danced all alone, to a music that only she heard. And Bollocks made love to Candy in a field near by.

Tuppe lay on his back in the corn circle and gazed up at the stars. 'It's good here, isn't it?' he sighed.

'Splendid.' Cornelius lay beside him, chewing on a corn stalk. 'I could really get into this kind of life.'

'Oh could you?' Tuppe made a doubtful face. 'Really?'

'I could. Life on the road, you know, like Jack Kerouac. The sun never going down on you in the same place twice. The road beneath. The sky above.'

'Away with the raggle-taggle gypsies-oh.'

'That kind of thing, yes.'

'A life of romance. And rheumatism. You'd hate it.'

'I would not.'

'*I* did. Listen, Cornelius, I spent my childhood on the road. If you've never done it, it seems like a good idea. If you have, it ain't. To quote your lost love, it sucks.'

'You were just little then,' said Cornelius.

'I'm still little,' said Tuppe. 'And it still sucks.'

'You're not little.' Cornelius touched his heart. 'Not in here you're not.'

'Oh please.' Tuppe mimed two fingers down the throat. 'You would hate a life on the road. Believe me. You would.'

'I know. But it's good for now.'

'It's good for now, yes.'

'They're good people.'

'They're great people.'

'Great people.'

'So what are *we* great people going to do?'

'We're off to see The Hairdryer.'

'That's not what I mean and you know it.'

'I know it.' Cornelius raised himself on his elbows. 'Is this a *real* corn circle, do you think?'

'As opposed to what?'

'An unreal one, I suppose.'

'And what exactly would be the difference?'

'I don't know.'

'This one's a Thoroughgood,' said Tuppe knowledgeably.

'A Thoroughgood? What's that?'

'Tubby Thoroughgood. He's a wee man, like myself. One of the Thoroughgood clan. They do most of the circles round here.'

'They what?'

'The Thoroughgoods do up here. The Rimmers do Wiltshire. The Dovestons do Wales. I forget who does Sussex. The McCartneys I think.'

'*What?* You mean they're all fake?'

'Of course they're not fake. It's all real corn.'

'That's not what *I* mean and *you* know it.'

'I don't know what you mean,' said Tuppe. 'They are circles in cornfields. They're art. They mystify. They intrigue. They excite controversy and debate. They entertain. And above all, they are beautiful to behold.'

'But some people think—'

'Some people think that hedgehogs fall out of the sky – your dad for one. Whatever some people think, is up to them. As long as they pay the one-pound admission fee, that's all right with the farmer. He respects the artist's right to remain anonymous, and gives him ten per cent of the take. You can make more money exhibiting corn circles nowadays than harvesting the crop.'

'That's outrageous,' said Cornelius.

'I know. In my opinion the artist should get fifty per cent of the take.'

'And that's not what I meant either.'

Big Bone appeared on the scene with two flagons of cider.

'I've got some scrumpy,' he said. 'Where's Bollocks?'

'He's in the next field, shagging your wife,' said Tuppe helpfully.

'We'll save him some for later then,' said Bone. 'He'll need it.'

'Outrageous,' said Cornelius once more.

'You haven't tasted it yet,' said Bone.

'That's not what I . . . Oh, forget it.' Cornelius grinned. 'It's good here, isn't it?'

'Splendid.' Bone passed the cider flagon round.

'Pity Rosie's not here.' Tuppe took a big sip and passed it on to the tall boy.

'Tell me, Bone,' said Cornelius, 'what do you think about corn circles?'

'I love 'em. This one's a Thoroughgood, isn't it? Big centre, plenty of room for the art lovers to mill about. But I reckon it's a right stitch-up, the artists only getting ten per cent of the take. Don't you?'

'Outrageous.' Cornelius took a great big swig of cider. 'Outrageous.'

Inspectre Hovis sat alone in his garret. He was reading a copy of *The Book of Ultimate Truths* and he was making copious notes. Again and again he referred to the big fat file on Hugo Rune. And again and again he made notes. Occasionally he delved into certain books of occult lore, which had been in his family for twenty-three generations. And then he made more notes.

Once in a while he drank from a Thermos flask containing iced ether, and having so done he uttered things such as 'I feel that I am nearing a solution' or 'The Crime of the Century right in the bag' and sometimes 'I am a little grey Bakelite tram and my name is Barnacle Bill'.

And every so often he fell off his chair and struck the floor with a bang. And when he did this, the lady who lived downstairs whacked her ceiling with a broom handle and threatened to call the police.

*   *   *

'Enjoying the cake?' asked the king.

Arthur Kobold was up to his elbows in it. 'Very much,' he said with his mouth full.

They were seated in great big ornate chairs at the great big banquet table in the king's great big hall. The king was drunk.

'We don't get out as much as we used to,' he said.

'Not as much?' Arthur wiped his mouth on his sleeve. 'Not at all, in fact.'

The king poured something potent into Arthur's glass. 'And we don't laugh any more. Know what I mean?'

Arthur pushed more cake into his mouth. 'You're drunk,' said he.

The king looked crookedly at the generous array of unbunged barrels. 'I hardly touch the stuff. You're the one who's drunk, Arthur.'

'I have every excuse to be drunk. Pressure of work. You only work once a year, or, you're supposed to. You don't even do that any more.'

'Would you want to work on *your* birthday?'

'I wouldn't mind if I had the rest of the year off, like you do.'

'Kings are not supposed to work. Especially on their birthdays. Kings delegate, that's what kings do.'

'If you let me delegate a bit, we could get out once in a while.'

'Where's my friend Hugo?' asked the king.

'Gone,' said Arthur. 'We went through all that last night. Remember all the fuss about . . .' Arthur paused and studied the king's blank expression. He didn't remember. About his favourite car getting stolen and Rune escaping and the other cars getting blown up and the special birthday spell getting broken.

'Well?' said the king.

'Nothing,' said Arthur.

'Hugo and I used to go out together and have big laughs.'

'That was nearly twenty years ago, before you and he fell out.'

'Did we fall out, Arthur? Did we?'

'You did. A little matter of him getting your daughter pregnant, in the hope that you'd make him marry her and he could then become Prince Hugo the First of Fairyland.'

'Cad!' said the king. 'And did he marry her?'

Arthur shook his head. 'Your daughter refused. But she had the child. The weird one. The deviant. Called himself the Campbell and ran away to become a Scotsman. Then tried to get back here and assassinate you.'

'Cad! Whatever happened to him, do you think?'

'We blew him up. With The Train of Trismegistus.'

'My poor dear grandchild.' The king put his face in his hands and wept tears of ale.

'You told me to do it. You called it being "firm but fair". You hated him.'

'I did not.'

'You did too.'

'Well, he was half human, and the only thing I hate more than a half-human is a whole human. Have some more cake, Arthur, do.'

207

'Thanks.' Arthur Kobold carved himself another slice.

'So,' said the king. 'At least you're here. I can rely on you.'

'You can rely on me,' said Arthur cakely.

'That's good,' said the king. 'That's very good.'

'Good cake.'

'Good cake and good company and I can rely on my good friend Arthur.'

'You certainly can.'

'I can rely on him to get back my favourite car, make good all the damage done to the other four, fix my special birthday spell that he broke and bring in Hugo Rune before he wreaks chaos on the lot of us. More cake?'

Arthur was choking on the piece he already had. 'Not for me,' he spluttered.

'Not for me, *what*?'

'Not for me, *sire*.'

'Not for me, thank you.' Polly put her hand over her wineglass. She was dining with Prince Charles at a most exclusive restaurant. 'It's getting very late.'

'I do so appreciate you coming out to dinner with me,' said the prince, dropping the royal 'one'. 'It's been really interesting talking to you about trains and everything.'

'It was kind of you to ask me. You're a really nice man.'

'Thank you.' The prince did that nice smile he does. 'I'm not very good at this kind of thing, but, would you care to come back to my place and see

208

my priceless collection of LWR sleeper-ties?'

'Not really,' said Polly. 'But if you want to come back to my place and have a shag, I'm up for it.'

'Hey, Bollocks.' Cornelius raised his head from the cider flagon. 'Come over here.'

'What am I missing?' Bollocks stumbled into the corn circle, zipping himself into respectability. 'What's happening?'

Cornelius handed him the flagon. 'We were just discussing the corn-circle phenomenon.'

Bollocks gulped cider. 'Pretty weird stuff,' said he, wiping his chin.

'So you don't know how they're done?' Cornelius made a hopeful face.

'Mystery to me,' Bollocks took further sips.

'A mystery?' Cornelius grinned.

'Complete mystery.' Bollocks finished the cider. 'How do the Thoroughgoods get them so perfectly round?'

'Good night,' said Cornelius Murphy lapsing from consciousness. 'And God bless you, Tubby Thoroughgood.'

19

Tuppe was up with the larks. And the dogs. The dogs were doing a lot of barking and the farmers who owned these dogs were adding to the canine cacophony with loud barks of their own. And they weren't smiling.

Cornelius, upon whom Tuppe had curled himself up for the night, awoke in some confusion. He went immediately for the tried-and-tested 'Where am I? What's going on?' routine, with the addition of 'Get off me, Tuppe, and shut those dogs up.'

'What is happening?' he continued, when his senses had got themselves all back together.

'Dogs are barking,' said Tuppe informatively.

'But why are they barking?'

'You have me on that, I'm afraid. I can tell you why pigs grunt. But I doubt if that would be helpful right now.'

Cornelius crawled over to the open door of the happy bus and gazed out. The sun was shining bravely, but it shone down upon a scene which was sadly lacking in the rural-bliss department.

Three fierce-looking red-faced men, in tweedy caps, waxed jackets, hardy trews and Wellington boots, were remonstrating with Bone and Bollocks. Louise and Candy stood with their backs to the bus.

The children clung to them fearfully. There were dogs all around. Big dogs and close.

'What's happening?' called Cornelius.

'Bugger off, boy,' a tweed-capper called back.

'Ah,' said Cornelius. 'I think I get the picture.'

'Stay inside,' called Bollocks. 'You're not involved in this.'

'On the contrary.' Cornelius climbed to his feet and climbed down from the bus. 'You stay here,' he told Tuppe. 'Those are very big dogs.'

'You have my moral support,' called Tuppe. 'Use it as you think fit.'

'Now,' said Cornelius smiling all around.

A big fat tweed-capper nudged a similarly proportioned compatriot in the padded-rib area. 'That the new scarecrow you ordered for your top field, Harry?'

'I see.' Cornelius continued to smile. 'Is there some problem here?'

'Not for us, boy, but plenty for you if you don't get your shit heap and your scabby mates off my land.'

'Shit heap and scabby mates?' Cornelius raised an eyebrow. Two large black dogs began to sniff around his slender ankles.

'Ain't much on the bone for you, fellas,' the farmer told them.

'Go back in the bus,' said Bollocks.

'It's OK.' Cornelius raised a calming hand. 'Would you kindly call your dogs to heel?' he asked the farmer. 'They're frightening women and children. That isn't right.'

'Oh, we've got a *right* one, have we?' The farmer laughed hideously and fixed Cornelius with a bitter stare. 'Get your scum off my land.'

'We were leaving anyway,' said Bollocks, ushering Louise, Candy and the children back into the bus. 'Come on, Cornelius, let's go.'

'We're not going anywhere yet,' the tall boy replied, when all were safely on board. 'We haven't had our breakfast.'

One of the farmer's colleagues rolled some unspeakable phlegm around in his mouth and spat it at Cornelius. 'There's your breakfast,' he said with a sneer.

And then Tuppe appeared in the bus doorway. 'Did someone say breakfast?' he asked.

'*What?*' The spitter of phlegm gaped at Tuppe. 'It's a bleeding dwarf. Got Snow White in there, have you?'

'That's enough,' said Cornelius, who was no longer smiling. 'You may spit at me if you choose. But you will not insult my friend. He is immune to such crassness, but I find it extremely offensive. Would you care to apologize?'

'Would you care for me to set my dogs on you?' the farmer asked.

Cornelius reached down and stroked the neck of the Pit Bull that was sniffing around his ankles. It looked up at him and lolled its tongue.

'Nice boy,' said Cornelius Murphy.

'Seize him, Prince!' ordered the farmer.

Prince, however, seemed disinclined to do any seizing. He snuggled against the Murphy leg. Cornelius bent down and took the dog's head gently between his hands.

'He's very good with animals,' Tuppe whispered to Bollocks.

'Seize him, Prince!' went the farmer.

Cornelius smelt the dog's breath. 'Prince hasn't eaten since yesterday afternoon,' he informed the now fuming farmer, 'and then it was on bad meat. Now that isn't right, is it?'

'I don't feed bad meat to my dogs.' The farmer took a step forward, but Cornelius ignored him, he had now turned his attention to the fellow who made the scarecrow remark.

The tall boy drew a deep breath through his nose. 'Still poisoning badgers?' he said.

And he said it quietly, because the dogs were no longer barking. They were sniffing silently about Prince, the leader of the pack. And Prince was licking the tall boy's hand.

'Badgers?' The fat fellow made a face of alarm. 'What do you mean?'

'You tell him,' Cornelius told the last of the three. 'You were with him. You supplied the poison. Chemicals are really your thing, aren't they? Those concoctions you pump into your cattle will get you into trouble one day.'

Three mouths hung open. There was a bit of an unholy silence.

Then, 'What? What? What?' went the farmers three.

And, 'Seize him, Prince!' went up the cry once more.

But Prince remained disinclined.

'Perhaps Prince would prefer *Winalot* to the sheep's heads you feed him,' Cornelius suggested.

'Now just you see here . . .'

'No,' said Cornelius. 'You see here. I have no axe to grind with you people. Although I think what you do is obscene, it is actually none of my business. So, I'll tell you what I'll do, I'll forget all about informing the authorities . . .' he paused.

'If?' said the big fat farmer.

'If you apologize nicely and furnish us all with a bit of breakfast. How does that sound?'

Cornelius had never smelt pure hatred before and he didn't like the smell of it one little bit.

The farmers stared at Cornelius and Cornelius stared back at the farmers.

'And I think, as a gesture of good will, you might raise Tubby Thoroughgood's share of this year's take to fifty per cent,' was the tall boy's closing shot.

They all tucked into the wholesome fare the farmer's wife delivered.

. 'How did you know all that stuff?' Bollocks asked.

Cornelius tapped his aquiline proboscis. 'Good clean air and farmers who never change their jackets. Mind you, I took a chance on the chemicals. He stunk of cattle and hormones and stuff. I just put two and two together. Him being so fat and all.'

'Brilliant.' Bollocks ladled fried eggs on to the tall boy's plate. 'If the kids hadn't been there, I would have punched their lights out.'

'The dogs would have had you.' Cornelius got stuck into his breakfast.

'How did you do that with the dogs? Calm them down and everything? That was brilliant also.'

'Dogs don't hate,' said Cornelius between mouthfuls. 'Only people hate. People think they can train dogs to hate, but they can't, the animals don't understand the concept. Dogs do what their masters tell them, for love. Animals do respond to love. I just showed a little love, there was no trick there.'

'That's bollocks,' said Bollocks.

'Of course it is,' Cornelius replied. 'Actually, I am in possession of a talisman of protection, that has been in my family for twenty-three generations.' He grinned through his toast.

'That's more like it.' Bollocks loaded up a plate for himself. 'I knew there was a logical explanation. Brilliant. You're quite brilliant, Cornelius.'

'He's the Stuff of Epics,' said Tuppe.

'I'd like to bear your children,' said Louise.

'Me too,' said Candy.

Cornelius grinned a bigger grin than ever. 'If I can square it with your husbands, I shall be honoured to oblige,' said he.

The sun, which had so recently risen upon Cornelius, Tuppe and the folk of the happy bus, rose also upon Inspectre Hovis.

The man from The Yard lay prone upon the garret floor, smelling strongly of ether and a dire cocktail of illegal substances. The great detective, whose greatness had yet to be proved to many minds, had just

215

the two days left to solve The Crime of the Century. That crime of crimes, which, as yet, possessed the substance of a ghost's fart in a force-ten gale. Just two days left, before redundancy and goodbye, Mr Hovis. No knighthood, just goodbye.

The Inspectre dragged himself into the vertical plane. 'I will survive,' he told his wash-basin. 'I will triumph,' he informed his unmade bed. 'I will succeed!' he shouted to the four grey walls.

Thump! Thump! Thump! went the broom handle on the ceiling below.

Other people were waking up upon this fine and sunny morning and some in the strangest of places.

Mickey Minns opened his eyes and stared at the ceiling. 'Where am I?' he asked.

His wife rolled over and smacked him right in the face. 'Get back in your bloody wardrobe,' she told him.

Anna Gotting woke up. She stumbled from her bed and bashed her fist on the wall. 'Keep it down in there!' she shouted.

Polly Gotting tried to keep it down. But 'taking tea with the parson' can get pretty loud.

'Sorry,' said Prince Charles. 'Was one making too much noise?'

'You might cut out the train whistles. But other than that, you're doing fine.'

'This is much more fun than polo,' said the prince.

'I wouldn't know about that,' Polly replied. 'I've never read any of Jilly Cooper's books.'

'Just like that. Just like that,' went the prince.

'I'm sorry?'

'Tommy Cooper. He used to say, "Just like that." '

'I don't think I quite understand.'

'It's a sort of joke thing,' the prince explained. 'When you said Jilly Cooper, I pretended that I'd thought you said Tommy Cooper. So I went, "Just like that". In a zany, goonish, madcap kind of a way.'

'Why?' Polly asked.

'Because you make me so happy,' the prince replied.

20

There are twenty-three really wonderful things in this world, and being tall, young, handsome, well-endowed and the multi-millionaire lead singer of a world-famous rock band, probably accounts for a good half-dozen of them.

Or possibly not. Because as someone once said, 'Money can't buy you happiness.' And being world-famous means that you can't travel on the London Underground any more, which must be a real bummer!

Or possibly not. Although it is to be noticed that a good many rich and famous folk claim to be deeply miserable.

Of course, they may all be lying through their expensively capped teeth, to make the rest of us feel better, or it might just be true.

The lead singer of Gandhi's Hairdryer was deeply miserable, but then he'd always been like that. Tall, young, handsome, well-endowed and a multi-millionaire perhaps. But still a miserable sod.

At least he could, in all truth, claim that success hadn't changed him at all. But whether this would have cheered him up much remains in doubt.

On this particular morning, as upon so many

others, the lead singer awoke to find himself in yet another Holiday Inn.

And it will come as no surprise at all that he awoke flanked all about by naked females and the debris of yet another night without shame. Because, let's face it, the wanton excesses of a rock band on tour have been chronicled many times before.

The frenzied debaucheries, the reefer madness, the whole kith and caboodle and the roadie's spaniel. We have come to expect these things. Nay, even to demand them. It's a tradition or an old charter or something.

And as such, the fact that the lead singer awoke all alone, wearing nice green pyjamas, in a neat and tidy room, with his clothes on a peg and his orange juice and Bran Flake breakfast on its way up, accompanied by a copy of the *Daily Telegraph*, came as a serious let-down.

But then, as has been mentioned, the lead singer was a miserable sod.

And on this particular morning, as upon so many others, the lead singer lay in his bed, with his hands behind his head, and dreamed about trains.

Because, though all the world might know him as Vain Glory, drug fiend, monster of rock and deflowerer of virgins, he was just plain Colin to his mum.

And, as Colin lay in his bed with his hands behind his head and dreamed about trains, a very strange thing happened. The corners of his mouth turned upwards into a kind of crooked rictus. Muscles which had scarcely seen service were brought into play. A smile appeared upon his face.

Colin was feeling decidedly gay.

Not in the shirt-lifting sense of the word, of course. He'd tried to be a homosexual, but he'd only been half in Earnest. And although his mother had made him a transvestite, he'd swopped it at school for a train set. Et cetera. Et cetera.

Decidedly gay. Because Colin had finally decided, once and for all, to give up rock music and devote his life to the restoration of pre-war GWR rolling stock. He would announce this at the gig tomorrow night. It would come as a big surprise to his fans and to the other members of The Hairdryer. But he felt sure they'd understand and wish him well. He felt sure they would.

The happy-busers had now finished their breakfast belly-buster. The children were outside, frolicking in the Thoroughgood. Cornelius was up the back end of the bus, enjoying the hospitality of Candy and Louise. That is, having sexual intercourse with them. Whether 'tea' was being taken 'with the parson', it was impossible to say. The bandages had come off the tall boy's head and all that could be seen was hair.

Bollocks was tinkering with a radio set.

'Wotcha doing?' Tuppe asked.

'Checking to see where everyone is.'

'Ah.' Tuppe wiped his eggy mouth on his sleeve. 'I often wondered how all the travellers know where to meet up. CB, is it?'

Bollocks shook his head. 'BBC.'

'BBC? How's that?'

'Well.' Bollocks made conspiratorial gestures. 'The

220

BBC organize all the big festivals. Then they broadcast things like, thirty thousand travellers are expected this weekend at such and such a place.'

'You're winding me up,' said Tuppe.

'I'm not. There're two broadcasts, see. The first is to confuse the police, this announces a false location for the festival, so the police set up road blocks all round it and use up their manpower. When this has all gone ahead, the BBC broadcast the real location of the festival. What they say is, "Thousands of disappointed travellers, turned away by police from such and such a place, are now believed to be heading for—" And that's where the gig really is. And we end up there before the police arrive.'

'But what about all the punch-ups with the police?'

'Well, you can't make the operation run too smoothly. The police would eventually suss that they were being had. So what happens is, the BBC arrange for there to be some violent skirmishes. It makes the police look like they're doing their job, and it provides the BBC with some great footage for the six o'clock news. Everybody's happy.'

'But your blokes get beaten up.'

'Not our blokes. They're all actors working for the BBC. Check it out next time you watch it. You'll recognize a few old faces: ex breakfast TV presenters, that bloke who used to be on *Blue Peter*.'

'Incredible,' said Tuppe. 'So who is it at the BBC that organizes the festivals?'

Bollocks shrugged. 'Probably some old reprobate who remembers the good old days before the war, when the BBC used to make up *all* of the news.'

'That rings a bell.' Tuppe scratched his head. 'I've read that somewhere.'

'I read it in *The Book of Ultimate Truths*.' Bollocks twiddled the dials on the radio set. 'Written by a forgotten genius, guy called Hugo Rune. Ever heard of him?'

'I do believe I might.' Tuppe suddenly became aware that the bus was beginning to rock violently.

'Keep it down back there, Cornelius,' the small fellow shouted. 'We're trying to get the BBC.'

Arthur Kobold sat in his dingy little relocated office, deep somewhere in a Forbidden Zone. He was fed up.

'I'm fed up,' he said.

'*You're* fed up? How do you think *I* feel?' This question was addressed to him by the big deflated green thingy, which now lay in a wrinkly heap on the guest chair, looking not unlike one of Ed Gein's hand-stitched evening suits.

'Stuff you,' said Arthur.

'If you'd be so kind. Yes please.'

'What are you doing here in my office anyway? You retrieved the diamonds. What do you want?'

'I want my money.'

'Money? What money?'

'My time and a half for after midnight. And there were some out-of-pocket expenses. I've filled in a chitty.'

'Filled in a chitty? Have you gone stark raving mad? You don't get any time and a half after midnight. You're a conjuration. Moulded from etheric

222

space by a process of controlled resonance, involving the use of certain restricted words of power. Imbued with a rudimentary intelligence and the physical wherewithal to achieve a certain end. To wit, the reclamation of the diamonds. This you have achieved. Hence, your work is done.'

'You're making me redundant,' complained the wrinkly heap of skin.

'You are redundant,' said Arthur Kobold.

'Then I want my redundancy money.'

'I don't think I'm making myself clear.' Arthur rose from his chair, plodded around his desk, plucked up the swathe of skin, tucked it to his chest, folded it once, folded it twice, smoothed out the wrinkles and folded it a third time. Then he went over to his filing cabinet, opened the top drawer, dropped the neatly folded redundant conjuration into a vacant file and slammed shut the drawer.

'Get the picture?' he asked.

'Let me out,' cried a muffled voice. 'Unfold me at once, you fat bastard. Let me out, I say.'

Arthur Kobold returned to his chair. 'Put a sock in it,' he said. 'Or it's the paper shredder for you.'

Inspectre Hovis was in the Portakabin. He was shredding paper, loads and loads of paper. He had already shredded the important case notes for no less than twenty-three big unsolveds. Not to mention a quantity of vital documents, bound for the desk of Chief Inspector Lytton, which had turned up on his by accident.

Hovis was thoroughly enjoying himself. When the

telephone began to ring, he had considerable difficulty in finding it.

But when he had, he picked up the receiver and said, 'Inspectre Hovis speaking,' the way that only he could say it.

'Sherringford, my dear fellow,' said a voice. 'None the worse for your regrettable wetting, I trust.'

'Who is this speaking?'

'It is I. Rune.'

'Rune? I don't believe I know any Rune.' Hovis floundered frantically amongst the shreddings. He had to find another phone, get this call traced. 'Rune, you say. How do you spell that please?'

'As in Rune, you buffoon. You know me well enough. My file lies before you. Somewhere beneath the shreddings, I have no doubt.'

'I do believe your name rings a small bell.' Hovis ceased his foolish flounderings. The Portakabin did not possess, amongst its many hidden charms, another telephone.

'A *small* bell?' roared the voice of Rune. 'How dare you, sir. My name is a clarion call. A mighty chime of hope, issuing from the tower of Ultimate Truth. For such as was, is now, and shall be ever more.'

'Quite so,' said Hovis. 'How may I help you?'

'Help *me*? Help *me*? You think that you can help the man who has brought succour to the crowned heads of Europe? The man who taught the Dalai Lama to play darts? The man who shared his sleeping-bag with Rasputin, J. Edgar Hoover and Sandra Dee? The man who once scaled the Eiffel Tower in

224

fisherman's waders, to win a bet with Charles de Gaulle?'

'What do you want, Rune?' asked Inspectre Hovis.

'Do you still have my diamonds?' Rune enquired.

'What diamonds are you referring to?'

'Oh wake up, Hovis, do. The Godolphins. I sprayed the damn street with them. At no small risk to my health and well being. Thought they might stir up your interest. Tickle your fancy. Do you still have them?'

'No,' said Hovis. 'I don't.'

'Nabbed by the blighter who reduced you to your underwear. Am I right?'

'You are.'

'Of course I am. I always am. You will meet me this afternoon. Three of the *post meridiem* clock. At The Wife's Legs Café, Brentford. There we shall discuss matters and you will stand me a buttered muffin and a pot of Lapsang. Come alone and unarmed. Your knighthood depends on it.'

And then the phone went dead.

Hovis thrashed shreddings from his chair and flopped into it. This was a turn up for the book and no mistake. Rune calling *him*. This put the cat amongst the pigeons and the nigger in the woodpile. It was a fine kettle of fish.

Hovis took out a small greasy clay pipe, filled it with opium and rolled plug tobacco and lit it with a lucifer. This was a regular three-pipe problem and no mistake.

He tossed the match carelessly aside and it fell into a waste-paper basket. Here, in the final moments of its short, yet brilliant career, that match passed on that thing which Prometheus stole from Olympus, to a screwed up Kleenex tissue.

This tissue would smoulder gently away for quite some time. And it would be several hours before the fire began in earnest (not to be confused with the other Earnest). But when this fire did get started, it would rip through the Portakabin, reducing it to blackened ruination, in less than ten minutes.

Sadly, Inspectre Hovis would not be around to enjoy the conflagration. He would be in Brentford. In The Wife's Legs Café, drinking *Château La Swasantnerf* and listening to the words of Hugo Rune.

Mad and mysterious be the ways of fate that shape our ends. Yet the veil that covers the future's face may well be woven by the hand of mercy.

Some say.

'. . . and the minister denied that recent allegations of sexual misconduct, illegal appropriation of Government funds and direct involvement in the sale of nuclear weapons to a Third-World power, had anything to do with his resignation. He merely wished to spend more time with his wife and children. Dreaming about trains.

'Upwards of twenty-three thousand travellers are expected to attend the summer solstice festival in Gunnersbury Park on the border of Brentford tomorrow, where world-famous rock band Gandhi's Hairdryer will be performing. Lord Crawford, whose family have owned historic Gunnersbury House and its landscaped grounds for the last two hundred and thirty years, said that he hoped everyone would have a jolly good time and that if anyone got caught short, it was OK for them to use his toilet.'

Bollocks switched off the radio set. 'There you go,' he said.

Tuppe bounced up and down. 'I'm trying to follow this. The festival is not really going to be in Gunnersbury Park.'

'No. That's to fool the police. The festival is on Star Hill. We know this because Bone is a friend of the Gandhi's drummer and he heard about it months ago.'

'Whacky stuff,' said Tuppe. 'I love it.'

Cornelius came bumbling down the bus.

'Watcha,' said the small fellow. 'Finally broken surface?'

'Yes thanks. Did I just hear that the gig's been moved to Gunnersbury Park?'

Tuppe tapped his nose. 'It's all a secret. I'll tell you later.'

'Good shag?' Bollocks asked.

'Very nice thank you.'

'Hope you wore a condom. We're all rotten with the clap.'

'Of course.' Cornelius grinned. 'It pays to play safe.'

'But I thought you were supposed to be fathering children,' said Tuppe.

Cornelius did not reply to this. But he spied Bone at the wheel and realized for the first time that the happy bus was moving once more. 'Where are we now?' he asked.

'Heading for Brentford.' Bollocks skinned up a joint. 'Tell me, Cornelius, who are you really?'

'Really? What does that mean?'

Bollocks smiled. 'Well, you're *somebody*, aren't you? We could all suss that when we picked you up. Then the business with the farmers. And now your big hair. Famous people always have big hair. There's no point in denying that.'

'He's the Stuff of Epics,' said Tuppe. 'I told you.'

'Is this an epic we're in now, then? I mean, because we picked you up and you helped us out. Does this mean we're in the epic with you?'

Cornelius rammed large quantities of big hair down the back of his shirt. It appeared to have grown considerably during the short period that his head had been bandaged. 'I suppose it would mean you were in it too,' he said, 'if *I* was still in it myself. But I'm not.'

'He quit,' Tuppe explained.

'That's a bit of a cop-out.' Bollocks rolled a roach. 'Why did you quit?'

'His bottle went,' said Tuppe.

'It did not. I became, er, disillusioned.'

'Bottle job.' Tuppe made obscene little pinchings with his thumb and forefinger.

'Tell me about it.' Bollocks slipped in the roach. 'Your epic, what went wrong, why you became disillusioned. Perhaps the bus and us could help.'

'I don't think you could.'

'Well, tell me anyway.'

Cornelius shrugged. 'All right, I'll tell you the lot.

I doubt if you'll believe me. You'll probably think it's all bollocks.'

'Probably,' said Bollocks, twisting the joint's tip and preparing to light up. 'Everything else in this world is.'

The Wife's Legs always hummed in the warm weather. Midsummer and the Vent Axia on the blink again. Fag smoke fugged the air, chip fat ran down the windows, but the tea was spot on, and the fried slices.

Inspectre Hovis entered to no applause. He fanned before his face. The fug stuck. And he in his last suit. It would never do.

Big men filled the chairs. They enjoyed cigarettes and gave not a hoot for government health warnings. Several rose from their seats upon sighting the Inspectre and made off with talk of pressing business elsewhere.

Hovis waved them fond farewells. And sought Rune.

The mage sat in the corner. In the shadows. Enigmatic. *Outré*. Spacious. Before him on the table, an ashbowl contained the butts of three South American cigars. A bottle of *Château La Swasantnerf* lacked its label and a third of its contents. Two large hands, their fingers sheathed with exotic rings, toyed with an empty wineglass. Rune's head was lost in darkness.

'Come,' called the voice of Rune.

Hovis came. He pulled up a chair and settled down at Rune's table.

'Drink?' The mage poured wine and pushed the

glass towards Hovis. 'Tell me what you think.'

The Inspectre raised the glass to his nose, turned it, took a sniff, held the glass to the light, put it to his lips, took a sip, then gargled.

'A fine nose,' said he. 'Good firm body. Milk white thighs.'

'Milk white thighs?' Rune asked.

'*Château La Swasantnerf*,' said Hovis. ' '69, of course. West end of the vineyard and trodden by the owner's niece. Milk white thighs.'

'Correct. Sherringford, why did you become a policeman?'

'Why did you become a wanted criminal?'

'No criminal I,' said Rune. 'Common laws are for common people.'

Hovis sipped from his glass. 'Why have you invited me here?'

'We share a common, and here I use the word advisedly, a common craving. Recognition for our genius. You for yours and me for mine. You are the best The Yard has to offer. I am the greatest that mankind has ever seen. Together we might achieve a certain celebrity.'

'Would you care to elucidate?'

'The Crime of the Century,' said Rune. 'What else?'

'Hugo Rune, I am arresting you on suspicion. You are not obliged to say anything, but anything you do say may be taken down and used in evidence.'

'You silly arse,' said Hugo Rune. 'You'll empty the entire café. Be still now and listen. I have much to say to you. And by much, I mean a great deal.'

'You knocked me into the Thames,' the Inspectre complained.

'I did it to save your life. You will be for ever in my debt. But now sit comfortably and know a joy that sadly *I* can never know.'

'What joy is that?'

'The joy of listening whilst I talk.'

'. . . of listening whilst I talk.' Rune's words went down on tape. And his actions were observed, through the telephoto lens of Chief Inspector Lytton's regulation police-issue surveillance camera.

Because, of course, the Portakabin telephone had been bugged. Rune's call to Hovis had been recorded and during the time between the phone call and the meeting, The Wife's Legs had also been bugged.

Chief Inspector Lytton put aside his camera. He stood upon the flat roof of a building opposite the café. He was a very furious chief inspector. A chief inspector who, not one hour before, had received a telephone call from Prince Charles himself, requesting the reinstatement of Inspectre Hovis and that Lytton pass on the good news of his forthcoming knighthood.

Chief Inspector Lytton glanced down at the junior officer who knelt beside him. This officer had his finger poised above the firing button of an anything-but-regulation police-issue 7.62 mm M134 General Electric Minigun.

'Fire as soon as I give the order,' said Chief Inspector Lytton.

The junior officer, whose name was Constable Ken Loathsome, did a big thumbs up. 'Who eats the lead, Chief?' he asked.

'Two men,' said Brian Lytton. 'A large bald one and a not quite so large gangly one. The large bald one is a serial killer. Twenty-three children. Pulled their still-beating hearts out with his bare hands. And ate 'em.'

'Urgh!' went Ken.

'The not so large, gangly one. He's a much nastier piece of work.'

'Blimey,' said Ken.

'So just make sure you don't miss. Do the job right and you might well find there's a promotion in it for you.'

'Right on,' said Constable Ken.

Police Constable Kenneth Loathsome wasn't much of a shot. But then, he wasn't much of an anything really. Distinguished only by a crummy mock-American accent and the desire to shoot people, Chief Inspector Lytton couldn't really have chosen a better man for the job.

It was a little after five of the late-afternoon clock, when two figures, one large and bald and one not quite as large, but gangly, stepped out from The Wife's Legs Café and stood upon the pavement. They were shaking hands at the moment Chief Inspector Lytton gave Constable Ken the order to fire.

Ken flipped up the safety cover and rammed his thumb hard down on the firing button. The 7.62 mm M134 General Electric Minigun did what it did best.

Dispensed 7.62 mm x 51 shells at the rate of six thousand a minute.

Rapid fire! The constable was hard put to keep the killing end of the mighty weapon trained on anything even vaguely resembling the targets. But at that range, and with such an awesome piece of hardware, you really can't miss.

21

Hugo Rune took a dozen rounds to the head. The force lifted him from his feet and drove him back through the window of The Wife's Leg's Café. Hovis turned in horror, tried to run. Bullets raked across his chest. Riddled him from head to foot.

Somehow Rune was rising. He came forward, his great arms outspread. But bullets rained into him, and he fell across the now lifeless body of Inspectre Hovis. Late of Scotland Yard.

When Constable Ken finally released his trigger finger, twenty-three seconds had passed. Two thousand three hundred rounds had left the minigun. The police had run up a bill for twenty-three thousand pounds in damage claims. And two men lay dead on the pavement.

'So long, suckers,' said Ken briefly. And then he was violently sick.

'Oh my God,' he continued, and, 'what have I done?'

'You've done a man's job, sir.' Brian Lytton looked upon all that he had made, and found it pleasing.

'Bleeuugh!' went Ken, on to the chief inspector's trousers.

A crowd had already begun to form around the two dead men. Appearing, as if from nowhere. Those who have read *The Book of Ultimate Truths* will recognize this as Spontaneously Generated Crowd Phenomenon. Those who have not, will not.

The big men, who had taken cover when the killing started, were now climbing to their feet, dusting themselves down and squaring their shoulders in rugged manly ways.

The wife was already receiving far more comfort than she actually needed.

Chief Inspector Brian 'Bulwer' Lytton smiled an evil smile and led the blubbering constable away down the fire escape.

'You chuck up in the car and you're for it,' said he. 'And you can foot the bill to have my trousers dry-cleaned.'

Prince Charles was taking tea. But not with 'the parson' this time. With Polly and her mum. In their kitchen. He hadn't mentioned to Polly yet about making the phone call to have Hovis reinstated, he thought he'd save that for later. Be a nice surprise for her.

Polly put the kettle on. She never minded doing it at home. Her mum whispered away at her from behind a tea cosy imaginatively fashioned to resemble the head of John the Baptist.

'You know who he looks like?' she asked Polly.

'No,' said Polly.

'Jeff Beck,' said her mum.

'He does not.'

'He does too. My friend Mrs Murphy played bass for Jeff on "Hi Ho Silver Lining". She showed me this picture. Jeff had more hair then. But the ears are the same.'

'Don't you have a meeting of the Chiswick Townswomen's Guild to go to?'

Prince Charles made that curious jaw movement that he does when he's feeling lost. 'This is a charming kitchen,' he said. 'Are these Hygena units?'

'They're Pogue and Poll,' replied Polly's mum, drying her hands on a dishcloth printed with the image from the Turin Shroud. 'My husband Colin fitted them. They came in a flat pack.'

'Were they difficult to erect?'

'Yes quite. The instructions were in Danish. Happily my husband is cunnilingual.'

'The worktops look very easy to wipe down,' said the heir to the throne. 'Is that a *faux*-marble finish?'

'No, it's Formica.'

'How interesting,' said the prince. 'And do you have any labour-saving devices?'

'Yes, we have a microwave oven.'

'Ah yes.' Prince Charles scratched his ear. 'My friend Mark Knopfler used to sing a song about those. Although I forget how it went.'

'There you are,' whispered Polly's mum behind the Baptist's head. 'I know a balding middle-aged ex-muso when I see one.' She took herself over to the table and sat down next to the prince. 'Are you in the music business yourself, Mr . . .'

'Windsor,' said himself.

'Windsor? You're not related to Barbara Windsor, by any chance?'

'Barbara?' The prince adjusted his double-breaster.

'Busty Babs, the loveable cockney sparrow. Star of countless *Carry On* films.'

Charles looked bewildered. He was bewildered.

'Would you care for a slice of Black Forest Gâteau, Mr Windsor?' Polly's mum passed the plate.

'Yes please.'

'Mr Windsor is my new employer,' said Polly, bringing over the kettle and warming the pot.

'How nice. And did you say you were in the music industry, Mr Windsor?'

'Not really.' Prince Charles suddenly seemed to have cake all over himself.

'But you do know Mark Knopfler. Do you know anyone else? In "the biz", as it were?'

'Phil Collins,' the prince ventured.

'Not fanciable Phil, loveable cockney sparrow and star of countless Phil Collins films?'

'And Bob Geldof. I met him once.'

Polly's mum smiled at the prince. 'Excuse me a mo',' she said. Rising from the table, she took Polly by the arm and guided her back to the cooker. 'He's a real no-mark, this bloke,' she whispered. 'A right name-dropper.'

'Oh, and I know the lead singer of Gandhi's Hairdryer.'

'*What?*' Polly's mum returned to the table. 'You know Vain Glory?'

'Oh yes indeed. We're very good chums. We share a common interest in steam trains.'

'Get away,' said Polly's mum.

'Truly,' said the prince.

'Vain Glory,' sighed Polly's mum.

237

'Would you like to meet him?' asked the prince. 'Only he sent me some stage passes for his concert tomorrow night. Perhaps you'd like to have them.' He patted at his pockets in search of them, but he only did it for effect, because, as those in the know, know, the royals do not have real pockets, because they never have to carry anything around with them. 'They're outside in the Aston Martin,' said Prince Charles. 'I'll go and get them.' And so saying, that's just what he did.

Polly's mum winked at her daughter. 'Aston Martin *and* he knows Vain Glory. You've fallen on your feet this time, my girl. This bloke's a God-damn prince.'

Cornelius had finally done with the telling of his epic tale. He didn't think he'd left anything out. He'd told of his search for the missing chapters from *The Book of Ultimate Truths* and how Arthur Kobold had conned them from him; of his discovery that Hugo Rune was his real father and that mankind was secretly controlled by a race of non-humans inhabiting the Forbidden Zones.

Of what happened when he and Tuppe entered one of the zones. Of the MacGregor Mathers and of the time spell and of Hugo Rune. And of Hugo Rune's diabolical stratagems.

He concluded his soliloquy with words to the effect that, bad as the beings in the zones might be, far worse were the consequences of their sudden exposure to an unsuspecting world. To whit, the complete and utter collapse of civilization as any of them knew it.

Something that he personally, did not want on his conscience.

Bollocks just sat there, the joint still there between his fingers. He hadn't even lit it. His mouth hung wide and his face lacked for an expression.

'Is he still breathing?' Tuppe asked.

'Only just.' Bollocks let out a long low whistle. 'And you two really went through all of that?'

'All of that.' Tuppe nodded vigorously. 'And so here we are.'

Bollocks stared into the face of Cornelius Murphy. 'You bastard,' he said.

'You what?'

'I said, you bastard. You know that you're the Stuff of Epics. You get involved in something as incredible as all that, you go through all that you've gone through, and then you quit? You just quit? You bastard.'

'It's far more complicated than you think—'

'Oh no it isn't,' said Bollocks.

'Oh yes it is,' replied Cornelius.

'Oh no it isn't,' chorused everyone on board the happy bus. For they had all been listening to the tall boy as he told his tale.

'I'm sorry,' said Cornelius. 'But I quit.'

'Bastard.' Bollocks threw up his hands. 'You bastard. Get off our bus.'

'No, Bollocks, wait.' Candy dropped down on to the cushions beside Cornelius. 'You know you can't quit really,' she said. 'You can't quit being who you are. Being what you are. And knowing what you know.'

239

'I can,' said Cornelius. 'And I have.'

'Off,' said Bollocks.

'No,' said Candy. 'Cornelius, listen. You have to go on. See it through to the end. You have to. Not just for yourself. But for all of us. For the children.'

Cornelius looked up at the children. They sat before him in a wide-eyed row. A small one with curly hair blinked back a tear. 'Are you going to save us from the bad fairies?' she asked.

The tall boy groaned. He really didn't need this.

The small child scrambled away and Candy said, 'You have to, Cornelius. You just have to.'

'I can't. I just . . . '

The small child returned. Sunlight angling down through the windows caught her golden hair to perfection. She had large tears in her eyes now and she held in her hands . . . an ocarina.

'This is my daddy's,' she said. 'Will you take it and stop the bad fairies?'

Cornelius Murphy buried his face in his hands. 'All right! All right! I give up.'

The king was pissed again. It *was* late afternoon after all, and he *was* the king.

'You do have everything under control now, don't you, Arthur?' was the question that he asked.

'Certainly do.' Arthur availed himself of the royal cakes without being asked. 'I have just had a call from a chief inspector of police that we have on our payroll. He informs me that Hugo Rune is no longer a threat to security.'

240

'You mean he's—'

'Very,' said Arthur.

'Shame,' said the king.

'Oh, don't start all that again.'

'Do you know,' the king poured himself another drink, 'sometimes I wonder if it's all really worth-while? This buggering up of mankind that we do. Holding them back. Messing them all about.'

'They would thank you for it if they knew,' Arthur unreliably informed his king.

'Would they really thank me?'

'Of course they would. They love you, don't they?'

'Do they still love me, really?'

'They adore you. You still have an enormous fol-lowing.'

'Tell me about my following,' said the king. 'Tell me, Arthur.'

'They still perform The Ceremony of the Sacred Sock.'

'Do they?' asked the king. 'What is that by the way?'

Arthur sighed. 'The sacred ceremony, where they pray for you to bestow gifts upon them.'

'And do they still call me by my name?' asked the king.

'Oh yes,' said Arthur Kobold. 'They still call you good old Father Christmas.'

The crowd closed in around Cornelius Murphy. There were tears of joy and kisses and smiles and cuddlings. And things of that nature generally. Touching? Heart-warming? Sentimental overkill?

241

Steven Spielberg could not have directed it better.

Tuppe, who had in fact directed it, paid off the small golden child with a fifty-pence piece. 'You done good, kid,' said he.

'We agreed a pound,' the child replied. 'And two for the ocarina.'

'Just call me good old Father Christmas,' said Tuppe.

'Good old Father Christmas,' said the king.

'Good old you,' said Arthur Kobold.

'And they still hang up their socks?'

'They still hang them up, but you don't put anything in them any more.'

'No,' said the king, 'I don't. Why don't I?'

'Because', said Arthur, 'you got fed up with it and you said, "Stuff the lot of them, it's *my* birthday and it's *my* magic birthday spell. And I'm going to use it having a good time and the parents can fill up their kids' stockings themselves." '

'I said that?'

'You did. And at the end you said, "So there!" And you stuck out your tongue. I remember that quite well.'

'Stuck out my tongue?'

'And said, "So there!".'

'I did that?'

'You know you did. The special birthday spell was formulated so you could travel all around the world dispensing joy and goodwill and presents, before one second of real time had passed.'

'So that's how I did it. I always wondered.'

'That's how you *did* it. But you don't do it any more.'

'Because that other bloke stole my birthday,' said the king in a sulky voice.

'That *other bloke? Jesus*, you mean! You can't even bring yourself to say his name.'

'He ripped me off,' Father Christmas complained. 'Just because he was born on my birthday. He even named himself after me. Jesus Christmas! Doesn't sound right anyway.'

'I have tried to explain to you about him before,' said Arthur. 'I don't know why you get so worked up. You're both gods, aren't you? In as many words, and as near as makes no odds. But you're a far more popular god than him really.'

'Am I?' asked King Christmas.

'Of course you are. I keep telling you. Christmas Day. Which god would you choose, if you were a kiddie? The squalling brat in the manger, who's getting all the presents, or the jolly red-faced man, with the nice white beard, who's bringing *you* presents?'

'I know which one I'd choose,' said the king.

'And me,' said Arthur.

'So do you think I should use my special spell to bring joy and goodwill and presents once more to the world of men?'

'Nah,' said Arthur. 'Stuff the bastards is what I say.'

'My opinion entirely,' the king agreed. 'I'm the guvnor. I'm in charge. And I'll run the world my way.'

'Quite so,' said Arthur. 'You do it your way.'

'I will,' said the king. 'And, Arthur, as you have

done so well, I am going to promote you. From now on you are my chief of security.'

'Oh goody goody gumdrops,' said Arthur Kobold through gritted teeth.

'And I want a bit of peace and quiet, Arthur. No more horrible humans stealing my cars. No-one trying to bring down my kingdom. You take care of that for me and we shall all live happily ever after. Is this Murphy creature going to be a problem?'

Arthur shook his head. 'Not unless he manages to raise an army against us. And I can't see where he'd get one of those from, can you?'

22

'. . . Twenty-three thousand travellers are expected to attend the free festival at Gunnersbury Park tomorrow. Lord Crawford, interviewed this afternoon at Heathrow, shortly before his departure for a long weekend in Antigua, said that he deeply regretted that he would not be able to attend the festival in person, but hoped that everyone would have a jolly fine time. And make their own toilet arrangements. A police spokesman said that the area surrounding the park would be closed off and that no travellers would be allowed through. He did not expect any trouble, although there was always, what he described as 'a hard core', who turned nasty. The regular policy of meeting violence with violence would be adopted. On-the-spot film of the skirmishes will be shown tomorrow on *News at Six.*'

Bollocks turned off the radio. 'Uncanny,' said he.

The happy bus was rolling merrily along. Tuppe stood on the back seat and watched the world that passed behind. 'It looks like we've got us a con-voy,' he said.

Cornelius sat beside him. He whistled while he worked. He had the ocarina in one hand and a skewer in the other.

Tuppe dropped down beside him. 'How's it

coming?' he asked. 'And careful with that skewer,' he went on. 'You nearly had my eye out.'

'Do these new holes look in the right places to you?' Cornelius handed Tuppe the ocarina.

Tuppe gave it a looking over. 'They do to me. Can you remember the order to play them in?'

'No need,' said Cornelius. 'As *you* will be doing the playing.'

'Oh yes? And when will I be doing this?'

'Tomorrow evening. At the festival. On Star Hill. We know there's a portal there, don't we?'

'We don't know exactly whereabouts though. It's a big hill. It could take a lot of blowing.'

'Oh I think we can get the hill to meet us halfway.'

'You have a serious plan in mind, then?'

'Certainly do.' Cornelius tapped his nose with the skewer and nearly put his own eye out.

Tuppe was certainly right about the con-voy. As the happy bus bowled along, other buses fell into line behind it. Not all of these looked particularly happy though. Most looked dark and dire and altogether intimidating. And, it had to be said, their occupants didn't look a bundle of laughs either. Morose was probably the word. Down right evil were three more.

But they weren't, of course. Anything but. These were middle–class university graduates, with first-class honours degrees in sociology and psychology and philosophy and 'the humanities' (whatever they are). All those qualifications which aren't worth that afore-mentioned bogeyman's bottom burp in the economic climate of today.

246

Not that it was the failure to secure work in their chosen fields of endeavour that drove these people into a life on the road. Oh no, it was a shared wish to make the world a happier place to live in.

Now at first glance, or even at second or third, shaving lumps out of your hair, dressing in evil-smelling rags, dragging small dogs around on strings and generally carrying on in the vilest imaginable manner, might not seem the way to go about making the world a happier place.

But not so. Throughout history, society has forever looked to find a scapegoat in times of crisis. When trouble looms, there's nothing people like better than to find some minority to blame. It's a tradition, or an old charter, or something.

It leads to pogroms and ethnic cleansing. It is most unpleasant.

And this is where the travellers come in.

At a secret congress in the early 1980s, a group of socially aware unemployed young graduates sat down and set out a manifesto. They would form themselves, they said, into a band so despicable, so foul and unspeakable, that they would become the universal scapegoat.

It worked like a dream, and does to this day. When the travellers appear in town, old scores are forgotten, the community bands together in perfect harmony against the common foe.

It unites. And it remains united. And bit by bit the world becomes a happier place.

Or so it says in *The Book of Ultimate Truths*.

★   ★   ★

Arthur Kobold tucked the king into bed. Good old Father Christmas, the Guvnor, Secret Ruler of the Whole Wide World, snored soundly.

Arthur stood over the sleeper and made a gun with the fingers of his right hand. 'Bitow bitow bitow,' he went as he mimed the assassination.

'The King is dead. Long live King Arthur the First.' He blew imaginary smoke from his gun barrel forefinger. 'King Arthur, d'you hear that, punk?'

The king stirred in his slumbers, mumbled something about chimney pots and lapsed into loud snorings.

Arthur Kobold slunk from the room.

Prince Charles returned to Buckingham Palace. He returned in the company of Polly Gotting. There was no way he was going to let *her* out of his sight. They were made for each other. He just knew it. There was the age difference, of course. And the class barrier. But one of the best things about being a member of the royal family was that you could pretty much do anything you wanted. That was the whole point of being 'a royal', wasn't it?

Charles could never understand why the Press made such a fuss when one of his family went off the rails (an expression which was something of a favourite with him). Surely it was a 'royal's' duty to do just that. In private, naturally. Not where it might frighten the horses.

Polly followed the prince through the palace corridors. She gazed up at the historic walls, with their historic paintings hanging above the historic furniture. Although there could obviously be no moral justification for so very much wealth being in the hands of so very few people, there was something almost comforting about it. Its permanence, perhaps? She certainly wasn't a royalist, teenage royalists are not exactly an endangered species (they're much rarer than that), she was simply a person.

And as a person, and being here, it was quite clear that there was more to the monarchy than just the sum of its parts.

Prince Charles led her up a sweeping flight of steps, which might well have been the very one on which Cinderella dropped her slipper. He opened the door of his private apartment and smiled her inside. A telephone was ringing and he went off to answer it.

Polly sat down on an enormous bed and took in the room. There was another opportunity here for a pretentious and not particularly amusing architectural description, but as a running gag, it hadn't really proved its worth.

So Polly looked all around, wasn't all that keen on what she saw and waited for the prince to return.

When he did he said, 'That was my equerry, Leo Felix. Dark chap. You met him when you came for the interview.'

Polly nodded.

'Leo says that I've been invited to host the concert that Gandhi's Loincloth are giving tomorrow.'

'Hairdryer,' said Polly.

'I don't think I have one,' said the prince.

'Gandhi's *Hairdryer*. You said Loincloth.'

'Did I?' asked the prince. 'That's funny, because

249

Colin, that's the lead singer, he's a chum of mine. Loincloth? I wonder why I said that.'

'You were looking at my legs when you said it.'

'Ah,' said the prince. 'One was, was one?'

'One was, I'm afraid. Are you going to host the gig, then?'

'I really don't know. What do you think? Would it be the done thing?'

'Would you like *me* to be the done thing again?' Polly asked the prince, which was pretty excruciating, but people do say things like that when the relationship is still at the hot-and-horny stage. And at least they hadn't started giving each other nauseating little pet names yet.

'Toot toot,' went the prince. '*Big Boy* is coming into the tunnel—'

'Don't be a prat,' said Polly.

'I'll tell you what,' said Tuppe, when Cornelius had finished outlining his serious plan, 'that is a serious plan you have just finished outlining there.'

'So, what do you think?'

'Well, let me get it straight. What you are suggesting is, that, as Bone knows the Gandhi's drummer, he swings it for me to get up on stage in the middle of the gig and play the magic notes through the megawatt sound system. Then, when the portal opens, you do a sort of Pied Piper routine and lead a twenty-three-thousand-strong peace convoy through the portal and into the Forbidden Zones.'

'Exactly. Overwhelm the blighters with a single unexpected and peaceful invasion. I don't want to

250

wipe them out, Tuppe, I just want them to leave mankind alone to get on with its own business.'

'And you really think Kobold's bunch will agree to *that*?'

'Well, if I suddenly found twenty-three thousand travellers in *my* front room, I'd agree to pretty much anything in order to get them out. Wouldn't you?'

Tuppe grinned a wicked grin. 'And I'd be prepared to reward, most handsomely, the enterprising young man who could get them out.'

Cornelius winked. 'My thoughts entirely. Arthur Kobold owes us substantial damages. We won't be taking a cheque this time. So, what do you think, a blinder of a plan, or what?'

'Well.' Tuppe screwed up his face. '*I* think it's a real blinder. But, I do have to say, that if Anna were here, I have the feeling that she just might say that it was a very *sad* plan and possibly that it sucked. No offence meant.'

'None taken, I assure you. So, do we, as they say, give it a whirl?'

'As they say, we do.'

The sun went down upon Gunnersbury Park and no lights showed from the big house, home of the Antigua-bound Lord Crawford. There were plenty of lights beyond the walls though. These were of the revolving variety and adorned police car roofs. Roofs that had those big numbers on them for helicopter recognition during riot situations.

Not that there were any riot situations on the go at present. Oh no. The police cordon that ringed the park around and about, and blocked off lots of vital roads, showed not the vaguest hint of riot.

The officers of the law lounged upon bonnets, smoking cigarettes, filling in their expense chitties and discussing the sort of thing that policemen discuss when in the company of their own kind.

The TV news teams had all departed several hours before, having got all their required footage. And the anarchic travellers, who had put up such a violent struggle trying to break through the police cordon, now sat in cells, smoking cigarettes, filling in their expense chitties and discussing the sort of things that actors discuss when in the company of their own kind.

Of the twenty-three thousand genuine travellers, there wasn't a one.

Mickey Minns was in his shop, checking his equipment.

He had just returned from The Flying Swan.

The patrons of Brentford's most famous watering hole were taking their pleasures outside on the pavement this particular evening. In deckchairs. They were viewing the borough's newest arrivals: the travellers.

Now, as anyone who has ever spent any time there will tell you, Brentford is not as other towns. Anything but. And the previously related concept, of the travellers as universal scapegoats, didn't amount to much hereabouts. In Brentford camps which were divided, stayed divided. And camps which were together, remained together.

The pubs, for instance, being the very linchpins of local culture, had long ago picked up sides regarding most things. The arrival of the travellers didn't alter much.

The Shrunken Head, whose takings had been down of late, due to a new landlord with a penchant for a pub quiz, put up the TRAVELLERS WELCOME sign immediately.

Neville at The Flying Swan put it to the patrons. 'Yes or no?' he asked them.

Norman the corner-shopkeeper said 'no'. He had already put up the barricades and was preparing himself for the holocaust to come.

Old Pete was of the yes persuasion. 'They're a free-love mob, aren't they?' was his argument.

There were yes-folk and no-folk and don't-know-folk and don't-cares. And when Neville finally called for a show of hands, it was fifty-fifty.

Which left Neville with the casting vote. Something Neville really did not want.

And then, out of the blue, or, as many cynical fellows were later to remark, right on cue, in walked John Omally, resident drinker at The Swan for more years now than he cared to think about and a man always ready and willing to give his all for the common good.

John thought for a moment and then came up with an inspired compromise. A vetting system, whereby he personally would undertake the responsibility of deciding who was worthy to enter the hallowed portal of The Swan and who was not.

Neville was delighted with this, because if

anything went wrong, he could put all the blame on Omally.

The patrons were delighted with this also, because if anything went wrong, they could put the blame on John Omally.

And John Omally was delighted with it, because he intended that nothing would go wrong. Not with him outside, carefully vetting the potential customers. That is, selling the entry tickets.

'It is called the spirit of free enterprise,' he told his best friend Jim Pooley.

'I thought that was a car ferry which sank,' replied Jim. 'But I've got all those rolls of raffle tickets you asked me to buy this morning. Red ones and green ones.'

'Jolly good. Red ones are admission to The Swan, ten bob a head. Green ones are, sorry The Swan's full up, but would you like to buy a ticket for the festival, two pounds a head.'

'I thought it was a free festival,' said Jim.

Omally offered him that 'nothing is free in this world' look. 'You'd better start the ball rolling, Jim,' said he. 'Do you want a ticket to get into The Swan, or what?'

The happy bus had reached Brentford. It was parked down by the Grand Union Canal. Opposite Leo Felix's used-car emporium. The natty-dreader had left his business empire in the hands of his brother-in-law, him working full time for the prince and everything.

Cornelius stretched out on a whole lot of cushions and viewed the stars.

'It's funny to be home, but not really to be home,' he said.

'I suppose it must be.' Tuppe made himself comfy.

Cornelius yawned. 'It's going to be a big day tomorrow.'

'And then some. If you can pull this off, you'll change the whole world.'

'And the whole world will never know about it. That's the beauty of the thing, Tuppe. Kobold's bunch will be forced to surrender, due to the sheer weight of numbers. And afterwards, who would believe anything the travellers said anyway?'

'Inspired,' said Tuppe.

'Thank you,' said Cornelius.

And they both settled down to sleep. Each secure in the knowledge that the other believed wholeheartedly in the plan.

Which, naturally, they did not.

It would have slipped past many people, probably because it has not been mentioned before, that the following day was *The Queen's Unofficial Birthday*. She had her *real* birthday, of course. And her *Official* birthday. But this was something new. Her special *People's* birthday.

It was an innovation, conceived by certain advisers and publicity people at the palace. These folks studied a lot of history and recalled the time, chronicled in *The Book of Ultimate Truths*, of a pre-war period, when the King's coronation was broadcast 'live', three times in a single year, as a morale booster. And morale boosters such as that, the world could always do with.

And hence, these palace people had had big meetings with certain bigwigs in the TV industry. And a live nationwide broadcast had been given the big thumbs up.

There wasn't going to be much to it. All the Queen had to do was come out on the balcony, read a small prepared speech and wave at everybody.

It had been scheduled for eleven in the morning. But now the bigwigs were having a bit of a rethink.

There was this Gandhi's Hairdryer gig, you see. The big free festival. It had been eating up a lot of headlines and was also going out live, as a worldcast. If the Queen's balcony wave could be made to coincide with this, perhaps during a break between numbers, while the Gandhi's were off-stage laying groupies, or something, it made sound financial sense. Two for the price of one. And word had reached the bigwigs' ears, via a certain Rastafarian equerry, that Prince Charles had agreed to host the Gandhi's gig.

However, the question did arise as to how the change of schedule might be 'sold' to the Queen. Her Majesty not being a personage that is lightly messed around with.

And so three bigwigs sat about a boardroom table in one of those Modernist carbuncles, thrashing the matter out.

'Right,' said the first. 'Selling the proposition to HRH. Ideas anyone?'

'Tell her the whole world will be watching,' said the second. 'After all, it will.'

256

'Won't impress *her*,' said the third.

'Tell her it's for the good of her people,' said the second.

'Who do we know that could tell her that *and* keep a straight face?' asked the first.

'Not *me*,' said the second.

'Tell her it's for her own good then,' said the third. 'Which it is.'

'Perhaps if you took her a bunch of flowers when *you* told her,' the first suggested.

'And some chocolates,' the second added.

The third man shook his head and whistled the *Harry Lime* theme.

'I say, guys,' said a fourth man, who had entered without knocking, 'I think I have the solution.'

The three men turned to view this unannounced arrival. He was a dubious-looking cove, with a camera strung about his neck. A camera with a big long lens.

'Phone up her son Charlie and get him to ask her,' said this fellow. 'Tell him that I have certain photographs of him in my possession. Photographs of him and a certain Polly Gotting, taken from a bedroom window across the street from her house. Mention the words 'tea' and 'parson', that should swing it.'

23

The Brentford sun rose from behind the water tower at the old pumping station and brought a golden dawn to the borough. Birdies gossiped on the rooftops. Roses yawned in the memorial park. Pussy-cats stretched themselves and annelid worms of the class *Polychaeta* manipulated the bristles on their paired parapodia.

Norman at the corner-shop numbered up his newspapers and passed the bag through the hatchway of the security grille to Zorro the paper-boy. 'Go with God,' said Norman.

A milk float jingled to a halt before one of the flatblocks and Mr Marsuple freighted a crate of Gold Top towards the lift. He was whistling. Moments later he would return to find that the remaining twenty-three crates had been stolen.

For, although this was a golden dawn that promised a day of likewise hue, it was a day that the folk of Brentford would long remember.

It was the day the travellers came to town.

Cornelius awoke to the smell of frying bacon. Three streets away, at The Wife's Legs Café. He chivvied Tuppe into wakefulness.

'Care for a serious fry-up?' he asked.

'We don't have any money.'

'Leave that to me. Let's go.'

They left the happy-busers to sleep on and wandered out into the day. Cornelius stretched his long legs and Tuppe stretched his short ones.

'It's good to be back.' Cornelius made futile attempts to bat down his hair.

They walked up from the canal, through the historic Butts Estate, along Albany Road and around the corner to The Wife's Legs.

It was a bit of a mess.

The windows had been boarded over and curious man-shaped outlines had been chalked on the bullet-pocked pavement outside.

'What is all this?' Tuppe asked.

'Let's go in and ask.' Cornelius pushed open what was left of the door and they went inside.

The wife was turning pink sausages in a frying pan. Big men sat around tables, reading their small newspapers, tugging upon mugs of tea and discussing the sort of things big men discuss when in the company of their own kind.

'Morning, big men,' called Cornelius.

'Morning, Cornelius,' the big men called back. 'Morning, Tuppe.'

'Morning, big men.'

'I'll order breakfast,' Cornelius said. 'You tune up the big men. Find out what happened here.'

'Okedoke.'

Cornelius ordered breakfast. The wife looked decidedly shaky, but quite pleased to see him. She gave him the cream of the milk. Cornelius told her he was expecting a postal order.

'By the end of the week, or you're barred,' the wife told him.

The tall boy smiled warmly and freighted the mugs of tea to his favourite table by the window. It was a bit short on view this morning. Tuppe soon joined him.

'You would not believe what happened here,' he said as he scaled a stool. 'Someone opened fire on the place with a minigun.'

'A minigun? You're kidding.'

'I am not.'

'You mean a 7.62 M134 General Electric Minigun?'

'I do.'

'7.62 mm x 51 shells? 1.36 kg-recoil adaptors?'

'And a six-muzzle velocity of 869 m/s. That's the one.'

'Capable of firing six thousand rounds per minute?'

'Correct. Was all that supposed to be funny, by the way?'

'Search me. So what exactly happened?'

'Well,' Tuppe sipped tea, 'as I say, someone opened up on the place yesterday afternoon and shot two men dead.'

'Blimey,' said Cornelius.

'Blimey is right. One was a policeman, well known in these parts. Inspectre Hovis.'

'Never heard of him. What about the other?'

'Ah,' said Tuppe.

'Ah? What is, Ah?'

'Ah is, I'm sorry.'

'Why, what have you done?'

'I haven't done anything.'

'Then why are you apologizing?'

'I'm not apologizing. I'm saying I'm sorry.'

'Is *this* supposed to be funny?' The tall boy sipped his tea.

'It's not funny. Listen, Cornelius. The other man who got shot, no-one got his name, but he was a great big heavily built man. With a shaven head. And he was wearing a nineteen-thirties Boleskine Tweed plus-fours suit.'

Cornelius spat his tea all over the table and all over Tuppe.

Mickey Minns awoke in the wardrobe. There had been some more unpleasantness in the Minns household, but it was better left undwelt upon. The Minns bore an arm-load of clothing away to the bathroom. He really intended to enjoy the gig tonight and he wanted to look his very best.

The trouble was, as he stood in front of the mirror and struggled to get his arm down the narrow sleeve of a cheesecloth shirt, a-shade-of-green-that-dare-not-speak-its-name, none of the fab old gear seemed to fit any more.

It seems like one of those really wonderful ideas, keeping all of your old clothes. To still possess those faded purple moleskin *South Sea Bubble* hipster loon pants, with the patch pockets and the twenty-three-inch bottoms, the ones you wore to your first Happening. And the tie-dye five-button grandad vest that you threw up all over.

Wonderful idea? I don't think so.

Mickey returned to his wardrobe and pulled out the *Giorgio Armani* suit that he had been saving for when he was invited to attend The Rock and Pop Awards.

Outside the horn of his van went Beep! Beep! Honk! Mickey peered out of the window to see Anna waving up at him.

Polly Gotting awoke in the bedroom of Prince Charles.

The ringing of the telephone woke her.

The prince reached over and picked it up.

'One,' said he.

Certain words came to his ear and these he answered with polite ones of his own.

More followed and the prince replied to these also. 'Yes,' he kept on saying. And then, 'Goodbye.'

'Whatever's happened?' asked Polly. 'You look terrible.'

'Ah,' said Charles Philip Arthur George, no relative of Barbara. 'I think I'd better go and have a word with my mum.'

'I don't know what to say.' Cornelius didn't. 'Except I'm sorry I spat my tea over you. But he's dead. Rune is dead. I can't believe it.'

'Of course it could just be another great heavily built man, with a shaven head and a penchant for nineteen-thirties Boleskine Tweed plus-fours suits.'

'You really think so?'

'Not really, no.'

262

'I can't believe it. I just cannot believe it. Did anyone see who did the shooting?'

'One of the big men says a friend of a bloke his brother knocks around with's mate heard someone say that the police did it.'

Cornelius whistled. 'You can't argue with evidence like that.'

'Can't you?'

'Of course you can. Why would the police shoot one of their own?'

'I don't think they did. You see there's something else. When the ambulance arrived, the bodies had gone. They'd literally vanished.'

Cornelius looked at Tuppe.

And Tuppe looked at Cornelius.

'*Them!*' they both said.

A very bitter expression appeared upon the face of Cornelius Murphy. 'I think we can forget about the peace convoy plan,' said he. 'This time it's war.'

BRENTFORD: A TOWN UNDER SIEGE

screamed the banner headline on the front page of the *Brentford Mercury*.

'Keep the noise down, you're giving me a headache,' said young Zorro, pushing the rowdy news-sheet through the wrong letter-box.

Actually Brentford was looking rather untidy. Which did not befit a borough that regularly swept the board with all the *Best Kept* awards. But untidy was definitely the word. There were all these shabby-looking buses. They seemed to be parked on every

263

corner and down every alleyway and on every vacant plot of land. There were at least a hundred of them on the waste ground behind Moby Dick Terrace.

But there was none in Gunnersbury Park. The cordon was holding like a dream. There'd be promotions in this.

The media were enjoying it. The SIEGE had even found its way on to breakfast television.

'Mr Omally,' said the bright-looking lady presenter, crossing her long legs before the sofa. 'You represent The Brentford Residents' Committee.'

Since I formed it last night, thought John. 'As long as there has been one,' he said.

'So, I suppose it must come as something of a shock to have twenty-three thousand travellers turning up on your doorstep.'

'Blitz spirit,' said John, who'd heard old Pete use the expression. 'And dig for victory.'

'But it must be imposing a terrible strain on the community.'

John nodded thoughtfully and kept his best side to the camera.

'We live in troubled times,' he said. 'Unemployment. Homelessness. These are difficult days for us all.'

'Please go on.' The lady presenter recrossed her legs.

'I will.' John moved closer. 'You have very beautiful legs, by the way.'

'Why thank you.'

John smiled. 'Difficult days. Millions of young

264

people on the dole. No jobs, no hope, so they take to the road. I'm sure *you* understand.'

'I do,' replied the lady presenter, somewhat breathlessly.

'I knew that you would.' John placed a hand on her knee. 'It's tragic. We in Brentford welcome these people. We say, send us your tired and huddled masses. Let us share your grief. Come share our bounty . . .'

'Wonderful.'

'Come share our bounty,' John went on. 'Be with us. Take a beer at The Flying Swan. Eight fine hand-drawn ales on pump. Convivial atmosphere. Sandwiches and light snacks available at the bar. Unrestricted parking in the Ealing Road. Would it be impolite of me to put my tongue in your ear?' he asked the lady presenter.

All around and about Brentford, the travellers were doing their best to make their presence felt. Fences became campfires. Ozone-friendly graffito was being sprayed. Defecation was all the rage.

It was not their wish to be welcomed to Brentford as tired and huddled masses. These people had a vocation. And just because John Omally was selling the virtues of The Flying Swan and preparing to enjoy those of a prominent breakfast television presenter, that wasn't going to change anything.

Prince Charles went in to have a word with his mum.

He spoke many words and all of them in a tone of deep regret and apology. And when he was done he made a hopeful face, studied his reflection in his polished toecaps and waited for the axe to fall.

It didn't. 'You are a very naughty boy,' said the Queen. 'But no naughtier than your father or your grandfather I suppose. And let us face it, it's the duty of a royal to go off the rails every once in a while.'

Charles smiled his charming smile.

'I will agree to do my birthday wave during this pop concert thing, but on one condition.'

Charles made the face that asked, 'What's that?'

'I want you to present this Polly person to me tomorrow. If she is as wonderful as you say she is, you shall have our blessing. I am having The Archbishop of Canterbury over for tea. Bring her along then.'

'To tea?' Charles asked.

'To tea.'

'With the parson?'

'What are you grinning about?' asked the Queen. 'And where's my birthday present?'

24

Everything begins with a word. Everything. The scriptures are quite clear about this.

In the beginning was the word and the word was with God and the word was God.

This, of course, is the principle of High Magick. The word and the power of the word. The intonation. The resonance. The vibration. Things of that nature.

The word came to the travellers on the one o'clock news. It came from the BBC.

The word was that twenty-three thousand travellers, disappointed at being turned away from their festival at Gunnersbury Park, were now heading for Star Hill.

And, in approximately the time it takes to turn a key in an ignition, or at least get a bump-start going, they were.

Magic.

'Hang about,' called John Omally. 'What's all the rush? Come back.'

'*One two. One two,*' went Anna Gotting through one million watts of power.

'Shiva's sheep!' Mickey Minns covered his ears. 'I think we can give that the thumbs up. Would you look at all those buses.'

They rose up the hill from the place where the other buses (the ones with the numbers on the fronts and the regular places to go) turn around. The first was a technicolor dream of a thing. Bollocks sat at the wheel.

'This is some nice hill,' he said to Tuppe.

'We like it.'

'What's up with Cornelius? He hasn't said a word since the two of you got back from breakfast.'

'He had a spot of bad news,' Tuppe whispered. 'I think there may well be a great deal of unpleasantness when he meets up with Arthur Kobold.'

Men in official Gandhi's Hairdryer World Tour T-shirts waved the happy bus to a halt and put up their thumbs. Bollocks switched off the engine, opened the roof hatch and put up a ladder. 'You'll see the show a whole lot better from up here, Tuppe,' he said.

'Brilliant.' Tuppe scaled the ladder, climbed out on to the roof and took it all in. And there was a lot to be took.

Upon the crest of the hill, upon the very spot where the concrete memorial plinth of the Reverend Kemp had until so recently stood, was a massive erection. And *what* a massive erection it was.

A mighty stage rose above the tree line. Flanked by two Herculean hairdryers, fifty feet in height and housing speaker systems of sufficient power to stagger the senses of that legendary stable-swabber himself.

Moored between these titanic structures and bobbing gently in the breeze (which came as ever from the east), was a shining dirigible, cunningly fashioned to resemble the head of a not-altogether-unknown Mahatma. Glasses, big grin, the lot.

And, lest some confusion still remained in the minds of the less mentally alert regarding the name of the band scheduled to play, huge letters of the HOLLYWOOD sign variety lined the back of the stage. They spelled out the words G AND HIS HAIRDRYER.

No doubt the road crew would sort that out later.

Tuppe was very much impressed.

Cornelius wasn't. His hair appeared through the roof hatch, followed by his head. He took one look up the hill, went, 'Bleugh,' and vanished back into the bus, taking his hair with him.

Tuppe remained impressed. A massive erection never left a bad taste in *his* mouth.

And Tuppe continued with his looking. He spied out the big generator trucks, the lighting gantries with their laser flares and Super Troupers, the control box, where all the technical hocus–pocus went on, the small housing estate of luxuriously appointed artistes' caravans. And he wondered whether the Gandhis were already inside these, gargling champagne, munching steak sandwiches, and doing rude things with groupies.

And in the latter part of this wondering, Tuppe spied out a golden window of sexual opportunity. And so he shinned back down the ladder to see if he could spy out Mr Bone.

Mickey Minns sat on the edge of the great pink stage, sharing a joint with Anna Gotting. Mickey was dreaming about Woodstock.

He sighed in a lungful of Ganja smoke and said, 'Did I ever tell you about the time I . . . ?'

'Yes,' replied Anna, recognizing that far-away look. 'But you can tell me again, if you want to.'

The sun shone on down and the trucks and buses kept on coming. The greensward became black with them. They paved it over.

And when the common ground was all full up, the men in the official Gandhi's Hairdryer World Tour T-shirts began waving them on to the golf course.

It was now three in the afternoon. No, stuff that. It was now six in the evening. No, stuff that also. It was now nine o'clock at night.

And The Sonic Energy Authority came on stage. Lasers criss-crossed the sky. Super Troupers did their thing and the band launched into their first number.

Now, if you've never seen SEA, and nobody really has, getting the measure of their music can be a tricky business.

The lead singer, Cardinal Cox, when asked by the presenter of a TV arts programme to describe it, said, 'Basically, like, the music is *diatonic*. Based upon any scale of five tones and two semitones produced by playing the white keys of a keyboard instrument, especially the natural major and minor scales, as these form the basis of the key system in most of Western music, like. But, naturally, this can be seen as a metaphor. Whilst the five tones represent man's five senses, the two semitones represent the dualistic proposition that reality consists of just the two basic principles, mind and matter. Like.'

'Pretentious prat,' muttered the presenter. 'Well, let's take a break there, and coming up in part two . . .'

The Sonic Energy Authority did play pretty loud though. Because as we all know, 'If it's too loud, you're too old.'

Their first power chord, a diminished A7th with a flattened ninth on the F string, which was largely symbolic of the euhemerist theory that the gods arose out of the deification of historical heroes, was an absolute stonker.

It blew Tuppe straight off the bus roof.

'Look out below,' he called as he tumbled through the hatch. Bone caught him.

'Mr Bone,' said Tuppe. 'I gave up looking for you. What say we look up your friend the drummer and see if he might introduce us to his friends the groupies?'

'Good idea.' Bone hefted Tuppe on to his shoulders and struck out for the good-time girls. 'Let's rock 'n' roll,' he said.

'Hello,' called the Cardinal, between philosophical key-shifts. 'Is there anybody out there, or what?'

'*Cheer*', '*Hoorah*' and '*Yeaaahhhhhh!*' went the crowd.

'Then let us Rock 'n' Roll!' The Cardinal, a striking figure in latex drainpipes and a chain-mail tank top, and with slightly less hair than Cornelius Murphy (but not much), gave his guitar a piece of his mind. 'This one's called "Hi Ho Silver Lining",' he bawled.

'Let's go, Tuppe,' said Cornelius. 'Tuppe? Where are you?'

'What is all that bloody racket?' cried the king.

'I don't know.' Arthur Kobold crossed his heart. 'It's not my doing.'

'Well it's going on right over my head.' The king pointed towards the high fan vaulting of the great hall. 'And it shouldn't be doing that, should it?'

'No, sire, it shouldn't.'

'Then kindly go up and see what it is, Arthur. And stop it, right away. I run this planet and I will not have a lot of human rubbish making a racket over my regal head. Put a stop to it. Right now.'

'As if I didn't have anything else to do.'

'What did you say, Kobold?'

'Nothing, sire.'

'Now just let me get this straight.' Chief Inspector Brian Lytton was speaking into a police-car microphone. 'The festival is *not* going to be held in Gunnersbury Park? It is actually on the go a mile away at Star Hill, at this very moment?'

'Well,' said a fellow officer of lower rank, 'we're in the mess room here at The Yard, watching it live on TV. So I suppose it must be.'

'Well,' said Brian. 'What a turn up for the book. Whoever would have thought it? Thank you very much for mentioning it, officer. Over and out.' He replaced the police-car microphone. '*Bastards!*' he screamed. He picked up the microphone again and said, 'All cars in the Gunnersbury Park vicinity now proceed at once to Star Hill. Illegal rock concert in progress. Arrest everyone.'

'Let's burn rubber.' Constable Ken, now fully recovered from the events of the day before (crime is a disease and *I* am the cure) and looking forward to his promotion, brrrmed the engine. 'Let's go kick some ass,' he said. 'Which way *is* Star Hill, Sarge?'

'Possibly *that* way.' Reliable Ron Sturdy pointed towards the great display of lasers lighting up the sky. 'Just follow the noise.'

'Are you all having a good time?' called the Cardinal, because rock stars always call out things like that. A need for reassurance, probably.

'*Yeah!*' the crowd replied.

'Then this one's for you. It's off our last album. It's called "Weren't the Sixties Fab?". Thank you.'

'I like this one,' said Mickey Minns to Anna.

'What exactly were *The Sixties*?' Tuppe called down to Bone.

'Search me,' said Bone.

'Knock on the door then.'

Bone squared up before the door to the Gandhis' luxury artistes' caravan. 'How did we manage to slip unseen past the teams of hired heavies, whose job it is to prevent people like us doing things like this at rock concerts?' he asked Tuppe.

'Does it matter?'

'Not to me.'

'Knock then.'
Knock knock knock, went Bone.

At a Holiday Inn which might have been anywhere, because they all look the same and Status Quo have stayed in them all, the Gandhis were preparing themselves.

Colin, the lead singer, zipped himself into a con-toured black leather jump-suit of Caped Crusader credibility, strapped on a steel codpiece which might have seen the Elephant Man all right as a crash helmet, and became Vain Glory.

'Are we ready to rock?' he enquired of his fellow musicians.

Fearsome personages with hair and studs and straps and boots and pierced nipples with their room keys dangling down.

'We're ready,' said they all.

Atop the Holiday Inn, a helicopter stood with its blades gently twirling. The pilot's name was Colin. He was dreaming about planes.

'Tuppe,' called Cornelius into the crowd.

'Prince Charles,' said Prince Charles, smiling through the open window of his limo. 'I'm with the band.'

'Stage pass,' demanded the fellow in the official Gandhi's Hairdryer World Tour T-shirt.

'Ah,' said the prince. 'I did have one of those, but I gave it away.'

'Piss off then,' said the fellow.

'Oh,' said the prince.

'Well?' said the king. 'What is it?'

'It's a rock concert,' replied Arthur Kobold.

'Right above my head? My royal, regal head?'

'I'm afraid so, sire.'

'Well put a stop to it, Kobold. Pull out its plug.'

'Yes, sire.'

Copter blades picked up speed. Colin the pilot dreamed about Concorde. The Gandhis had lift-off.

'This will be a gig to remember,' said Vain Glory. 'Trust me on this. I'm telling the truth.'

But the rest of the band weren't listening. They were real Rock 'n' Rollers. They were taking drugs, gang-banging the groupies and eating steak sandwiches.

Why do they always eat steak sandwiches?

'Tuppe.' Cornelius wandered on. 'Tuppe, where are you?'

'Oi!' shouted a traveller from a bus top. 'Shift your hair. We can't see the band.'

And the band played on. The Sonic Energy Authority launched into 'Johnny B Goode'. Why 'Johnny B Goode'? Because it's such a blinder of a song, that's why. And the crowd loved it.

Twenty-three thousand pairs of feet stomped out their appreciation. Right over the head of the king.

Fancy his great hall just happening to be inside Star Hill.

*   *   *

'Left at the bottom here,' Chief Inspector Lytton told his driver, as they reached the place at the bottom of the hill where the buses turn around. 'Bloody Hell,' he continued. 'Would you look at all that lot?'

A hired heavy in an official Gandhi's Hairdryer World Tour T-shirt, which bulged somewhat about the shoulder regions, finally answered the door to the artistes' luxury caravan.

'What do you want?' he asked, without charm or interest.

'We're friends of Andy the drummer,' said Bone.

'*We?*' asked the heavy.

'I'm down here,' said Tuppe.

'Piss off,' said the heavy.

'But we're friends of Andy.'

'Well *he* is,' said Tuppe. 'I haven't been introduced yet. Would it be OK if we came inside and had some group sex?'

The heavy scratched his head. 'If you promise you'll take me to dinner afterwards. Or maybe to a show.'

'What? Just for letting us in?'

'No, for the group sex. There's only me here. But I'm quite versatile. Who wants to be the parson?'

'Cor look,' said Tuppe. 'Here comes a helicopter.'

And here it did come. Caught to perfection in the searchlights. It dropped down on to the hill. That Holiday Inn can't have been very far away then!

If you're going to be a famous superstar – and let's face it, which of us who've ever played the tennis racket and stood in front of a bedroom mirror, isn't going to be? – you have to do it right. Your helicopter has to land at exactly the correct moment.

The Hairdryer's did. Just as the Cardinal and his band were leaving the stage to Olympic Stadium applause. Guitars held high. Fists up. Victory signs.

It's all like that when you're rich and famous.

You can't go wrong.

'I am Prince Charles,' said Prince Charles. 'I'm supposed to host the concert. I would have been here earlier but . . .' He grinned foolishly back at Polly. 'Should I explain why we're late?'

'Certainly not.'

'Back up and piss off,' said the fellow. He was still wearing the same T-shirt.

'What's going on here?' asked Polly's mum. Who just happened to be passing.

'Chap in the T-shirt won't let me up to the stage.'

'Leave it to me, dear.' Polly's mum took the T-shirt wearer away to one side and spoke urgently into his ear. The T-shirt wearer came back over to the prince's car and gave the prince a big long stare.

'Blimey,' said he. 'It's really him. Sorry, mate. Go right on up.'

'Many thanks.' The prince drove on.

'Never recognized him,' said the wearer of the T-shirt, as the limo departed. 'Fancy that!'

'He's lost a lot of hair,' said Polly's mum, 'but I knew him by his ears.'

'Jeff Beck,' quoth he-that-did-the-T-shirt-wear. 'And I never got his autograph.'

'I could get it for you, if you'll give me that T-shirt.'

'More than my job's worth. Piss off.'

Gandhi's Hairdryer – the band, the legend, and the official World Tour T-shirt – hit the stage. The crowd erupted as they strapped on their guitars, gestured rudely at their audience, grinned at one another, went 'one two' into the microphones and pansied about generally.

Arthur Kobold had a good view from the side of the stage. He had lately emerged from one of those secret passageways, like the ones they always have in *Rupert Bear* that come up in the middle of gorse bushes. Arthur was very impressed by the sheer scale of the entire enterprise.

'It must have a very big plug,' said Arthur.

'One-two-three-four, one–two–three–four,' went Vain Glory. They were going to start off with a fast one. 'Let me hear you say—'

But that was as far as he got. There was a brief moment of feedback and then all sound died on the stage. Vain Glory lashed out at his guitar and cried unheard into his microphone. The drummer went bump bump bump. Band members stared lamely at one another. The crowd began to boo.

Arthur Kobold looked on. He hadn't done anything.

'We will have to take a short break there,' came a voice nobody knew. It was the voice of a media bigwig. It came full blast through the sound system. It came from the control box where the bigwig sat.

278

'A word from Her Majesty the Queen,' it continued, as a big screen rose above the HOLLYWOOD letters. 'Live from the balcony of Buckingham Palace.'

'Booooooooo!' went the crowd. 'Boo. Boo. Boo.'

'That's not very nice,' said Prince Charles to Polly, as they mounted the steps to the stage. An enraged Vain Glory was just coming down them.

'Char-lee,' said the lead singer, wringing the prince's hand. 'You got here in the nick of time, *Big Boy*. Sort this shit out, will you?'

'The peasants are booing the *mater*,' said Prince Charles.

'Bloody helicopter pilot's fault,' moaned Vain. 'We weren't supposed to arrive until the speech was over. I told my manager, If we don't headline above the Queen, we do not appear.'

'Should I go up and have a word with everybody?' the prince asked.

'The Queen's special unofficial people's birthday speech,' boomed the voice of the big-wig.

'Bollocks!' cried Bollocks and pretty much everybody else.

'Best do it now then,' said Vain. 'Before they storm the stage.'

'I'll have a go.' Prince Charles smiled at Polly. 'Wish me luck.'

'Good luck.' Polly kissed him on the cheek.

Now, the prince had made many speeches before in his life. But never to a mob like this. They saw him stroll onto the stage, with his hands behind his back. And *they* knew he wasn't Jeff Beck.

279

'BOOOOOOOOOOOOOOOOO!!!!!!' they went.

'Applause *please*,' said the voice of the bigwig. 'Or I regret I shall be forced to pull the plug on this gig.'

'Now, where is that voice coming from?' Arthur asked himself.

Pull the plug? The travellers became silent. But this was not a peaceful silence. This was a silence which carried about itself such an air of menace, that you could almost cut this silence into strips with a knife and use it to frighten Pit Bull Terriers with.

The bigwig in the control box felt it. He saw his whole life passing right before his eyes.

Prince Charles waved and said hello. But the centre-stage microphone was still switched off.

The crowd prepared itself mentally for the storming of the stage.

'Applause please,' cried the bigwig. They were the best famous last words he could think of.

And suddenly the crowd welled into applause.

'Thank you,' said the prince. But it wasn't for him. Vain Glory had appeared once more on the stage. The bigwig in the control box hastily switched the centre-stage microphone back on.

Vain came up behind the prince and put his arm around his shoulder. He tapped the microphone. 'Listen up,' he said.

'Cheeeeeer!' went the crowd.

'Listen up. This guy is a buddy of mine. And his mum's gonna say a few words. It's sound, OK? Then the Gandhis are gonna rock 'til dawn. What d'you say?'

'We say yeah,' said the crowd.

'Er, let me hear you say yeah,' said the prince.

'Yeah,' said the crowd.

'Yeah?' said the prince.

'Yeah,' said the crowd.

Vain Glory whispered at the prince's ear, 'The secret is in knowing when to stop. Introduce your mum, then leg it.'

'Ladies and gentlemen, boys and girls,' said the prince, 'Her Majesty the Queen.'

There was silence. Vain Glory put his hand to his ear. 'Did we hear you say yeah?'

'Yeah,' went the crowd. And three people clapped.

And the big screen behind the stage lit up to display a picture of the prince's mum, on the balcony at Buckingham Palace.

Cornelius ceased his fruitless search for Tuppe and sat down to watch.

The Queen put on her spectacles and read from a prepared speech.

'Peoples of the world,' she read, 'it affords us much pleasure to speak to you all on the evening of our special birthday. These are difficult days for us all.'

For some more than others, thought the crowd, to a man (or a woman, or a child, or a small dog on a piece of string).

'Caring look,' read the Queen. 'Oh, I see, that's a stage direction. Can we go for another take?'

'She's losing it,' whispered Charles to Polly. 'Should have abdicated years ago. The Queen Mother won't let her. Says she doesn't want to be referred to as the Queen Grandmother.'

The Queen received words of advice through an earphone. She made a caring face. 'And in these difficult, and troubled times, we all must—'

But that was all she said. Because one minute she was there, making her speech. And the next minute she wasn't.

A rumble went through the watching crowd on Star Hill. It was a 'What's going on here?' kind of a rumble.

'You don't suppose she's been shot?' Prince Charles tried very hard to keep that note of glee out of his voice.

'No look.' Polly pointed up at the image on the screen. Palace security men were now all over the balcony. They were pointing their guns in all directions and shouting things like, 'Where the *bleep* did she go?'

And then another voice rose above theirs. It was a deep and sonorous voice and it said, 'Attention, peoples of the world. Her Majesty the Queen has just been kidnapped.'

And then the screen went blank.

And then the travellers really cheered.

25

'Well,' said Prince Charles to Vain Glory, 'on with
the show then, Colin. Would you like me to introduce your first number?'

'What?' said Polly.

'Go for it,' said Colin.

'Rune.' Cornelius Murphy was elbowing his way
back to the happy bus and an appointment with
Bone's ocarina. With Rune alive, the metaphorical
goalposts had been moved once more. The peace
convoy, which had been translated in his mind into
a marauding army, had now become a peace convoy
once more. But one which had now better move very
fast indeed, if it was to do anything before Rune put
the rest of his diabolical scheme into action, came
forward as the Queen's saviour and led the forces of
law and order and retribution, along with all the
world's media, to the portals of the Forbidden Zones.

When Cornelius did reach the bus, he found
Bollocks at the door waiting for him.

'Your old man just kidnapped the Queen,' said
Bollocks. 'Just like you told us he would.'

'Is Tuppe with you?'

'He's in the back. He and Bone got duffed up by
a hired heavy.'

'What?' Cornelius made his way to the little man with the big lip.

'Tell me who did this and he will die,' said Cornelius Murphy.

'Bone did it,' Tuppe replied. 'I was running away. The heavy hit Bone and Bone fell on top of me.'

'The heavy wanted me to commit an unnatural act with him,' Bone explained. 'So I gave him head butts.'

'Did you see the broadcast?' Tuppe asked Cornelius. 'Your old man just kidnapped the Queen. I'll bet you're pleased to know he's not dead.'

'I'm ecstatic. Although I would have much preferred a simple postcard. Where's the ocarina?'

'Ah,' said Tuppe.

'Ah?' said Cornelius. 'Ah, again? As in, Ah, I'm sorry?'

'I'm afraid so. I was keeping the ocarina safe. But when Bone fell on me it got broke.'

'Oh perfect.' Cornelius threw his hands up into his hair. 'This is just perfect. What are we going to do now?'

'Er, excuse me.' Bollocks fluttered his fingers. 'But you know you said that if you were having an epic, then I could be in it.'

'We were and you were,' said Cornelius. 'But now it looks as if we're not again. I don't know exactly where this leaves you.'

'I'd rather like to build up my part a bit, as it happens. Because I have the solution to your problem.'

'You do?' said Cornelius.

'I do,' said Bollocks.

'Go for it,' said Tuppe.

Something, well it was two somethings really, moved invisibly through the corridors of Buckingham Palace. There was a large something, and a not-so-large something. The large something carried the not-so-large something, which was struggling, but unable to cry out, due to the Elastoplast dressing stuck over its mouth.

The large something was, of course, Hugo Rune. And the smaller struggling something, a somebody. *The* somebody. Her Majesty the Queen.

Rune's patent mantle of invisibility covered the two of them and hung down to the royal Axminster Nobody saw a thing as Rune slipped from the palace with his regal prize and crossed the car park bound for his silvery automobile.

Inspectre Hovis switched off his television set. As was the case with Hugo Rune, the great detective was anything but dead.

How so?

How so indeed?

'The Crime of the Century,' said Inspectre Hovis. 'My hand-tailored hat is off to you, Rune. Had you not spied out the glint from the barrel of the 7.62 mm M134 General Electric Minigun on that rooftop opposite The Wife's Legs Café, and then chosen to demonstrate the extent of your mystical powers by mentally projecting images of ourselves leaving the front door of the premises, whilst we, in fact, slipped out through the back, then our lives would surely have been lost.'

Oh *that's* how he did it!

Inspectre Hovis dusted down the creases in his immaculate tweed trousers and picked up his heavy pigskin valise. He had work of national importance to do. And now.

His conversation with Rune had stretched long hours into the night. Not that it could really be called a conversation. Rune had talked and Hovis had listened. And Rune had eaten. And Rune had drunk. And when Rune had consumed all the food and drink the Inspectre possessed, he had sent Hovis out to buy more. And when he had finally done with the talking and eating and drinking, he had taken himself off to bed. To Hovis's bed. And Hovis had been forced to sleep on the floor.

But the fruits of all this talking and eating and drinking now lent their weight to the pigskin valise.

There was a map of London, on which all the entrances to the Forbidden Zones were clearly marked, a number of ocarinas of the reinvented persuasion, complete with instructions for their correct use, a great dossier, compiled by Rune, of the crimes wrought against mankind by the denizens of the Forbidden Zones, a free pardon for Rune, regarding all his past misdemeanours (to be signed by Her Majesty at the time of her release) along with a long list of hereditary titles and privileges Rune claimed to be his, through virtue of certain traditions, old charters, and somethings. And so much more.

A solemn pact had been drawn up between the

policeman and the mystic, to the effect that each would protect the interests of the other. Rune, the mystic, would kidnap the Queen, in such a manner that his identity remained unknown, and keep her in a place of safety. Hovis, the policeman, would lead in the police and the Army and whoever else he could muster up, acting upon information received from Hugo Rune.

Each would live long and prosper.

Of course, there did remain the matter of whether Hugo Rune could actually be trusted. Inspectre Hovis did not think for one tiny moment that he could be. But he chose not to dwell upon Rune's possible treacheries. For now, as Holmes would have put it, the game was afoot. Hovis had to make his way directly to Scotland Yard, arouse the most powerful of the powers-that-be, yet-are-not-in-the-pay-of-the-blighters-in-the-Forbidden-Zones, and begin the assault. He and Rune had synchronized watches. It had been agreed Hovis should lead in the troops at the stroke of midnight.

'And so,' said the great detective, checking his immaculateness in the cracked old bedroom mirror, 'Scotland Yard at the double, and the Crime of the Century right in the bag.'

'It's an interesting plan,' said Cornelius to Bollocks.

'A veritable blinder of a plan,' agreed Tuppe.

'I'm glad you like it,' said Bollocks to the both of them. 'Shall we go out there and give the thing a try?'

And as neither of them had done it for a while,

Cornelius looked at Tuppe.

And Tuppe looked at Cornelius.

'Let's do,' they said.

'I want this thing handled delicately,' said Chief Inspector Lytton at the bottom of the hill, near to the place where the buses turn around. 'I want a volunteer to go up there and switch off the sound system.'

The policemen surrounding him turned their faces away and mumbled into their boots. They'd quite enjoyed the violent skirmishes of the previous day, because they did outnumber those travellers (the ones in the pay of the BBC) by about twenty-three to one. But this looked like a kamikaze mission. They weren't keen.

Mumble mumble mumble, went the officers of the law.

'Come on now,' said Lytton. 'Who's going to make me proud?'

Mumble mumble.

'Come on now . . .'

'Sir.' Sergeant Sturdy took a step forward and gave a smart salute.

'Good man, Sturdy,' said the chief inspector.

'Not me, *sir.*' Sergeant Ron pointed over his shoulder towards Constable Ken, who was picking his nose and examining the yield in a wing mirror. 'Him, sir.'

'Ah yes,' said Chief Inspector Lytton. 'The very man for the job.'

★   ★   ★

'Do you really think you can do this?' Cornelius shouted to Bollocks, as they made their way through the crowd. The crowd that was really rocking to the Gandhis.

'Computers,' Bollocks shouted back. 'I did computer studies at Essex University. Got my Master's degree there. They'll have all the state-of-the-art stuff up there in the control box. I probably even designed some of it. All you have to do is use the little mouse and draw your ocarina with its extra holes. I can then get the computer to translate your drawing into a 3D image and analyse it. The computer will then be able to play the new notes. From the control box we can pump them straight through the speaker system.'

Naturally Cornelius didn't hear much of this. Not with all the good rocking and everything. But he saw Bollocks put his thumb up, which seemed like a good sign.

'Of course we do have to get into the control box first,' said Bollocks, but Cornelius didn't hear that either.

The bigwig in the control box was in something of a lather. He was on the telephone.

'What do you mean, vanished?' he was asking. 'How can the Queen of England just vanish? What about that voice saying she's been kidnapped? Who was that? How was it done?'

The bigwig on the other end of the line (he had been the second bigwig at the meeting of bigwigs) did not know the answers to any of these questions. He did not know how the Queen could simply vanish from the balcony of Buckingham Palace with the whole world looking on. But he did not seem altogether concerned about the whos, hows and whys. He seemed far more concerned about certain enormous sources of potential revenue. Product managers, who handled the accounts of companies who sold goods *By Royal Appointment*, were already flooding his switchboard with calls regarding the booking of prime TV slots during coverage of the situation to come.

'I'll get the contracts boys straight on to it,' said the bigwig in the control box, replacing the receiver and rubbing his hands together.

Bollocks, Cornelius and Tuppe crept in the direction of the control box. There were a lot of hired heavies about now.

'You don't happen to see the one that hit Bone, by any chance?' Cornelius shouted into Tuppe's ear.

'Does it matter?'

'Well, I just thought it might be fitting if he was the one we had to clout to get into the control box.'

'That's him,' said Tuppe, pointing to the one that just happened to be guarding the control box.

Coincidence? Synchronicity? The ten-thousand-decibel hairdryer of destiny? Call it whatever you will. But call it something, because there's a good deal more of it yet to come.

Like this next bit, for instance.

Inspectre Hovis hailed a black cab. 'Take me to Scotland Yard,' said he. 'At the double.'

'Right you are, guvnor,' replied Terence Arthur Mulligan.

Cornelius sauntered up to the fellow in the official Gandhi's Hairdryer World Tour T-shirt, who was guarding the control box.

'Back,' said this fellow, registering the tall boy's approach.

'I understand you recently smote a chum of mine,' said Cornelius.

'Smote?' The fellow lowered a beetling brow. 'What is smote?'

'Smote, as in smite,' said Cornelius. 'As in, to smite, to have smitten, and, to have been smitten.'

'As in smitten with love?' asked the heavy, eyeing Cornelius up and down and nodding with approval.

'No. As in, smitten with the fist.' And verily did Cornelius smite he that had smitten Bone and caused him to fall upon Tuppe and fatten his lip and break the reinvented ocarina, withal.

And verily the smiter of Bone did fall unto the earth.

'Nice smiting,' said Tuppe.

'Let's get inside,' said Cornelius.

The bigwig in the control box had the phone back at his ear. He was shouting into it about residuals and product placements and stuff like that. He didn't even look up as Bollocks, Cornelius and Tuppe walked in.

The sound engineer, who was supposed to be in charge of things, did though.

'Are you guys with the band?' he asked.

'That's right.' Cornelius offered a smile. 'I'm . . .'

'The Hairdryer's hairdresser,' said Tuppe. 'And this,' he waved up at Bollocks, 'is their new technical advisor, he's come to check out all the equipment.'

'And what do you do?'

'I write the songs that make the whole world sing,' said Tuppe. 'And I procure young women and send out for steak sandwiches.'

'Nice work if you can get it.'

'You can get it if you try,' said Tuppe.

'Get out at once, before I call for the hired heavies,' said the sound engineer.

'I think we're rumbled,' said Tuppe. 'Methinks 'twer' best this fellow be now smitten.'

'Smitten?' said the sound engineer. 'As in, smitten with the clap?'

'Close,' said Cornelius, smiting the sound engineer.

'Hold on there.' The bigwig watched as the sound engineer struck the floor. He didn't make any attempt to help him though. He put his hand over the mouthpiece of the phone and said, 'Keep the noise down, I'm in negotiation here.'

And thus it was that Cornelius did smite the bigwig also.

'Come on over baby, there's a whole lotta smiting going on,' sang Tuppe.

'Let's have a look at this computer system,' said Bollocks.

Constable Ken Loathsome plodded up Star Hill. He was taking the roundabout route. The route which did not have him finding his way into a traveller' cooking pot. Cannibals to a man Jack of them, those travellers, everybody knew that.

The constable's hand was in his right trouser pocket. It clutched the regulation police-issue pistol, of the kind they do *not* carry in their cars. He wasn't looking for trouble. But if trouble came looking for him, he'd shoot it.

'Now that's handy,' said Bollocks. 'This computer system is the very same as the one I worked on at Essex.'

Coincidence? Synchronicity? Told you.

'I should have this set up in a couple of minutes. Now, Cornelius, you see this screen? Well take this little thing, that's the mouse and—'

'Cornelius knows all about computers,' said Tuppe helpfully.

'Not all,' said Cornelius.

'Got a home system?' Bollocks asked.

'I did have,' said Cornelius. 'But there was a slight malfunction and I took off the cover and fixed it. But after I'd put the cover back on, I found I had a couple of small screws left over, so I—'

'That would be before you read *The Book of Ultimate Truths*?'

'Regrettably so.'

'Never mind. Computers are all bollocks anyway. Go on then, work the mouse.'

'We're going in the wrong direction, aren't we?' asked Inspectre Hovis.

Terence Arthur Mulligan glanced into the

driving mirror with hooded eyes. 'It's a short cut,' said he.

The Gandhis were going at it full tilt. Now, if you've never seen Gandhi's Hairdryer play live, and there may just possibly be some lost soul in Outer Mongolia that hasn't, getting the measure of their music can be a tricky business.

The lead singer, when asked by the presenter of a TV arts programme to describe it, said, 'Basically, like, the music is *diatonic*. Based upon any scale of five tones and two semitones produced by playing the white keys of a keyboard instrument, especially the natural major and minor scales—'

'I'll have to stop you there,' said the presenter.

'Why?' asked the lead singer.

'Because it wasn't funny the first time and I'm not sitting through it again.'

'Fair enough.'

Twenty-three-thousand souls were giving the ground some Wellie.

You really had to be there.

At the side of the stage, Polly said to Prince Charles 'What about your mum?'

'My mum?' The prince was tapping his toes and popping his fingers.

'Your mum. She's been kidnapped or something and you don't appear to be showing a lot of concern.'

Prince Charles made his 'concerned' face. 'There,' said he. 'See how concerned one is?'

Polly found the words of Michelet (who?) forming in her mouth. '*It is a general rule that all superior men*

294

inherit the elements of superiority from their mothers,' she said. 'And, to quote the Marchioness de Spadara, *The babe at first feeds on his mother's bosom, but*—'

'Let's go behind the big speakers and—'

'No way!'

Bollocks tapped all sorts of things into the computer. Cornelius moved the little mouse about.

'How's it going?' Bollocks asked.

'Fine. I've drawn Rune's reinvented ocarina, complete with all the new holes. So, if you can program the computer to analyse the new notes and play them out through the speaker system, I reckon we can open up the portal on Star Hill and storm into the Forbidden Zones.'

'I don't think that would be a very good idea at all,' said Arthur Kobold, entering the control box and shutting the door behind him. 'Put up your hands please and move away from that contraption. I have a gun here somewhere.' He fished into his pocket and pulled one out. It was a very big gun. It was not regulation police issue.

'Now, nobody move until I pull the trigger. Then you can all fall down. Dead.'

26

'I only came here to pull the plug out,' said Arthur. 'But it would appear that I am, as ever, in the right place at the right time.'

'I really hate him,' said Tuppe to Cornelius.

'Shut up, small person.' Arthur waved his big gun about. 'Now, let's get this shooting done and this noise turned off and I can go back and finish my cake.'

Bollocks chewed upon his lip, Cornelius had still to punch in the order of the notes. 'Excuse me, sir,' said he, stepping in front of the tall boy, 'but this really isn't anything to do with me, I'm just the sound engineer.'

'Really?' Arthur raised an eyebrow.

'Really, these two guys forced their way in here, knocking people out. They forced me to program some nonsense into the computer. Please don't shoot. I have a wife and three children. Well, two wives really.'

'Really?' said Arthur once more.

'Really.' Bollocks crossed his heart. Get on with it, Cornelius, he thought.

Cornelius would dearly have liked to have been getting on with it. And no doubt he would have been doing so. If he'd been able to remember the order of the notes. Which he couldn't. He knew that Tuppe could though.

'So you're the sound engineer?' Arthur did trigger cockings.

'That's me.' Bollocks put out his hand for a bit of a shake. It didn't get one.

'If you're the sound engineer,' said Arthur, 'shouldn't you be wearing an official Gandhi's Hairdryer World Tour T-shirt?'

'It's at the dry cleaner's. I spilt some steak sandwich down the front.' Bollocks smiled.

'How about a stage pass, then?' Arthur glanced down. 'Both these unconscious chaps are wearing them. See? The one on top has a stage pass marked *Big-Wig*. And the one underneath, the one wearing an official Gandhi's Hairdryer World Tour T-shirt, his stage pass reads *sound engineer*.'

'Get away,' said Bollocks. 'What a coincidence.'

'Just back up into the corner. Murphy, what are you up to?'

'Nothing,' said Cornelius, which was precisely correct. 'Now listen, Arthur. Let's be reasonable about this.'

'I am being reasonable. I'm being firm but fair. You present a serious risk to us. You'd do the same if you were in my place.'

'*I* wouldn't,' said Tuppe.

'Nor me,' said Cornelius. And they both shook their heads.

'Come out from behind that hair,' said Mr Kobold. 'And put your hands up.'

Cornelius put his hands up through his hair.

'Listen,' said he, 'there has to be some compromise. This can't go on for ever. Your lot will get found out sooner or later. Better it's done my way, peacefully, before Hugo Rune marches in with the army.'

'*Hugo Rune?*' said Arthur Kobold. 'Hugo Rune? Army? What? What? What?'

Hugo Rune was driving along in his silver car. Even if it didn't really run on water, it was still a wonderful thing. And it did go very fast.

And, as it was cloaked in a patent mantle of invisibility, no-one saw just how fast it did go. The guards on the palace gate didn't.

Rune didn't actually sing as he drove along, but he hummed to himself. Deeply. Majestically.

Her Majesty wasn't feeling particularly majestic. Hugo Rune had actually locked her in the boot.

Cornelius finished a hurried résumé of Hugo Rune's plan for the conquest of the Forbidden Zones.

'The bastard!' Arthur Kobold was appalled. 'I thought he was . . . er . . .'

'Dead?' Cornelius asked.

'The bastard. What shall we all do?'

'Well, you could stop pointing that gun at us for a start.'

Arthur wasn't keen.

'Look,' said Cornelius, 'I don't want to expose you and yours to the world. Really I don't. I just want you and yours to leave me and mine to run the world our way.'

'Can't be done.' Arthur shook his head. 'You'

298

make a complete hash of it. *Our* safety would be at risk.'

'Mr Kobold,' said Cornelius, 'if Hugo Rune gets his way, there won't be any of your lot left. There will be no safety to risk. You'll all be dead.'

'I will have to cogitate upon these matters.'

'Take your time,' said Tuppe. 'Come back in half an hour. We'll wait.'

Arthur Kobold shook his head sadly. 'I don't think so. Rather that I just shoot the two of you now.'

'*Two?*' said Bollocks. 'Does that mean I can go?'

'Shoot the *three* of you now.'

'Bollocks,' said Bollocks.

'I'm sorry, but there it is. Who wants to be shot first?'

'He does.' Three fingers pointed. Two of them pointed at Bollocks.

'Thanks a lot, lads,' said that man. 'Some part in his epic I had.'

'That's life,' smiled Arthur Kobold, aiming for the head.

Everyone! Up against the wall and spread'm!' Contable Ken blundered through the control-box door.

'What?' Arthur turned to meet him, gun in hand.

'Iraqi terrorist!' Ken pulled his pistol from his pocket and let fly. Everybody ducked. Especially Arthur Kobold.

'My hands are up,' said he, throwing down his gun.

'Yeah. Good. OK.' The young policeman had his gun between both hands and was doing his best to

299

point it at everybody. 'All of you, hands high and kill the power.'

'I thought there was never a policeman around when you needed one,' said Tuppe.

'How can we switch off the power if our hands are up?' Bollocks asked. Which was a fair enough question.

'Guy with the hair,' said Ken, 'turn out your pockets.'

'Why?' Cornelius asked.

'Because I like making people turn out their pockets,' said Ken, lapsing into English. 'It really humiliates them. Especially when I demand that they unroll their condoms.'

'Nice work, officer,' said Arthur Kobold.

'Eh?' said Constable Ken.

'Chief Inspector Kobold, Noise Abatement Division.' Arthur flashed something at the young policeman. It might have been a warrant card. It looked more like a beer mat.

'Sir?' said Constable Ken.

'You cut the power, Constable, I'll get some backup.' Arthur Kobold saluted.

Constable Ken saluted back – with his gun hand and nearly put his eye out.

'Now just hold on,' said Cornelius.

'Say sir in the presence of a superior officer,' Ken rubbed his forehead. 'I nearly put my eye out,' he said.

'But wait. Don't let him leave.'

'Any more lip from you scuz-bucket, and I'll blow your goddamn brains out.' But that was about tha for Constable Ken. Arthur Kobold struck him from behind. Right on top of the head. He collapsed on to the bigwig and the sound engineer. Shame really, but probably all for the best. Spared us any more of the duff Americanisms.

'Now,' said Arthur, pointing his gun once more at Bollocks. 'It was you first, wasn't it?'

'Could we have a recount?' Bollocks asked.

'This is not a short cut,' said Inspectre Hovis. 'This is Hammersmith.'

'Leave it to the professional,' replied the Mulligan. 'I'll get you to where you have to be.'

Hovis jumped forward in his seat. 'I know you,' he cried. 'What's your game?'

Arthur squeezed the trigger. Tuppe was covering his head. Cornelius was covering Tuppe's head. Bollocks was complaining that a condemned man should always be entitled to a final joint.

The gun went bang very loudly indeed. And Arthur Kobold fell to the floor.

Anna Gotting stood in the doorway. She had a rig-rigger's spanner in her hand. A spanner which had just dealt Arthur Kobold a devastating blow.

'I've been watching you guys come in here,' said Anna. 'I'd come in myself, if I could climb over all the bodies.'

Stop this cab,' demanded Inspectre Hovis. 'I have work of national importance to do.'

'Up yours, copper,' sneered the wayward cabbie.

'Then, Terence Arthur Mulligan, I am arresting you on the charge of abducting an officer of the law. You have no need to say anything, but anything you do say will be taken down and may be used in evidence.'

'We're on the road to hell,' said Terence Arthur Mulligan. 'And bollocks to you, by the way.'

Bollocks was back at the control desk, fiddling with the computer. Happily he hadn't been shot at all. The bullet had only wounded Cornelius. In the hair.

'It's all rather complicated,' the tall boy told Anna, as he helped her over the pile of bodies. 'I don't think I have time to explain right now.'

'You have another plan, don't you?'

'Well, it's Bollocks's actually.'

'That doesn't surprise me. It was the last time.'

'That's not what I meant.' Cornelius turned away

'Allow me to explain,' said Tuppe.

'Piss off,' said Anna.

'Give us a French kiss,' said Tuppe.

And Anna hit him with the spanner.

'Turn this cab around.'

'No way, copper.'

'You're nicked, Mulligan.'

'And you're in the deep brown stuff.'

'Right,' said Bollocks. 'What order do these notes go in, Cornelius?'

'Actually, I'm not altogether sure. But Tupp◄

knows. What order do the notes go in, Tuppe? Tuppe?'

But Tuppe didn't answer. The blow from Anna's spanner had sent him to join the sleepers on the floor.

'Tuppe, wake up,' said Cornelius. 'This is no time to take a nap.'

Anna made an innocent face. 'Could you tell me exactly what the latest plan might be?' she asked Bollocks.

'Sure,' said Bollocks, smiling upon the beautiful young woman. 'You must be Anna. Cornelius told me all about you.'

'Come on, Tuppe,' went Cornelius. 'Wakey, wakey.'

'Well,' said Bollocks to Anna, 'quite a bit's happened since you last saw Cornelius. He met up with his dad, Hugo Rune. But this Rune, it seems, is a total nutter, bent on some kind of world domination of his own. He's just kidnapped the Queen and he intends to lay the blame on the beings inside the Zones; lead in the army, with the whole world watching, and wipe the lot of them out.'

'I seem to recall that Cornelius had a not too dissimilar plan. Although his didn't include the Queen.'

'Yeah, well, you see Cornelius has had second thoughts. He's reasoned that if the whole world suddenly discovered that it had been tricked and manipulated all throughout history by these beings, fingers would be pointed, blames exchanged, society would break right down.'

'This also crossed *my* mind. Although I was too polite to mention it at the time.'

'Right. So anyway. Cornelius has come up with an ingenious plan: open up the portal on Star Hill and lead a twenty-three-thousand-strong peace convoy into the Zones, overwhelm the beings by sheer weight of numbers and demand that they cease their activities.'

'Tuppe's spark out,' said Cornelius. 'He's got a big bump on his head.'

'Perhaps he tripped.' Anna tucked the spanner into the back pocket of her jeans.

'You'll have to punch the notes in yourself then, Cornelius.'

The tall boy made a dubious face. 'I'll do my best. But I'm really not sure.'

Bollocks gave up his chair and continued his conversation with Anna. 'Cornelius reasoned that the beings in the Zones will surrender. Just like any other beings, they'll do anything to rid themselves of travellers.'

'Did I say that?' Cornelius asked. 'I don't remember saying that.'

'I'm sure you did. Now get on with those notes.'

'Quite so.' Cornelius did a sort of dip dip sky blue who's it not you.

'And,' said Bollocks, 'the beauty of the plan is that the world will know nothing about it. Nobody is going to believe a traveller telling him that he's been to the Middle Earth, or Fairyland, or whatever. And the travellers don't tell people anything anyway. It's quite an inspired plan.'

'I see,' said Anna.

'How are you doing?' Bollocks asked Cornelius.

'I think I'm almost done. Yes, I'm sure I'm done.' Cornelius crossed his fingers.

'Right.' Bollocks leaned over the computer console. 'We log it in here.' He pressed a button. 'See that, it goes up on the screen. Shiva's sheep, those are very strange frequencies.'

'They are?'

'They are. Now all you have to do is press that button and the sequence will play directly through the speaker system.'

'This button?'

'That button.' Bollocks indicated a big button. It was blood red. The way some of them are.

Cornelius considered the blood-red button. 'Right,' said he, 'well somehow I have to get up on the stage and tell the travellers I know of a land of milk and honey.'

Bollocks nodded thoughtfully. 'Say, perhaps, that you were able to fight your way through all those hired heavies and do that, I wonder how the travellers would react.'

'Probably stone him to death,' said Anna. 'I know I would.'

'I'll think of something.' Cornelius batted down his hair. 'I am the Stuff of Epics. Keep your ears open, Bollocks. I'll get up there and make my speech. And when you hear me say, "Behold the wonder", then you press the blood-red button.' The tall boy turned to take his leave. 'And look after Tuppe,' he said.

'Just one small thing', said Anna, 'before you climb over the bodies.'

'Oh yes?' Cornelius turned back.

'It sucks,' said Anna. 'Your plan. Sucks.'

'Somehow I just knew you were going to say that.' Cornelius turned away once more.

'But you don't know why.'

'And neither do I care.'

'You really should. It's quite important.'

Cornelius sighed and turned back once more. 'Go on then, say your piece.'

'OK. Now as I understand it, the essence of this inspired plan of yours is that the whole world will know nothing about it. Am I correct?'

'You are correct.'

'I see. Then don't you think it a bit of a problem that the whole world is sitting at home watching this gig live on TV?'

27

Terence Arthur Mulligan put his accelerator foot hard down. Inspectre Hovis fell back in his seat. 'Turn this cab around,' he shouted. 'Drive to the nearest police station and give yourself up.'

'Some chance.' Mulligan swerved around a corner, dislodging Hovis to the floor. 'You're supposed to be dead. My masters will pay me a big reward for you. I'll ask for it in diamonds.'

'Have at you, sir.' Hovis clambered up and swung his cane. It rebounded from the window dividing him from the cabbie.

'Bullet-proof glass,' crowed the Mulligan. 'And the doors have central locking. I'm taking *you* in.'

Hugo Rune was already in. But then he had re-invented the ocarina for that very purpose. Getting into the Zones had never been a problem for him. It was getting *out*, as the ocarina didn't work from the inside.

But he was in again now all right. The silver car was parked back on the spot where Cornelius had originally found it, in King Santa's private car park. The ice-cream van was still there too.

Hugo Rune drummed his plump fingers on the golden wood of the steering wheel. So much physical activity, it really wasn't his way at all. He, like the king, was a man for delegation.

On the back seat of the silver car stood a pedestal table. Its top covered by a silken cloth. Beneath this cloth was a perfect micro-cosmic representation of the interior of the car.

Hugo Rune didn't speak. When you possess the wherewithal to overthrow the secret King of the World, and have the Queen of England locked in your boot, you don't actually have to say anything to make people wake up and take notice.

'Wake up,' shouted Cornelius Murphy. 'Wake up and take notice.'

'I am woken up,' said Tuppe, rubbing the bump on his head.

'Not you. I mean Mr Kobold.'

'I've missed something, haven't I?' said Tuppe.

'Just a slight spanner in the works.'

'No, I'm sure I felt the spanner.'

'The peace convoy plan just went out the window.' Cornelius began to smack Arthur Kobold about the head. 'Apparently the gig is being broadcast world-wide.'

'First I've heard of it.'

'There was something about it on the BBC,' said Bollocks.

'So what's the plan going to be now?' Tuppe asked Cornelius.

'Mr Kobold is going to take us into the Zones and introduce us to his guvnor.'

'Does Mr Kobold know this yet?'

'No, but he will, as soon as we wake him up.'

Something moved invisibly through the corridors of the Forbidden Zones. Two somethings, in fact. A large something and a not-so-large something. The large something was carrying the smaller something. But you couldn't see either of them, because they were both invisible. Or something.

Anna poured the contents of the sound engineer's Thermos flask over the head of Arthur Kobold. The sound engineer wasn't going to need it, he was still out for the count.

'Oooh, ahhh. What's going on? Where am I?'

Cornelius knelt down beside Arthur Kobold and put his big non-regulation police-issue pistol against his head. 'You are in big trouble,' he said. 'Now get up and take me to your leader.'

'I certainly will not.'

Cornelius sighed. 'Mr Kobold,' he said, 'we have not known each other long, but I think we understand each other reasonably well. The way I see it, you have two options open to you. The first is that you take us at once, without trickery or complaint, straight to your "guvnor". Hopefully, between he and I some compromise can be reached that will spare your world and mine. The second is that you refuse. If you do, then I will shoot you dead, press the blood-red button over there and lead twenty-three thousand travellers into your guvnor's front parlour. Personally, I don't care which one you choose. But I'd be interested to learn your personal preference.'

'How prettily put.' Arthur Kobold made a brave face. 'And you're quite right, we understand each other well enough. You wouldn't shoot me in cold blood. You know you wouldn't.'

'I would.' Anna stepped into Arthur's line of vision.

'Allow me to lead the way,' said Mr Kobold.

'Allow me to lead the way,' said Terence Arthur Mulligan.

Hovis glowered up at the grinning cabbie, who now held open the taxi door. He would dearly have liked to strike him with his cane. But he felt discouraged to do so by the nature of Mulligan's two companions. They were big and green and muscly.

The taxi was now parked in a great Victorian warehouse of a place. Between an ice-cream van and Rune's silver car. The Inspectre viewed the latter with some small degree of comfort. But not much.

Mulligan viewed the former with some puzzlement.

'Where are you taking me?' Hovis asked.

'To the dungeon.' Terence made an evil face. 'The deep, dark dungeon.'

'But first to the torture chamber,' said one of the big green thingies. 'This is the sod who stuck his sword up my brother Colin's arse a couple of nights back on Kew Bridge.'

The Gandhis were still rocking. They hadn't stopped. The control box was soundproof, that's all. Arthur Kobold led Bollocks, Cornelius, Tuppe and Anna

310

away from it. They skirted around the hired heavies and were soon at the secret entrance in the gorse bush.

'OK,' said Anna, prodding Arthur Kobold with the big pistol, 'lead the way.'

'Guys,' said Bollocks.

'Yes,' said the guys.

'Guys, I think I'll pass this one up, if you don't mind.'

'Bottle gone?' Tuppe asked.

'Yes actually. I'm not into guns and stuff like that. But listen, I did my bit, didn't I? I was in your epic.'

'You certainly were.' Cornelius grinned. 'Enjoy the band. We'll get back to you later.'

'Good luck then, guys.'

'Good luck, Bollocks.' The tall boy shook him warmly by the hand. 'And thanks for everything.'

'Be lucky,' said Tuppe.

'You too.'

Arthur Kobold led the way down the flight of stone steps. 'This isn't going to get you anywhere,' he told Cornelius.

'Just move on. We'll see where it gets us.'

The steps went down and down, the way some of them do. Those that aren't going up and up. Although these could possibly be the same steps. It just depends whether you're going up or down.

Arthur Kobold's party were going down.

Inspectre Hovis was going down and the big green thingy, with the brother called Colin, kept kicking him as he did so.

311

'Is that your own cab?' the other big green thingy asked Terence.

'I lease it. It's the best way. The fares from the first day of the week pay the rental. From then on all the money goes into me own pocket.'

'Takings any good at this time of year?'

'Fair to middling. Lot of regulars on holiday.'

'But a lot of people take their holidays in London.'

'Oh yeah, you get the theatre trade and airport runs. But a lot of people come on guided tours and the Underground does good deals.'

'You wouldn't recommend cabbing as a profession, then?'

'It has its perks and you are your own man.'

'Never thought of going out on your own? Mini-cab or something?'

'Too much hassle. You thinking of taking up the trade, then?'

'Maybe. I've got some bonus owing to me. And there has to be more to life than just being a big green thingy. I thought I might buy a limo. Do weddings and stuff.'

Twenty-three thousand pairs of feet were now doing 'Hi Ho Silver Lining' right above the head of the Secret King of the World.

The far from jolly red-faced man poured a large libation of some alcoholic beverage into a mighty goblet and emptied this down his throat.

'*Kobold!*' roared the king. 'Stop that damn row. Kobold, where are you?'

Arthur stuck his head around the great door and smiled painfully.

'I'm here, sire,' he said.

And Cornelius Murphy stared above the shoulder of Arthur Kobold. And verily did he behold the hall of the hidden king.

'Holy sh . . .' The tall boy took a step backwards. The mind-boggling magnitude of the scene that lay before was a little bit much to come to terms with.

The sheer scale of the thing. Its solidity. Its grandeur.

The fact that it was right here. Under Star Hill.

This was Castle Gormenghast. Or the hall of King Arthur. Or something.

Tuppe peeped from behind the tall boy's left knee. 'I see that,' he whispered. 'You do see that also, don't you? It's not just me?'

'It's not just you. I see it.'

'And do you see *him*?'

Tuppe's right forefinger made wavery little pointings towards *he* that sat upon the throne. The big he. The he with the huge white beard and the huge red outfit, with the ermine trimmings. And that belt of his and those heroic black boots. That *he*. That *he* there.

Cornelius saw him. 'I see him,' he said.

And Anna saw him also. And she was somewhat stuck for words. No doubt this would not last for very long, and some would soon return to her. Words like 'suck' and 'sad'. But not just at this moment.

'Kobold,' said the king. Quite loudly. Very loudly. '*Kobold!* What are you doing about that noise?'

Anna gave Mr Kobold a kick in the backside. Arthur entered the court of the king at a greater speed

313

than he might reasonably have preferred and fell in an untidy heap.

'Why exactly did you do that?' asked the king.

'Er,' said Arthur, climbing to his feet, dusting himself down and slipping off his shoes. 'We have guests.'

'Guests? Guests? I didn't invite any guests.'

'They sort of invited themselves, sire.'

'No, no.' The king shook his mighty beard. 'That is strictly against all royal protocol.'

'Now call me a twat,' said Tuppe to Cornelius, 'but isn't that Father Christmas himself?'

'You're a twat,' said Anna. 'But it is, isn't it?' She stepped sharply forward and poked Arthur Kobold in the waistcoat area. 'Is this your guvnor?'

'It's the king.' Arthur smiled another painful smile towards his monarch. 'Your Majesty.'

'Well, tell him to put his hands up.'

Arthur Kobold now made the kind of face you make when you shut your fingers in a door. 'I'd rather not, if you don't mind.'

'I do mind.' Anna thrust Mr Kobold aside. 'You!' she shouted.

'I?' The king's eyes widened. They were somewhat bleary and bloodshot, but they certainly widened. 'Kobold,' said the king, 'there is a young woman thing here and she is pointing a pistol at me.'

'Anna,' said Anna.

'Anna?' said the king.

'Anna,' said Anna. 'As in *The King and I*.'

'*Guards!*' shouted the king. 'As in, call out the *guards*!'

314

28

The king's guards were otherwise engaged.

One of them was pushing a reluctant Inspectre Hovis through the doorway into the torture chamber. The other was discussing the pros and cons of the limousine-hire business with Terence Arthur Mulligan.

'You have to be careful with your clientele,' Terence said. 'Watch out for the piss artists who throw up in the back, or try and nick your car-phone.'

'I was going to ask you about the phone,' said the big green thingy. 'Should I get *Cellnet* or one of the others? I've sent for brochures, but I can't seem to make up my mind.'

'Get on that rack you,' said the other big green thingy to Inspectre Hovis.

When the king had finally tired with shouting the word 'guards', he poured himself another drink. 'Kobold,' he said wearily, 'take these *creatures*', he waved towards Cornelius and Tuppe, who were still skulking in the doorway, 'straight to the dungeon. And *her*,' he pointed a big fat finger at Anna Gotting, 'chop her head off.'

'With pleasure, sire.'

'Get real,' said Anna.

'And use a blunt axe,' said the king. 'A big one.'

'That's enough.' Cornelius stepped into the great hall. 'Stop it, all of you. Now listen, please.' He stared up at the big figure on the throne. 'Are you really . . . I mean, am I right in thinking that you are . . . that is to say . . . er—'

'Spit it out, boy!' roared the king.

'Are you Father Christmas?'

The king's enormous face split into an enormous smile. 'My boy,' said he with a hearty chuckle. 'My boy. I see, I see.'

'What does he see?' Tuppe asked.

'You've come to give me your Christmas letter. You've come to see jolly old Santa and give him your Christmas letter. Well, why not? Have you been a good boy this year?'

'Barking mad,' said Tuppe. 'This bodes well.'

Cornelius thrust his hands into his pockets and took a few paces forward across the flagstoned floor.

The king's smile froze. 'Shoes,' he said.

'What?' Cornelius asked.

'Shoes. Your shoes. Take them off.'

'Why?' Cornelius asked.

'Because it's protocol. And because I tell you to. Take your shoes off. Socks too.'

'No,' said Cornelius. 'I won't.'

'*Guards!*' shouted the king.

Arthur Kobold wrung his hands.

Sergeant Sturdy strode up Star Hill. He didn't take any roundabout routes. That was not his way of doing

316

things. Travellers danced to every side of him, but reliable Ron stared stoically ahead and marched right on. The crowd parted before him. He had a certain way about him, did Ron.

'Get on that rack,' said the big green thingy once more.

'By this steel thrice blessed,' cried Inspectre Hovis, unsheathing his blade.

The large something that carried the not-so-large something, continued to do so, invisibly.

Cornelius strode across the great hall with his shoes still on. His footsteps echoed and the sound put the king's teeth on edge. And when Cornelius pulled out a chair at the king's table and sat down upon it, the royal teeth began to grind.

'Murphy,' said the tall boy. 'Cornelius Murphy. Perhaps you've heard of me.'

'This is Murphy?' The king addressed these words to the cringing Arthur Kobold.

Arthur nodded. 'Bloody nuisance, so he is.'

'And what is all the hair about?'

'It's big hair,' Cornelius explained. 'All famous people have big hair. It's a tradition, or an old charter. Or something. You have a big beard. I expect it's the same thing.'

'I will have my guards hang you up by your big hair and roast you over a slow fire.'

'Not on Christmas Eve, I hope.'

'Kobold. Go out and find the guards. Tell them to

bring *two* big blunt axes,' the king glanced over at Tuppe, 'and one of those little metal things you chop up slabs of toffee with.'

Arthur Kobold looked at Anna. Anna shook her head. 'Which one would you like me to shoot first, Cornelius?' she asked.

'Shoot the king first,' said the tall boy. 'Arthur can take care of the paperwork.'

'Shoot the king?' Santa fell back in alarm. 'What are you saying? You can't shoot merry old Father Christmas. Think of all the dear little boys and girls.'

'I hate kids,' said Anna, pointing her pistol at the king.

'No, no, no.' The alarm the king fell back in, became absolute horror. 'Kobold, do something.'

'What, like offering to be shot first?'

'That might help.'

'Would it?' Arthur asked Cornelius.

'Not much. But I'll tell you what I'll do, I'll have Anna shoot you *and* the king, and I'll take care of the paperwork myself.'

'No,' said the king. 'No, no, no. Stop all this at once. I have no wish to be shot. Tell me what it is you want. A train set, is it? Or a radio-controlled car? You just tell Father Christmas and he'll see what he can do.'

'I want you to cease interfering with mankind. I want you to leave us to run things our way. No more tampering. No more control. It has to stop. Right here. Right now.'

'I don't understand.' The king plucked at his beard.

318

'Are you suggesting that I should stop ruling the world?'

'That is correct.'

'Oh no. Oh no, no, no. I cannot be hearing this. Someone tell me I'm not hearing this.'

'You're not hearing this,' said Arthur Kobold.

'Bless you, Arthur. The voice of reason. I must be having a bad dream. Plump up my pillows and wake me with a cup of tea at noon.'

The king closed his eyes.

'Can I have a piece of your cake?' Cornelius asked.

The king opened his eyes. 'He's still here. Arthur, do something. He's having my cake now.'

'Leave the king's cake alone,' said Arthur.

Cornelius pushed a large piece into his mouth. 'Hey, Tuppe,' he called, 'come and have a piece of Santa's cake.'

'It will end in tears,' said Tuppe, waddling over.

'Shoes!' shrieked the king.

'Now listen,' said Cornelius. 'The way I see it, you have two options.' Arthur hid his face. 'The first is, that you surrender to me now. Abdicate and cease all further interference with the world above. Should you choose this option, then I will do everything in my power to see that no-one from the world above interferes with you.

'The second.' As the king was quite speechless, Cornelius went straight on to the second. 'The second is that you refuse this. In which case, I will stand aside and let Hugo Rune march in here with the army behind him, take the throne from you by force and probably kill you into the bargain. Me, I'm easy. But I'd be interested to learn your preference.'

'Hugo?' spluttered the king. 'Hugo? Army? Force? Kill? What? What? What?'

'There's been a bit of a situation,' said Arthur Kobold. 'Apparently Hugo Rune has kidnapped the Queen and is planning to blame it on us and lead an army down here to wipe us all out. That's why Murphy's here, you see. Sort of.'

The king groaned and buried his face in his hands.

'I'm sure this must be very distressing for you,' said Cornelius. 'And I'm sure you'd like some time to think about it.'

'I would,' mumbled the king.

'But regrettably you can't have any. So what's it going to be? The first option, or the second option?'

'I think it will probably have to be the *second* option,' said the voice of Hugo Rune.

29

Father Christmas suddenly found his throne pulled from under him, and himself sprawling in a most unregal manner on the flagstone floor.

The throne then rose into the air, moved back a few feet and settled down. And Hugo Rune materialized upon it. He was smoking a green cigar.

'It is I, Rune,' said Rune. 'None other. So mote it be.'

'Get off my throne.' The king thrashed about on the floor. 'Help me up, Kobold. Help me up.'

Arthur Kobold hastened to oblige. 'Get off the king's throne, you blackguard,' he said.

Hugo Rune ignored the both of them. He took out his pocket watch, flipped open the golden cover and perused the hour. 'We have some time left to pass before the overthrow of this evil empire,' he declared. 'Now, how best might we pass it? I know, don't tell me, you would like me to entertain you with fascinating episodes from my life.'

'I wouldn't,' said Tuppe. Rune threw him the merest of withering glances. 'That would be nice,' said the small fellow, hanging onto his mouth.

'I recall a time in Brunei.' Rune settled back in the king's throne and puffed at his cigar. Arthur struggled to right the king, but wasn't making much of a job out of it. 'The sultan had taken on my services as financial adviser. He wasn't the sultan then, of course, he was a rickshaw repair man, called *Kwa-Ling*, that's Mandarin for Colin. Now, I say that he took on my services, this is not strictly true. For he did not know it then, nor has he ever known it.'

Cornelius was fascinated. Not by the tale. But by the man.

'Allow me to set the scene,' said Hugo Rune. 'A bar, roofed in bamboo and walled in native silks. It overlooks the South China Sea. I am seated therein, looking much as you see me today. Distinguished. Stately. In repose. The year is 1923.'

'Stop,' cried the king. 'Just you stop. Kobold, get me up.'

'I'm doing my best, sire.'

'Silence.' Rune stretched out his right hand and plucked at something in the air. A table materialized. It was a pedestal table. And this time it was not covered by a silken cloth. On top of the table was displayed a perfect representation of the great hall and all who sat, stood, or had fallen over and were being helped back up, in it.

'Oh dear,' said Cornelius Murphy.

'What's that?' asked the king. 'A present? Has Hugo brought his old friend a present?'

'Hugo has not,' said Hugo Rune. 'Now kindly do not interrupt me again. I am dining with a close chum of mine, Sigmund Freud. Our chosen fare, vichyssoise, Blue Point oysters, lobster tails with drawn butter, clam chowder and soft-shell crabs. Washed down with Iced Finlandia vodka and white Almaden. All brought in for me from Honolulu on the flying boat. In those days a gentleman was treated like a gentleman. The masses knew their place.'

'Those were the days,' said the king.

'Shut up,' said Hugo Rune. 'Now, where was I?'

'Dining out with Clement Freud,' said Tuppe. You were having crab sticks and jellied eels. You didn't say who footed the bill.'

'The meal was concluded,' Rune went on. 'We drank brandy and shared a pipe of opium. Siggy, as was his way, when three sheets to the wind and stoned as a six-day camel, asked me this question, "Guru," he asked, "what's it all about then, eh?"

'Now, I am not one to sing my own praises, but I pride myself that this is one question I can answer to complete and utter satisfaction.'

Cornelius wondered whether he should ask Anna to shoot Hugo Rune. Possibly just in the foot or something.

' "There are exactly twenty-three really wonderful things in this world," I told Siggy, "and always to be in the right place at the right time is one of them." Siggy sniffed at this *Ultimate Truth*. He had a touch of the tropical ague.'

'Kobold,' said the king, 'remove Rune from my sight. He has lost the last of his marbles.'

Hugo Rune reached over to the pedestal table and gave it a little shake.

The great hall shuddered. Tabards tumbled from the walls. All those standing fell to the floor. The king, who was almost half up, collapsed on to Arthur

Kobold. Cornelius clung to the king's table. Rune clung to his throne.

'Siggy sniffed,' said Rune, when some degree o normality had been restored. ' "Allow me to demon strate," I told him. "Pick the most useless individua you see in the bar." Siggy squinted all about the place his eyesight was never up to much, but finally h pointed to the said *Kwa-Ling*, rickshaw repair ma and town drunk. "Now," said I, viewing this speci men, "what say you if I could make this fellow th richest man in the world?" "I would say," Sigg replied, "ask him for the lend of fifty guineas, tha you might repay the loan I made you last year. Always the wag and the tight–wad, Siggy.'

The king had now manoeuvred himself to h knees and was wondering where Arthur Kobold ha got to. Arthur, for his part, was now lodged firml between the redly trousered cheeks of the king bottom.

Tuppe considered this quite amusing.

Arthur Kobold did not.

'Will you please stop?' the king implored. 'Yo have told me this story before. And nonsense it all i You uttered the words of some magic spell. Th rickshaw repair man stumbled into the street and immediately struck down by a passing car. The drive an American philanthropist, mortified by this, pa for his hospital bills and awards him a small sum money. The rickshaw repair man buys himself a pl of land. The land turns out to be rich in miner resources. He leases out the rights, buys more lan same thing happens, does it again and the same thi happens again and soon he's the richest man in the world. It's rubbish.'

'It certainly is the way you tell it. But true, nevertheless.'

'No it's not. Because the Sultan of Brunei is not the richest man in the world, I am. And *I* have all the best spells and even *I* don't have that one.' The king found his feet (yes, they were on the ends of his legs, I know). 'Ugh!' went the king, plucking Arthur Kobold from his bottom. 'And all this is quite enough. Down to the dungeons, the lot of you. Kobold, lead them out.'

Rune's hand strayed once more towards the pedestal table.

'If I might just ask a question,' said Cornelius Murphy.

'Yes?' said Rune.

'Where is Her Majesty the Queen?'

Inspectre Hovis had been thrusting and parrying for quite some time.

'Have at you,' he cried, taking up the classic fencer's position. Elbows on the desk, cigar in the mouth, and 'I know it's good gear, but the stuff's red hot and I can't move it on the open market, Plod would be down on me as quick as winking. I'll give you a "monkey" for it and no questions asked.'

The big green thingy scratched his head. 'Is that a misprint, or what?'

'Have at you, then.' Hovis took up the classic fencer's *pose*. Knees slightly bent, left arm back and crooked at the elbow, left hand dangling, swordstick held firmly in the right, parallel to the ground and level with the tip of the nose.

'Have at you.' Slice. Twist. Cut. Thrust.

'Grab his legs, Terence,' cried the big green thingy

'Leave me out.' Mulligan shook his head. 'I'm jus a cabbie. I don't get involved in no bother.'

'What do you do if someone cuts up rough?' the other big green thingy asked him.

'Bung on the central locking and drive then straight round to the nearest nick.'

'Central locking. I'll bear that in mind.'

'It's compulsory on a black cab now. You're no allowed on the road without it.'

Hovis kicked the other big green thingy in the teeth scattering many of these about the torture chamber.

'I know not of what you speak.' Rune flicked as from the end of his cigar. 'The Queen? What of this?

'If you've done anything to harm my wife,' roare the king.

'*His* wife?' said Anna.

Tuppe nodded. 'According to Rune, the Quee is one of *them*. She's not really a human being.'

'I never thought she was. She doesn't go to th toilet. Everyone knows that.'

'I knew it,' said Tuppe.

'The Queen is quite safe,' said Rune. 'Her exac whereabouts are known to myself alone.'

'You fiend!' cried the king.

Rune gave the pedestal table another little shake Walls shook and the king fell over again. This tim Arthur Kobold ducked well out of the way.

'As you must now be well aware,' said Hugo Rune, raising his bulk from the king's throne and positioning it behind the pedestal table, '*I* am in control here. I have but to reach a finger into this microcosm and squash any one of you, as I might an ant.'

'Squash her first,' said Arthur, pointing at Anna.

'Why don't *I* have one of those tables?' asked the king.

'Pay attention.' Rune raised a finger. Everyone paid attention. 'You,' Rune pointed to the king. 'I would address your people. Summons them here.'

'My people?' The king was still in the supine position.

'Your princes and princesses, lords and ladies, jugglers and fools. Your minions, underlings, peasants and peons. Elder statesmen, younger statesmen, artisans, maids in waiting, concubines, footmen. Your people.'

'They're all here really,' said the king, who was now sitting up. 'Except for a couple of guards and the woman who cleans on Tuesdays.'

'*What?*' cried Hugo Rune.

'Well,' the king explained, 'it's like this. Every generation there are fewer folk in the world. Take yourself. There is only one of you. Yet you had two parents, four grandparents, eight great-grandparents, sixteen great-great—'

'Shut up,' Rune raised the doom-laden finger. 'I know all that. I discovered it.'

'Well, there you are then. My missus walked out years ago and my daughter, who *you* got pregnant in your vain attempt to be made a prince, went with

327

her. My grandson became a Scotsman and got blown up. And Arthur never married.'

'Never fancied the cleaning woman,' said Arthur.

'And the guards aren't really guards at all. They're just conjurations.'

'And they're a right pain in the neck,' said Arthur. 'Always going on about overtime and bonus payments.'

Rune looked appalled. He was appalled.

Cornelius was appalled also. 'You mean to say that there's just you, Father Christmas, and his one little fairy left?'

'I don't like that term,' said Arthur. 'I'm a Kobold.'

'Who does your cooking, then?' Anna asked 'Who bakes the cakes?'

'Fortnum & Mason's,' said the king. 'Whoever did you think?'

'Fortnum & Mason's, eh?' Tuppe climbed up on to the chair next to Cornelius. 'Yum yum.'

'Try the Black Forest Gâteau,' said Cornelius.

'Get away from my cakes.' The king was finally back on his feet.

'Interesting situation,' said Cornelius to Hugo Rune. 'When exactly might we expect the police force and the army and the world's press to come bursting in here and arrest Father Christmas and his one little fairy?'

Rune took out his pocket watch once more and scrutinized its face. 'Quite shortly now. Doesn't time fly when you're having a good time? Do you know why, by the way? I wrote a rather erudite monograph on the subject.'

Rune smiled upon Arthur Kobold. 'How long would it take you to conjure up a few hundred guards? Put on a bit of a display of defence. Just for appearances' sake? You could do that, couldn't you?'

'I could, but I won't.' Arthur folded his arms.

Hugo Rune dipped into the microcosm on the pedestal table and twanged the head of the miniature Kobold. The full-sized version toppled sideways, clutching his skull. 'About five minutes,' he said.

'Well hurry off, then.'

'Now see here,' said Cornelius.

'Now see here,' said the king.

'No no,' said Rune. 'He that controls the magic table, controls all the "now see heres". The king must have his guards. He must be seen to be putting up a struggle. Can't disappoint the viewing public.'

The king stroked his whiskers. 'These policemen and soldiers and whatnot. They will all have guns, I suppose.'

'Of course.' Rune nodded his big bald head. 'Lots of guns.'

'Will they have swords at all?'

'Not in this day and age,' said Rune. 'Swords indeed.'

'Ah,' said the king. 'Tell you what, Arthur, why don't you conjure up *five* hundred guards and make a really decent show of it?'

Arthur and the king exchanged knowing winks. 'Let's make it an even thousand,' said Arthur Kobold, heading for the door.

'Help yourself to cake everyone,' said the king.

*　　*　　*

It was taking reliable Ron Sturdy rather a long time to get up Star Hill. He kept getting distracted. There were all these old buses, with bald tyres and out-of-date tax discs. And no-one seemed keen to help him with his enquiries.

The Gandhis were rocking on. Prince Charles had joined them on stage and was playing his cello. Polly was glowering at him.

Mickey Minns sauntered over to her. He thought she was Anna.

'Wanna dance?' he asked.

Inspectre Hovis was making reasonable progress. He was out of the torture chamber now and fighting his way up a flight of stone steps. The big green thingy, whose brother Colin the great detective had pranged, was putting up quite a show of force. But it was keeping its back to the wall, just to be on the safe side.

Arthur Kobold was back in his office. The filing cabinet was open and Colin was out.

Arthur was manipulating a foot pump.

'You're in for a bit of multiplication,' he told the green thingy that was growing bigger by the moment. 'Do your job properly and you'll get double-bubble, time and a half, a big wodge of folding in your old "sky rocket" and a golden handshake.'

'Did you have to stick the air pipe up my bottom?' the big green thingy complained.

★   ★   ★

'Mind if I sit back in my throne?' the king asked Hugo Rune.

'Be my guest,' said Hugo.

'So kind.' The king eased himself into it.

'Great cake,' said Tuppe. 'Are you really, truly, Father Christmas, by the way?'

'I am he,' said the king.

'Then what ever happened to my train set? I sent a letter up the chimney three years running. Don't tell me they all got lost in the Christmas post.'

'What's your name?' asked the king.

'Tuppe,' said Tuppe.

'As in *Tupperware*?'

'That's me.'

'I remember your letters,' said the king. 'Such neat handwriting.'

'Thank you,' said Tuppe. 'I did my best.'

'Caravan,' said the king. 'You lived in a caravan.'

'That's right.' Tuppe was very impressed. 'So why didn't you bring me a train set?'

'Because you're a bloody traveller,' said the king. 'And I don't give presents to bloody travellers.'

'What a shit!' said Tuppe to Cornelius. 'I reckon that dyslexic devil worshipper sold his soul to the right bloke after all.'

'Midnight,' boomed the voice of Hugo Rune. And on that cue Inspectre Hovis burst through the open door.

'Right on time,' said Rune. 'Magnificent.'

Hovis slammed the great door shut. Upon the fingers of the big green thingy. He shot the bolt into place and turned to gaze in no small wonder at all which lay before him.

'Well bugger my boots,' said the great detective.

And Rune smiled upon him. 'Has all gone as we arranged? I trust you have the police force and the army and the world's press with you. You didn't forget to phone the BBC?'

'I have called nobody.' Hovis brushed a cobweb from his shoulder. 'I made the mistake of hailing a black cab. You neglected to warn me about those. Some kind of secret organization, I understand. Are these the culprits?'

'Him.' Anna, Tuppe and Cornelius pointed to Father Christmas.

'The shit,' said Tuppe.

'Him?' The Inspectre sheathed his blade. 'But surely this is none other than—'

Crash. Crash. Crash, went something going crash crash crash against the great door.

'The army?' Rune made a hopeful face.

'A big green thingy,' said Hovis. 'One of the king's conjured guards I do believe. A right evil crew they are too. Can't be destroyed by normal means, guns and whatnot. Only respond to the kiss of the sword.'

'*What?*' Hugo Rune looked quite upset.

'Some you win, some you lose,' said the king, smiling hugely.

'No, no, no,' went Hugo Rune.

And crash crash crash went the great door with renewed vigour, almost as if the energies of a single big green thingy had been increased by a factor of one thousand.

332

Reliable Ron Sturdy had finally reached the control-box. He swung open the door and stared down at the pile of bodies.

'Hello, hello, hello,' he said. 'What's all this then?'

'At 'em, lads,' cried Arthur Kobold from the corridor. 'Storm the great hall. Free the king. Destroy Hugo Rune. And that bloody woman also. Off with their heads.'

'Double time after midnight,' said Colin. 'We did agree double time.'

And crash went the great hall's great door, tearing from its hinges and plunging to the flagstoned floor. And in poured a monstrous legion of big green thingies, not pleasing to behold.

The king clapped and cheered. Anna and Tuppe took shelter beneath the king's table and Hovis whipped his blade out once again.

Hugo Rune raised his hand to smite the micro-cosm.

Cornelius leapt from his chair and dived at Hugo Rune.

'Constable, are you all right?' Sergeant Sturdy shook the dazed Ken Loathsome.

'Someone hit me, Sarge.'

'What did you say? I can't hear you above that damn band.'

'Someone bopped me on the head.'

'Hold on a minute, lad, I'll switch them off.'

Of course he could have just closed the soundproof

door, but he didn't. He stepped over the 'officer down' and approached the computer console. 'Which button?' he asked himself. 'Probably this big blood-red one,' he decided.

And without further thought, that was the one he pressed.

Heaving muscular forms, all vivid green and primed for mayhem with promises of a big cash bonus, rushed across the flagstones.

The king slapped his gargantuan thighs and laughed uproariously.

Anna and Tuppe cringed beneath the king's table and Cornelius struggled to restrain Rune.

'They will kill us all,' cried Rune. 'Let me destroy them.'

'You'll destroy us as well. Leave the thing alone.'

Cornelius made a grab for the pedestal table.

Hugo Rune stuck his foot out. Cornelius tripped and fell against the table. Knocking it over.

And then all sorts of exciting things began to happen.

The Gandhis suddenly found themselves strumming dead instruments. Their speakers fed back and a strange ungodly wave of sound swept out from them. It crystallized into a sequence of notes, the like of which none present knew the names of. Haunting. Mysterious. Downright weird.

The ground beneath the stage began to move. One of the Herculean hairdryers tore from its mounts and bowled down the hillside, scattering travellers before

334

it. The stage shook. Prince Charles took a tumble. Polly took a tumble. Mickey Minns helped her up and offered her considerable comfort.

And then the stage began to sink, down into the portal that was opening right beneath it. As thousands looked on in amazement, the stage, with its HOLLY-WOOD letters, its video screen, the most famous rock band in all the world, and the Prince of Wales, vanished into the top of Star Hill.

There was a moment of silence, there always is, but then a great cry went up. And the travellers stormed the hilltop.

The king's table slid sideways, spilling off its cake. Much of this went into the lap of the king, who followed the sliding table on his own sliding throne. In accordance with its microcosm on the now fallen pedestal, the entire hall was turning on its side. Cornelius tried to right the magic table, but he too was sliding across a floor which was rapidly becoming a wall.

Rune rolled by, followed by a good many big green thingys, an Inspectre with a swordstick and Mr Arthur Kobold.

And in through the great doorway slid something rather wonderful. An entire pink stage, complete with four-piece band and prince, a selection of light-ng gantries, a control-box containing a white-faced Sergeant Sturdy, an utterly out-of-it Constable Ken and a sound engineer who didn't have much of a part, a number of HOLLYWOOD-style letters, which now spelt out H.R. IS A NERD, probably by accident rather than design, and a fifty-foot hairdryer.

'What the heck is going on?' shouted Chief Inspector Lytton to his troops at the place where the buses turn around. 'They're all running away.'

'They're making up the hill,' said a helpful officer. 'It looks like the stage has collapsed. Should I radio for an ambulance?'

'Radio for reinforcements. Men, to your cars. Let's get up there.'

'Should I radio for helicopters, sir?' asked the helpful officer. 'We can see how well the big numbers on the tops of our cars work then.'

'Good idea. Radio for helicopters. Now forward, men. After those travellers.'

'Shiva's sheep!' Vain Glory clung to his microphone stand. 'We've fallen into hell.'

A big green thingy struck him from his feet.

'How dare you smite my chum,' said Prince Charles, wading into the big green thingy with the business end of his cello.

Cornelius fought to keep hold of the pedestal table and get it back up the right way, but tumbling bodies engulfed him in a verdant maelstrom of flailing fist (and not a little purple prose).

The great hall took another turn for the worse then came to rest. Upside down. Those who still had places left to fall to, fell to them. Those who tried to get up found others knocking them down. There was some unpleasantness.

But it was nothing before the face of that yet to come.

Because now, in through the door, surged the travellers.

'Charge,' cried Bollocks, at the head of them.

Now there have been battles and there have *been* battles. You had the Somme and El Alamein, Goose Green and Desert Storm.

But you never had anything like this before.

The green legions of King Christmas, rising from the ceiling which was now the floor, offered up a battle-cry and launched themselves against the invaders.

The invaders, somewhat stunned by the enormity of their adversaries, decided to take flight. But as more and more of their number were pressing in through the inverted doorway, they were unable to do so.

The big green thingys, for their part, suddenly realized that these were no ordinary invaders, these were the dreaded travellers themselves, feared throughout the world. The big green thingys sounded the retreat.

And then came the police-car sirens.

Those travellers that were in, wanted out. Those that weren't quite in, wanted to see what was in, before they went out.

And those that really weren't in at all, and didn't have much of a hope of getting in, turned to confront the police.

And so on and so forth. And, as if a great mass mind had suddenly arrived at a single decision, every one and every thing fell on each and every other one or thing and began to beat the daylights out of it.

In a far corner Cornelius tried to right the pedestal table. But the microcosm had gone. The mechanism was smashed and the innards all hung out in a ruined mass. Curiously, they appeared to consist of nothing more than a couple of old tennis balls with nails stuck in them and a clockwork mouse in a little treadmill.

Tuppe crawled over to his friend. 'Do you think we should get out of here before we get killed?' he asked.

'The doorway looks a tad crowded. Perhaps we had better hide. Where is Anna?'

'I thought she was with you.'

'You did not.'

'No, you're right.'

Anna was nowhere to be seen. And Cornelius, even with his height to his advantage, could not make her out amongst the seething battle.

'She'll be OK,' said Tuppe.

'You wouldn't be just saying that.'

'I would, you know.'

DO DAH DO DAH DO DAH DO DAH, went the police-car sirens. Or is it, WEEEEEEEEEEEEEEEE EEEEEEEEE? It's WEEEEEEEEEEEEEEEEEEEE, think.

A police helicopter circled over Star Hill.

'Hey look,' said the co-pilot, 'you can make out all the big numbers on the tops of the police cars.'

'So you can,' said the pilot. 'I wonder what they're for.'

'Get moving,' said Arthur Kobold. He'd got his gun back and he was prodding Anna with it.

Prodding her along a stone passage. A secret stone passage. It led away from the great hall. Anna was in front. Arthur was behind her. And good old Father Christmas was bringing up the rear. It wasn't that large a secret passage, they're not usually, Santa was pretty cramped.

'What are we doing, Arthur?' he asked.

'Making our getaway, sire.'

'But getaway to where?'

'South America?' said Arthur.

'Why don't you just give yourselves up?' Anna asked. 'You're beaten and you know it.'

'Don't be absurd,' Arthur gave her a good hard poke with the pistol. 'True, the king and I and the cleaning lady may be the last there are in London. But that's just London. Our lot are all over the world. Few in numbers, but great in power. We'll live to fight another day. Now, as hostage-taking seems to be the order of the night, you are our hostage until we make our safe escape. Then I'll shoot you. It's nothing personal. Well, actually it is.'

'Cornelius will track you down, no matter where you hide.'

'He won't find us. The world is a very large place. Much larger than *you* think it is. Murphy is probably dead by now anyway. And even if he's not, there's no way he's going to find the entrance to the secret passage.'

★   ★   ★

'Hey look,' said Cornelius, 'isn't that the entrance to a secret passage over there?'

'Oh yes,' said Tuppe sarcastically. 'And surely that is a piece of Anna's T-shirt lying in the entrance.'

'No.' The tall boy flexed his nostrils. 'But that' the way she went, I can still smell her perfume.'

Inspectre Hovis was in the thick of the fighting. A lesser man would surely have perished, but not Inspectre Hovis. His blade was in play to pleasing effect.

The big green thingys that Arthur had so hastily conjured by the multiplication of Colin, weren' really up to the required standard. The great detectiv was cutting the proverbial bloody swathe through them.

'Have at you,' he cried time and again.

As no more travellers could possibly squeeze throug the portal and into the great hall, those that remaine outside, about twenty-two thousand of them, rushe back down the hill towards the police, who wer advancing up it.

Chief Inspector Lytton was leading the way. O foot.

'Retreat,' he shouted. And squad cars to each an every side of him, did just that.

'Lads,' called the chief inspector, suddenly all o his ownsome. 'Lads?'

'Kill the pig,' cried the voice of the multitude.

★   ★   ★

'Get in,' said Arthur Kobold.

'Get in?' asked Anna. 'To this?'

'It's an ice-cream van,' said the king. 'I don't want to get into an ice-cream van. Look, my nice silver car is back. Hugo must have returned it.'

'Trust me, sire,' said Arthur Kobold. 'We need to slip away unnoticed. Your nice silver car will only draw attention to us.'

'We could use my special birthday spell. Move faster than time.'

'I broke your spell. It won't work again for another year. Please get into the van.'

'Perhaps we could take a taxi or something.'

'Do you see a taxi, sire?'

'No,' said the king. Although in fact he really should have been able to see a taxi. Terence Arthur Mulligan's taxi. But the king couldn't see it, because it wasn't there any more.

'I don't want to be driven around in a rotten old ice-cream van.' The king stamped his foot.

'Stop!' shouted Cornelius Murphy, emerging from the secret passage with Tuppe puffing hard on his heels.

'All aboard,' said the king. 'Mine's a banana sundae.'

The portal door of the king's private car park swung open to the outside world and the ice-cream van passed through it.

'Quickly,' said Cornelius.

'I'm being as quick as I can.'

'Sorry,' Cornelius scooped up the Tuppe and

hastened towards Rune's silver car. 'We've got to ge
after them.'

'Another car chase,' said Tuppe. 'Oh goody goody
Just what I need.'

Cornelius flung open the car door and flung Tupp
into the passenger seat and himself down behind th
wheel. The keys just happened to be in the dashboard

'Up and away,' cried Cornelius Murphy.

Wheels went skid, the engine didn't go glu
glug, but roar, and the silver car streaked out into th
night.

'Arthur, are you really sure you know how to driv
this thing?'

'Of course I do. It's very fast for an ice-cream van

In the back the king lurched from side to sid
Anna ducked these lurches as best she could. Th
king was a real space-filler.

Arthur raked the ice-cream van along a row c
parked cars.

'I'm getting the measure of this, Your Majesty.'

'Oh no.' The king stared out through the bac
window. 'That Murphy is chasing us. And in m
favourite car.'

'The game's up.' Anna dodged the mighty po:
terior. 'Surrender now, before Kobold gets us ;
killed.'

'Don't be ridiculous.' Arthur dragged the steerir
wheel to the right and the van went round a corn
on two wheels.

'He's a nifty driver,' said Tuppe. 'For a fairy.'

'Watch this.' Cornelius put his foot right down.
'OooooooooooooooooooooooH!' went Tuppe.

'I'm getting travel sick,' said the king. 'Slow down a bit.'

'Not until we've lost Murphy.' Arthur pranged the pedal.

'Don't you chuck up on me,' said Anna.

'They're getting away.' Tuppe clung to the dashboard. 'Go faster.'

'Get real, Tuppe, please.'

Mulligan's Ices tore out into the high street.

'Open road ahead.' Arthur did a racing-change. 'We'll lose him on the straight.'

'Oh I do hope so,' said the king. 'This is becoming a proper *annus horribilis*.'

'Who are you calling horrible?' said Anna.

'Just keep calm, sire,' said Arthur Kobold. 'Nothing can stop us now.'

Put it back into first gear again,' said Terence Arthur Mulligan to the big green thingy who was thinking of going into the limousine-hire business. 'Go on. You're doing all right.'

'I really appreciate you giving me a driving lesson so late at night,' said the big green thingy.

'Best time for it, when there's no-one around. Back into first. No, that's reverse.'

'Sorry.'

'No problem. I only lease the cab. If you bugger

343

the gears, it goes into the workshop and I get another one. Try putting your foot on the clutch pedal before you change gear.'

'Sorry,' said the big green thingy.

'Ha ha,' went Arthur Kobold. 'The open road. Home and free. Rio here we come.'

'Faster,' said Tuppe.

'It won't go any faster,' said Cornelius.

'We're losing them,' went the king. 'Ha ha ha.'

'No, that's still reverse,' said Terence Arthur Mulligan.

'What's that up ahead?' cried Arthur.

'It looks like a taxi reversing across the road,' said the king.

'It *is* a taxi reversing across the road.' Arthur went for the brake. 'Oh no.'

'Oh no!' cried the king.

'Oh no!' cried Terence Arthur Mulligan, covering his face.

'Sorry,' said the big green thingy.

'They're slowing down,' said Tuppe. 'Overtake them.'

'I will,' said Cornelius. 'And I'll do it on the inside just to make it more exciting.'

'As you please.'

'More brakes,' cried the king. 'More brakes.'

'I don't have any more brakes.' There was kind of thud. The kind of thud that brakes make. When they break. 'I don't have *any* brakes,' said Arthur.

Anna preferred a brief chance to certain death. Sh

344

climbed out of the serving window and jumped for her life.

Right onto the bonnet of a streaking silver car.

Was *that* lucky or what?

The silver car shot right past Mulligan's Ices with only a bit of swerving, but not enough to dislodge Anna from the bonnet. The ice-cream van just couldn't swerve. Some silver car had cut it up on the inside.

'Ohhhnoooooo!' went Arthur and the king and Terence and the big green thingy. All at the same time.

And then it was KAPOW!

It was a significant explosion, in every sense of the word. The mushroom cloud billowed into the sky. Those few who saw it, and there were only very few, agreed that it was a curious mushroom cloud. So red in the middle and so white all round and about with the smoke. It was almost like a big red laughing face surrounded by a great white beard. A bit like . . .

Cornelius brought the silver car to a gentle standstill. He jumped from the car and helped Anna down.

She held up her face to his.

They kiss.

Lovely.

'Vom-it,' said Tuppe.

And that was all that he said for quite a long time. Because there came to his small and exceedingly shell-like ear a rustling behind the driver's seat.

'Could someone help one up here?' said the voice of Her Majesty the Queen. 'One seems to have fallen arse over tit.'

345

THE AFTERWORDS

The travellers have now gone from Star Hill. They
hung around for a few days, to make as much of a
nuisance of themselves as they possibly could. But
then they got the word from the BBC that they were
expected in Harlech, where a Mr Doveston was
organizing a festival in the grounds of the castle. So
they moved on.

Polly Gotting did not marry Prince Charles. She,
like her sister, harboured a secret passion for balding
ex-musos with beer bellies and bad breath (well,
anything's possible) and she moved in with Mickey
Minns.

This didn't upset Mickey's wife, because when the
Minns got home from the gig on Star Hill, he found
a note saying that she had gone off to live in Spain,
taking the contents of Minn's Music Mine with her.
She had apparently absconded with a Mr Patel who
ran the shop next door.

Inspectre Hovis did get his knighthood, but not
for solving The Crime Of The Century. He got the
one Prince Charles had promised, for his delicate
handling of that certain little matter regarding an heir
to the throne, a homeopathist called Chunky and a
Dormobile named Desire.

Cruel fate, as ever conspiring against the great

detective, saw to it that he did not become Lord Hovis of Kew. This title apparently being held by a gentleman called Rune. The Inspectre became Lord Hovis of Brentford.

The Queen remained kidnapped for two long weeks. Which might appear strange, seeing as Cornelius had delivered her straight back to the palace. But by then it would seem that the various bigwigs had signed so many lucrative contracts, and the world's sympathy for the poor kidnapped Queen had already grown so great, that it was considered prudent she remain kidnapped for just a bit longer. It was also suggested that she might care to be kidnapped on a yearly basis, to further increase her popularity.

Tuppe was interested to note that when the Queen was finally 'liberated', it was from a traveller's caravan on Hampstead Heath. And that the 'kidnappers' turned out to be the very same fellows who had engaged in the skirmishes with the police outside Gunnersbury Park. He even thought he recognized at least one ex *Blue Peter* presenter amongst their number.

The BBC hold exclusive world rights on the 'liberation'.

The lead singer of Gandhi's Hairdryer never did get to announce his retirement. After the holocaust on Star Hill, the band split up, due to 'artistic differences'. Some unpleasantness then occurred regarding the loss of all that uninsured stage equipment, the record company sued for breach of contract and the Inland Revenue joined in the hue and cry and stung the lot of them for three years' unpaid income tax.

The lead singer now works as a guard on British Rail. He's never been so happy. His chums at the depot call him 'Smiley' Colin.

The world has yet to discover the truth about the denizens of the Forbidden Zones. Certain grey bearded experts of the archaeological persuasion, who examined all that remained of the great hall (which wasn't much after the travellers had stripped it of its fixtures and fittings), declared it to be a folly. Probably the work of the Reverend Kemp. This was the local cleric who was buried on the very top of Star Hill standing on his head, so that when Judgement Day came and the world was turned upside down, he would be the first on his feet. Well, it had to be him really, didn't it? It being upside down and everything.

You can still visit the ruins. The local guide, a Mr Omally, is to be found at The Flying Swan (eight hand-drawn ales on pump, snacks available at the bar, unrestricted parking in the Ealing Road). He's there most lunch-times, and he'll be happy to show you around. For a small remuneration, of course.

Naturally there are some loose ends that just can't be tied up. The present whereabouts of Chief Inspector Brian 'Bulwer' Lytton, for example, last seen leading an abortive police charge against the travellers on Star Hill. His file remains open, it reads 'missing presumed eaten'.

Terence Arthur Mulligan still drives a cab, although not the one his brother's ice-cream van crashed into. Terence had managed to leap from that in the very nick of time. Which was lucky for him. As to the big green thingy in his cab and the occupants of the ice-cream van, nothing is known. No bodies were recovered. It was almost as if they'd vanished into thin air.

But what of Cornelius and Tuppe and Anna? And what of the enigmatic Mr Hugo Rune?

Cornelius Murphy now lives for part of the year in Miami, Florida. That's when he's not on his yacht, or at one of his English country residences. He lives with his girlfriend Anna, his best friend Tuppe, and a succession of lady friends that the small fellow keeps bringing home after parties. They are, as the expression goes, of independent wealth.

The tall boy made his first of many millions auctioning off the automotive contents of a certain king's private car park.

And, of course, if you happen to be the Stuff of Epics, and possess a reinvented ocarina, there are many other lucrative openings to be found in and around London.

As for Hugo Rune, what can be said? There are those who suggest that, like Father Christmas, Rune never really existed. But there are others who swear that they have seen him water-skiing with the Sultan of Brunei, arm-wrestling with the Pope and frequenting the swank offices of a certain illustrious West London publishing house. There may possibly be some substance to the last of these supposed sightings, as the word is out, in literary circles, that Rune is seeking to publish his memoirs.

If this is indeed the case, and it probably is, then the world has not yet heard the last of Hugo Rune, guru's guru, master of the arts magickal, reinventor of the ocarina and self-appointed scourge of the fairy folk.

There are twenty-three really wonderful things in this world.

Hugo Rune knows all of them.

And then some.

THE END

THE BOOK OF ULTIMATE TRUTHS
by Robert Rankin

'Extravagant, corny and sublime . . . a whirligig entertainment'
Daily Telegraph

He had walked the Earth as Nostradamus, Uther Pendragon, Count Cagliostro and Rodrigo Borgia. He could open a tin of sardines with his teeth, strike a Swan Vestas on his chin, rope steers, drive a steam locomotive and hum all the works of Gilbert & Sullivan without becoming confused or breaking down in tears. He died, penniless, at a Hastings boarding house, in his ninetieth year.

His name was Hugo Artemis Solon Saturnicus Reginald Arthur Rune. And he was never bored. Hailed as the 'guru's guru', Rune penned more than eight million words of genius including his greatest work *The Book of Ultimate Truths*. But vital chapters of *The Book* were suppressed, chapters which could have changed the whole course of human history. Now, seventeen-year-old Cornelius Murphy, together with his best friend Tuppe, sets out on an epic quest. Their mission – recover the missing chapters. Re-publish *The Book of Ultimate Truths*. And save the world. Naturally.

'One of the rare guys who can always make me laugh'
Terry Pratchett

'Take Douglas Adams, Donleavy, Moorcock, Cervantes, childish cartoons, B-movies, Munchausen and game shows, add a psychedelic twist and a jigger of detective action, shake dementedly, and the result may be something like Robert Rankin's latest book'
David Profumo, *Daily Telegraph*

552 13922 X

A LIST OF OTHER HUMOROUS TITLES
AVAILABLE FROM CORGI BOOKS

THE PRICES SHOWN BELOW WERE CORRECT AT THE TIME OF GOING TO PRESS
HOWEVER TRANSWORLD PUBLISHERS RESERVE THE RIGHT TO SHOW NEW
RETAIL PRICES ON COVERS WHICH MAY DIFFER FROM THOSE PREVIOUSLY
ADVERTISED IN THE TEXT OR ELSEWHERE.

All Corgi/Bantam Books are available at your bookshop or newsagent, or can be
ordered from the following address:
Transworld Publishers Ltd, Cash Sales Department,
P.O. Box 11, Falmouth, Cornwall TR10 9EN

Please send a cheque or postal order (no currency) and allow £1.00 for postage and
packing for the first book plus 30p for each subsequent book ordered to a maximum
charge of £3.00 if ordering seven books or more.

Overseas customers, including Eire, please allow £2.00 for postage and packing for
the first book, £1.00 for the second book, and 30p for each subsequent title ordered.

NAME (Block Letters)..

ADDRESS..

....